PRAISE FOR EMILY COLIN

PRAISE FOR THE SEVEN SINS SERIES

- WINNER of the 2022 Silver IPPY Award for Young Adult Fiction
- WINNER of the 2021 North Carolina Indie Author Award in Young Adult Fiction
- FINALIST for the 2021 and 2022 Foreword INDIES Award in Young Adult Fiction
- SHORTLISTED for the The Manly Wade Wellman Award for Science Fiction and Fantasy
- WINNER of the 2022 Gold Moonbeam Award for Best Book Series

PRAISE FOR SIEGE OF THE SEVEN SINS

This is easily one of the best books I've ever read. *Siege of the Seven Sins* has it all—heart-stopping action, breathtaking characters, high stakes, and a thrilling story, all wrapped up in beautiful prose.

— MADELINE DYER, SIBA-AWARD-WINNING
AUTHOR OF THE *UNTAMED* SERIES

Thrilling, heart-wrenching, and blood-pumping.

— KARISSA LAUREL, AUTHOR OF *THE
STORMBOURNE CHRONICLES*

With an intriguing world, an impossible love story, and characters I both loved and loved to hate, the stakes are high. What if love was a death sentence? ... A series everyone should know about.

— M. LYNN, *USA TODAY* BESTSELLING AUTHOR OF
THE *QUEENS OF THE FAE* SERIES

PRAISE FOR SWORD OF THE SEVEN SINS

A hot, fast-paced, beautifully written story you won't want to miss!

— CAITLIN SINEAD, AUTHOR OF *HEARTSICK*

A romantic dystopian with a fantastic—and unexpected—twist ... *Seven Sins* is powerful, sexy, hopeful, and unsettling.

— HEIDI AYARBE, AWARD-WINNING AUTHOR OF
FREEZE FRAME

A rollicking ride through forbidden love and deadly adventure. ... I haven't ached for love like this to conquer all since Tris and Four. Eva and Ari forever.

— LEIGH STATHAM, AUTHOR OF THE *DAUGHTER*
TRILOGY

Amazing characters and a fast plot that will keep you on the edge of your seat!

— S.E. ANDERSON, AUTHOR OF *THE STARSTRUCK*
SAGA

A beautifully crafted story with so many intense moments I couldn't stop reading. This is the best book I've read in a long time.

— MICHELLE MACQUEEN, AUTHOR OF *WE THOUGHT WE WERE INVINCIBLE*, FOR *YA BOOKS CENTRAL*

Sword of the Seven Sins ... offers a new take on the dystopian genre. Colin's characters push the plot forward, while her writing immerses the reader in a rigid world on the brink of change.

— *BOOKSTACKED*

An absolutely mind-blowing, spine-tingling, action-packed extravaganza ... an electrifying, imaginative, phenomenally well written book. The tension, banter and angst blazes.

— *EMERALD BOOK REVIEWS*

Much of the fun here is watching Colin build her world ... The chapters move swiftly... The book should prove a hit with fans of *The Hunger Games.*

— WILMINGTON *STAR NEWS*

Sizzling hot and exploding with tension.

— LISA AMOWITZ, AUTHOR OF *BREAKING GLASS*

An absolutely wild ride ... I couldn't stop reading.

— *THE WORD TRAVELER*

[A] richly emotional tale . . . a writer to watch.

— JOSHILYN JACKSON, *NEW YORK TIMES*
BESTSELLING AUTHOR OF *A GROWN-UP KIND OF*
PRETTY

SHADOWS
OF THE
SEVEN
SINS

SHADOWS OF THE SEVEN SINS

A SEVEN SINS STORY COLLECTION

EMILY COLIN

Colin, Emily. 1975-.
Shadows of the Seven Sins: A Seven Sins Story Collection/ Emily Colin
ISBN (Ebook.) 978-1-961469-05-1
ISBN (Paperback): 978-1-961469-08-2
1. Science Fiction. 2. Young Adult Fiction. 3. Fantasy Fiction. I. Title.
813'.6
v.230611

Published by Black Orchid Books
A division of Emily Colin Consulting
Wilmington, NC
Cover Design by Lisa Amowitz

GLUTTONY

"A HEART FIERCE AND FALLEN"

CHAPTER ONE

Cordelia Navarro was born to blood and sacrifice.

She was also born to love cherry puff pastries, especially the ones from Dev Adelman's family's bakery on the City Road. The recipe was a secret, but as a skúmaskot—a shapeshifter of legendary power, considered royalty by all four of the Houses—Cordelia could have compelled Mrs. Adelman to tell her exactly what it contained. Still, she chose not to. Some things, she had decided, were better off remaining a mystery. The perfect blend of the cherries' tartness and the sugary flakiness of the dough felt like delicious, impossible magic, and she had no desire to break the spell.

She and Dev sat side by side on the footbridge that spanned the River Silber, which cut through the city, dangling their legs over the side. The wind gusted, misting them with a fine spray of water, and Cordelia clutched her pastry protectively, as if the breeze might snatch it from her fingers.

Next to her, Dev laughed, the sound carrying through the warm spring air. Like Cordelia, he was twelve, but in the past few months, his voice had begun to deepen. "I brought more," he said, holding up the bag by his side. "Imma gave me a whole batch. She knows you love them—and who could refuse you?"

Imma was what Dev called his mother. It had something to do with the heritage from which he was descended. Cordelia didn't know much about it, except that it involved lighting candles on Friday evenings—she'd seen Mrs. Adelman do this, reciting a blessing afterward—and that for a week in the spring, the Adelmans couldn't eat the delectable pastries they baked. That week had just passed, and Dev had delivered the puff pastries with glee, handing one to her and then biting into his own with an exaggerated zeal that sent powdered sugar flying everywhere.

Cordelia's own ancestors had come to Vik from far away, surmounting the wall that was built to keep them out when the rainforest burned and the southern continent flooded. Their customs had long since faded from memory; the only legacies they had left her were her dark hair, her skin that turned a burnished golden-brown in the sun, and the gift that flowed through her veins, in the form of her skúmaskot lineage—giving her the power to transform into a wolf at will, with the aid of her familiar.

Two centuries ago, the skúmaskot had been the ruling class of the entire Empire. Then there had been a terrible war, and in a battle called the Twilight Massacre, the High Priests who would go on to found the Commonwealths—where people lived and died by the laws of the Seven Deadly Sins—had risen up and murdered most of the skúma. All these years later, her kind's numbers were still recovering...and the Houses and Commonwealths coexisted in an uneasy peace, separated by geography and fundamental ideological differences. The High Priests thought the skúma were unnatural, sinful creatures who didn't deserve to live, and the Houses' governing Council of Nine considered the Commonwealths to be primitive backwaters, unworthy of their attention.

One day, there would come the war for which Cordelia was training—where the skúma and their familiars rose up against the Commonwealths, backed by their regiments of guards—but not yet. Here in Vik, Minneska's capital, the threat of conflict loomed on the horizon, like rainclouds always on the verge of bursting. They all lived in its shadow. But to mobilize a true offensive, all of the Houses would have to be united in their purpose...and though House Minneska was attuned to the need for revolution, the other three—Satrizona, San Fraesco, and Montyorke—tended toward complacency.

The Houses might hold differing views on inciting conflict with the Commonwealths, but they had one thing in common: most people worshipped both the many-headed gods and skúma like Cordelia, which was discomfiting and flattering in equal measure. Perhaps because of his family's faith, Dev was the only one who didn't treat her like she was made of spun glass—a precious resource that might fracture if it was held too tightly. He saw her not for what she could do, but for who she was. He always had, from the first time they'd met in the courtyard of his parents' bakery, when they'd been just six years old.

She'd been bored to pieces, sitting there, sipping her nettle tea. Everyone else had been coddling her, waiting on her, bowing to her—but not Dev. He'd sidled up to her when no one was looking and pressed a tiny box into her hand...and when she'd opened it, expecting a tribute of some kind, instead a little metal man had popped up, complete with a tiny fist that punched her in the nose when she'd peered at it closely. Her tutor, Gertrud, had been furious, demanding to know where such a thing had come from. But Cordelia had never told—and from then on, she and Dev had had an unbreakable bond, rooted in his mischievous nature and her desire to have a real, true friend.

She had her wolf, of course—who she'd named Asta; it meant 'divine strength,' in Greek—but the wolf was part of her. Though Cordelia knew she could always rely on Asta to protect her, that was different than having someone who'd chosen her—and who she'd chosen in return. She'd picked Janus to be her familiar, but that hardly counted; he'd relinquished his free will when he agreed to spend his life in her service. Dev was the only person in her life who'd always—from the very first day they'd met—

treated Cordelia just like anyone else. He didn't care about Asta, or her royal responsibilities, or even the fact that, if she lost her temper, Cordelia could shift into her wolf form and rip his head right off. He liked her; he trusted her. And from the very beginning, she liked and trusted him in return.

Over the six years since, many people had looked askance at their friendship—not that they would have the gall to say such a thing to her directly. Still, Cordelia had heard the mutterings of the staff at the House of Echoes, the shining white palace where she lived. She had no parents to speak of: her mother had died giving birth to her, and her father had given over the raising of her to Gertrud and a series of nannies. Skúma married for political alliances and procreation rather than love, and once Cordelia had made her way into the world, her father clearly believed he'd done his duty. They had a cordial relationship, but rarely spoke. He had no idea how she spent her time, and left her discipline to others.

Parents or no parents, Cordelia knew well that skúma could only marry each other, for the sake of continuing the bloodline; such a thing had been drilled into her since she was old enough to sit at table. Even without romantic intent, close friendships such as the one she had with Dev were discouraged, since the two of them were of such different social classes. But there was no rule against it; and though Cordelia knew she would one day have to marry another wolf—that was her duty, as a skúma of House Minneska—she and Dev were only twelve, years away from worrying about such things.

Today in particular, Dev had something else on his mind. He and his parents were leaving for the self-named capital city of far-off House San Fraesco tomorrow, bearing with them some of their most prized wares to trade. Dev had never left Vik before, and he'd been talking of little else for weeks. In fact, he was talking now, and with a pervasive sense of guilt, Cordelia tore herself away from thoughts of marriage and obligation to listen.

"—and can you believe San Fraesco is an underwater city?" he was saying, his eyes lit with anticipation. "Well, half underwater, anyhow. They say some of the streets are made of water, and everyone travels from one place to the next in boats. And there are tunnels that take you beneath the surface, to the place where the selkies live. Plums and mulberries grow wild, overhanging the canals, so that as you drift by in a boat, you can reach up and pluck as many as you like. And if you're lucky, you can still find veins of gold, the way there used to be centuries ago..."

Dev was a storyteller at heart. He went on and on, telling Cordelia everything that he imagined San Fraesco to be, half-fancy, half-reality, and she didn't have the heart to interrupt him. As a skúma, she'd been studying the history of the four Houses since she was old enough to walk. Her earliest toys had been a small wolf, selkie, panther, and falcon—the skúma that called each of the Houses home.

But everything she'd learned had been from the perspective of strategy and political alliance, not the realm of imagination and beauty that Dev painted for her. She liked listening to him, even if not everything he said was strictly true. Gertrud always said there was no room for pretending in Cordelia's life—that that was a childish luxury skúma didn't have—but when she was with Dev, she felt like anything was possible. Like she could have the things normal kids dreamed of, not just the regimented life of a royal warrior.

Dev jostled Cordelia with his shoulder. "I heard," he said, brushing his hands together to dust off the powdered sugar, "that there are ships buried beneath the city. Underneath the ground. How amazing is that?"

Savoring the last bite of her puff pastry, the cherry filling dark and sweet on her tongue, Cordelia hummed her assent. She'd known that about San Fraesco; in fact, she even knew how the ships had come to be there. Another day, she might have taken pride in telling him the truth. But today, for some reason, she found herself distracted by the play of the sunlight on his chestnut curls and the mischievous way the corners of his lips curled up when he smiled, as if he was in possession of a fabulous secret. Maybe it was because she'd been dwelling on thoughts of marriage and obligation, but she found her gaze lingering on Dev as he spoke, wondering what it would be like if she could choose him for her own.

At twelve, Cordelia had never kissed a boy, never wanted to—or a girl, either, for that matter. Her life had been comprised of two things: Her intensive skúmaskot training, under Gertrud's ruthless tutelage, and her stolen time with Dev—poaching pastries from the kitchen of his parents' bakery, riding horses through the woods that rimmed the city, sneaking out to prowl the streets of the Shadow District after dark. Anything else had been irrelevant. But now, listening to him talk about selkies and mulberries and gold, his eyes bright with exhilaration, she felt a flash of quicksilver desire—not for love, in general, but for *him*.

Was that terrible—wrong? Could he possibly feel the same way for her? What would anyone make of it—a member of the skúmaskot royalty and a shopkeeper's son?

Cordelia felt ashamed that she'd consider what other people thought, even in an scenario that could never come to be. This was *Dev*—her friend, brave and loyal and kind. What did it matter who he'd been born to? He hadn't chosen his circumstances, any more than she'd chosen hers. So what if he couldn't change form, if he'd never live in the House of Echoes or have a familiar, like she had Janus. Did that make him lesser, somehow?

She couldn't believe that was true. She'd been born to wage war; Dev was gentle and generous, with an open heart. He smoothed her rough edges, taught her how to dream of things beyond the confines of her world. He was always there for her.

But now—if she wanted him this other, new way—would it ruin everything?

"Cor." Dev tugged at her sleeve, frowning. "You're not listening to me."

She forced herself to focus on his face. His dark eyebrows were knitted in puzzlement, and she fought the urge to smooth them. "Sorry," she lied. "I just got distracted. Gertrud's got me working with Janus tonight again, in the woods—she wants us to simulate real-world battle conditions. I guess I'm just…worried."

His familiar smile was back, quirking one corner of his mouth and revealing the dimple in his cheek. "Not everything is about bloodshed, Cor," he said, teasing her. "Sometimes things are about—"

"Plums and mulberries and gold. I know." She got to her feet, doing her best to return his smile. It felt forced, and she was sure he'd see right through it—but what could she do?

"You're laughing at me," he said, grinning up at her. "Just wait until I come home with fruit and gems for you. Maybe I'll bring you a piece of buried treasure."

"Even better," Cordelia suggested, swallowing around the lump in her throat, "you'll come back from San Fraesco rich, with gold bars and plum pits in your pockets, and build yourself a place as grand as the House of Echoes. You'll plant the pits in an orchard, and the trees that grow from them will grant wishes from anyone brave enough to sample their fruit."

Dev's grin widened. "That's the spirit." He stood, too, facing her. The wind whipped through his curls, and he combed his fingers through them, scooping them back. Seeing him this unexpected, new way—how tall he'd gotten this past summer, how broad his shoulders had become—she had to make an effort not to stare.

"I have something for you," she said, trying to make her voice sound normal. "To take with you on your trip."

He cocked his head, shifting from foot to foot. "Oooh, a present?"

Dev loved gifts—giving them as well as getting them. It was one of the many endearing things about him. She had to suppress a smirk at his impatience as she reached into her pocket and pulled out what she'd brought him.

It was a small figurine of a wolf, dangling from a silver chain.

At the time, when she'd had the metalsmith make it, it had seemed innocuous enough: the wolf was the symbol of House Minneska. But now, her gift seemed to hold a deeper symbolism —as if she was staking a claim on Dev. As if her wolf was marking him as hers.

Mute, she held out the necklace, letting the chain dangle from her fingers. It swayed left and right, buffeted by the wind.

Dev's eyes—a blue so dark, they were nearly black—widened. Then he took it from her without a word and fastened it around his neck. The wolf nestled into the spot beneath his collarbone as if it was meant to be there. Seeing it, Cordelia felt an unmistakable sense of *rightness*. Inside her, Asta gave a contented, territorial growl; Dev belonged to her, and now everyone would know it.

Panic swept over Cordelia. This wasn't what she'd meant by the gift, but now it was too late to take it back.

Or was it? Deep down, had some part of her always wanted to make Dev her own? That was a fool's errand. She could never marry him. The most he could be was a royal consort—and surely he would never want such a thing.

She felt the blood rise to her cheeks, but refused to drop her eyes. Skúma didn't cower. Instead, she breathed deeply, trying to steady herself.

The wind gusted, bringing with it the scent of the crustaceans that crawled on the river's muddy flats. Beneath them, the bridge creaked and whined. Cordelia noted these things—she'd been trained to be aware of her surroundings at all times—but they were distant, reaching her as if through a layer of opacity. All she could see was the doubt and wonder in Dev's midnight-blue gaze.

He spoke at last, breaking the silence that had settled between them. "It's beautiful." For once, the teasing tone was absent from his voice. "You had this made… for me?"

Cordelia wanted desperately to lie. To say it was just something she'd found lying around the House of Echoes. But that would be doing Dev a terrible disservice; they were friends, and friends didn't lie to each other. Instead, she tried to make light of it, which felt almost as deceptive.

"How many cherry puff pastries have you brought me over the last six years?" Her voice sounded awful, sticky-sweet with false cheer—like the time Mr. Adelman had gone on a diet, and Mrs. Adelman had put some kind of fake sugar in all the pies. She'd said no one would be able to tell the difference, but Cordelia's horrified expression had given everything away. "I figured I owed you something good."

He snorted, bringing a hand up to touch the silver charm. "I could bring you puff pastries until we were both ancient, and it wouldn't come close to this. I'll wear it with pride, Cor. Thank you."

"It's to keep you safe," she said, feeling the need to explain. "While you're gone. And—so you'll think of me."

By the many-headed gods. Why had she said that? It was true, she'd wanted to give him a parting gift. But it was meant to be something given from one friend to another, just a trinket until they saw each other again, not a portent of something more.

He gave her another smile, but this one was uncharacteristically sad. "I could never forget you."

That was all he said—but behind his words, Cordelia couldn't help but hear the rest: *Can the same be said for you? In a few years, when you take your place with the adult skúma—when you serve on the front lines of the war you're meant to fight, with your familiar by your side and your wolf husband's ring on your finger—will I be nothing but a distant memory?*

Pain lanced through her at the thought, and she bit her lip, trying to contain it. That was something she'd learned in training —that sometimes physical discomfort could detract from emotional distress. But this time, it didn't help. When she thought of being apart from Dev forever, not being able to lose herself in his fanciful stories or laugh at his ridiculous pranks, it hurt her in a bone-deep way that no amount of distraction could erase.

His eyes narrowed, peering into hers, as if he was trying to divine what she was thinking. He reached out, taking one of her hands in his. He'd touched her a hundred times—drawing her attention to something, gripping her hand in his as they jumped from the roof of the barn where Vik's horses lived—but something about this felt different. Special. As if he was seeing her the same way she was seeing him.

"Cor," he said, his voice soft, "if I really had an orchard like the one you said—where the fruit granted wishes—what would you wish for?"

Her heart pounded, louder than the sound of the river lapping at the pilings of the bridge, far below. Louder than the roar of the wind. Deep inside, she felt the same sort of visceral urge that preceded her shifts—as if something larger than herself, an infinitely powerful force over which she had no control, was tugging at her. She sucked in a deep breath, but that didn't help: the breeze had shifted, and now Dev's scent filled her lungs, redolent of cherries and sugar and the salt-sage scent that was his own.

"I—" she began, with absolutely no idea what she planned to say. *I would wish for a world where people wouldn't judge us for being together. For a place where my power didn't come at the expense of my choices. For you to kiss me before you go, just once, so I could know what it feels like.*

"Cor." His fingers tightened around hers, and his lips parted. He drew breath, as if to speak.

Cordelia couldn't bear to think of what he might say. What if it was something that they could never take back again? What if it destroyed the friendship between them—the only pure thing in her life, the one path she'd chosen for herself?

"I have to go," she blurted, and tore her fingers from his.

She left him standing on the bridge, staring after her. And the next day, when he and his parents left for San Fraesco, she was too cowardly to say goodbye.

CHAPTER TWO

Dev was meant to be gone for two weeks. Each day, while she trained with Janus, learning to master her shifts at will rather than being driven to them by an excess of emotion, Cordelia thought of what she would say to him when she got back.

The more time passed, the more she began to think that maybe everyone was right. Perhaps people like them, who were so different, shouldn't be friends. Perhaps it could only bring both of them pain.

Now that she had seen Dev this strange, new way, she couldn't imagine going back to how things had been. And she didn't want to be a false version of herself with him. She had to tailor herself to fit her position all the time; it was the defining characteristic of her life. *Skúma don't show fear. Skúma don't lose control. Skúma always put their House and their duties before anything else.* Her friendship with Dev was the one place where she could be her true, genuine self. If that was gone—if she had to put on a front for him, too—it would break her.

No, it was better for them not to see each other anymore. He wouldn't like it, but he would understand.

I'm sorry, she would tell him when he got back. *But we're not children anymore, and it's time for us to put away childish things.*

Each day, she resolved anew to follow through on this commitment, even though the thought sent a visceral agony spiraling through her, like a greedy vine twining around her heart, squeezing it tight. As the clock ticked down to the date of Dev's return, and she tried to imagine how their conversation might go, she felt worse and worse. All she could think about was how happy he would be to see her, even if they hadn't parted on the best of terms. How they'd meet on the bridge, their special place. How he would give her his beautiful, impish smile, the one that lit his eyes. How he would have brought a gift back for her, just like he'd promised. And how betrayed he would be when she rejected all of it—his present, and *him.*

She couldn't do this. She *couldn't.*

But she had to.

The day that Dev and his parents were supposed to come back, Cordelia was ready. She had rehearsed her speech twenty-seven times, looking in the mirror of her grand room in the House of Echoes to make sure she'd gotten her expressions exactly right. She had hardened her heart. She had made a list of all the things she loved about him and all the reasons they couldn't be together, then burned it in the fireplace in her room— feeling as if she was burning, too. And then she had turned away, resolved.

She was ready. But the day of his supposed return came—and then went again.

Things could happen on the road; Cordelia knew that. Horses could throw a shoe; weather could delay travel. But when a second day passed, and then a third, she began to worry.

She told herself this was silly: Vik was hundreds of miles away from any of the Commonwealths, where their enemies dwelled. The Commonwealths were clustered in the south of what remained of the Empire, near the weapons caches from before the Massacre. Minneska, by contrast, was close to the northwestern border, and San Fraesco was further west still, at the very edge, bordered by the ocean.

Perhaps she was foolish to be concerned. Though recent intelligence indicated that the largest enemy settlement, the Commonwealth of Ashes, was growing in size and power, it did not yet pose a credible threat. And rogue exiles—those who had been cast out of a Commonwealth for sinning—did roam the Borderlands, but they rarely ventured this far west. Besides, Dev's father had been raised in San Fraesco; he knew the way well. Their trip was an adventure, an opportunity for trade, and a homecoming of sorts. Nothing should have gone wrong.

But then where were they?

As a fourth day passed, and then a fifth, Cordelia could no longer concentrate. She knew she was supposed to be telling Dev goodbye—but how could she do that, if she never saw him again? What if that time on the bridge, when she hadn't even let him say whatever he had in mind, was the last chance she'd ever get to speak to him?

She tried to talk to Gertrud about it, but her tutor dismissed her worries. Gertrud had made it clear that as far as she was concerned, Dev was a distraction from Cordelia's purpose, a frivolity that was to be tolerated because of her status—and because, for some reason, the Council of Nine had turned a blind eye to their capers. If he were to vanish, that would be unfortunate—but perhaps it would be for the best. He and his family were beneath Cordelia, and not worth her time. The way Gertrud's scent changed whenever Cordelia mentioned his name, tinged with the faint, acrid aroma of anger, told Cordelia everything she needed to know. It didn't matter what had happened to Dev; Gertrud couldn't care less, and was irritated that Cordelia would devote so much valuable time to thinking about it.

Gertrud's indifference inflamed Cordelia, especially because she was sure the Council shared it. No one cared what had befallen Dev and his family—mere shopkeepers who might've met with an unfortunate accident. They were unimportant, irrelevant—to everyone except Cordelia.

Asta was as disturbed as Cordelia was—though for a different reason. Dev was *hers*, part of her pack. Now he was missing, and the wolf wanted to leave Vik and find him, so the pack could be whole again. It was a constant discordant note playing in the back of Cordelia's mind, where her wolf shared thoughts with her own.

Her distraction didn't go unnoticed. Gertrud was becoming more and more aggravated with her; on several occasions, Cordelia had tried to shift during simulated battle conditions, with several of the guards charging at her, pretending to be the enemy, and failed. Even Janus, sworn to obey Cordelia in all things and bound to her very soul, was beginning to look annoyed.

These people are yours to protect, Cordelia thought miserably. *Just as Dev is. And you've let all of them down. You're ruining everything.*

On the morning of the seventh day after Dev was supposed to have returned, Cordelia was in the House of Echoes' training room, Gertrud's icy blue gaze fixed on her as she knelt on the wooden floor next to Janus. The crimson curtains were flung wide and the windows were cracked open, letting a fresh spring breeze blow through the room. It ruffled Janus's black hair, which he'd tied back with a rawhide band, and carried with it the scent of basil and mint, from the culinary gardens. Normally, this would've made Cordelia happy; spring was her favorite season, and Mrs. Adelman made the most delicious mint ice cream, something to look forward to after training was done.

But Mrs. Adelman wasn't here, and the scent of the mint just made Cordelia sad—and more worried than ever. It reminded her of everything that was wrong.

Today's lesson was about transforming a single part of her body at will—staying in human form while shifting her hand into a paw or forcing her canines to elongate, the way they did when she took Asta's shape. As he always did, Janus knelt to her left, guarding the side that would be her weaker one in her human body. Cordelia closed her eyes, centering herself, as he spoke the words of the ritual that anchored her shift—*I am your familiar. No harm will come to you while I am here.*

The words felt like a mockery. Why was she worthy of such protection when Dev was not?

Pushing the thoughts from her mind with an effort, she reached down, down, down into herself, calling on Asta—but the wolf just lifted her great head, her eyes glowing amber in the dark hollow of Cordelia's self, and refused to rise. Cordelia could hear Asta's thoughts, not nearly as articulate as her own human speech, but clear enough: *Waste of time. Useless. Must find Dev.*

I can't, Cordelia thought, miserable. *I'm not allowed to leave Vik, not without an escort—and no one would let me risk myself for him. I have to wait.*

The wolf growled, baring her teeth. When she spoke again, her sentences were less clipped, but just as pointed. *You have abandoned your pack. You are a poor excuse for an alpha.*

The accusation stabbed deep, and Cordelia caught her breath. What would happen if Asta turned on her? She'd never heard of such a thing—a skúma at odds with themselves. Would they tear each other to pieces?

Maybe she and Asta weren't at odds after all, though— because in her heart, Cordelia knew going after Dev was what she wanted. She just wasn't brave enough to do it.

But maybe she could be. Maybe she *should* be. Because if their roles were reversed, Dev would never use convention as an excuse. He would do whatever he could to find her, even if it meant incurring the wrath of his parents, the Council, and the many-headed gods.

Maybe she ought to—

"Cordelia!" Gertrud snapped. She grabbed Cordelia by the shoulder, her fingers digging in. Gertrud had an iron grip, and Cordelia had to fight not to wince. "Where are you? How many times have I told you that your training has to come first—that when you're here, you need to put all else from your head?" She shook Cordelia. "You're wasting my time and Janus's. Pull yourself together at once."

Ashamed, Cordelia bowed her head. "Yes, Gertrud."

Her tutor's silvering hair had come loose from its bun; with a series of harsh, jerky gestures, she pinned it up again. "Your behavior reflects poorly on all of us. You know I have to give the Council weekly reports on your progress—and you're far from the only skúma I train. Layla and Riley don't act this way, coasting on their charm, thinking they can bend people to their will with a smile. They're focused on their studies, devoted. Why are you the only one?"

Cordelia gritted her teeth. She hated being compared to the other two skúma in Vik who were close to her age; the rest were adults. Gertrud was always going on about *Layla this* and *Riley that*. It was all *Layla managed to shift in midair while three guards were charging at her* and *Riley shifted into wolf form three times in a single day, and he wasn't even tired*. For Cordelia, she had only harsh words and criticism…as if wanting there to be more to life than training, or liking people and wanting to be liked in return, were grievous faults.

Gertrud was glaring at her, arms folded across her chest, and Cordelia squared her shoulders, resigned. "I'm sorry," she said. "I'll do better. I—"

Her words stuck in her throat—because the wind had gusted once again, stirring the crimson curtains, and this time it brought with it the unmistakable scent of blood. *Dev*, she thought, her heart picking up speed.

Gertrud wasn't a skúma; her sense of smell wasn't heightened, the way Cordelia's was. She stared down at Cordelia, looking more peeved than ever. "You *what?*" she said. "At least finish your sentences."

But Cordelia ignored her. She shot to her feet, head tilted back, sniffing the air for all she was worth. The House of Echoes was high up on a hill, a white stone edifice set back from the City Road, but a moment later she heard it just the same: a commotion, drawing ever closer, along with the scent of old, dried blood. She could hear voices, raised in shock and horror—and soon Gertrud heard them too. Her tutor's eyes narrowed, fixing on Cordelia and Janus.

"Stay here," she said. "I'll go and figure out what's—"

But Cordelia didn't give her the chance to finish. Summoning the preternatural speed that skúma could possess even while in human form, she charged past her tutor, wrenching the door to the training room open so hard, it smacked into the wall, denting it. Plaster dust settled onto the wooden boards, making Cordelia cough as she ran down the hallway, following the noise and the scent of blood. Perhaps exasperated by Cordelia's defiance, Gertrud didn't follow.

She dashed down the winding staircase to the second floor, where she found a cluster of guards and eight of the nine Council members outside the tall, carved mahogany doors that led to the Great Hall. Dev was nowhere to be seen—but this had something to do with him. She knew it. She *felt* it.

Putting her shoulders back and summoning her best regal air, she approached the closest guard—Kinsley, she believed the woman's name was. There were many guards, and it was easy for them to seem interchangeable; but a good royal always knew their underlings by name. Cordelia had implemented tricks to help herself remember; Kinsley was distinctive for her intricate braided hairstyles, which Cordelia would have loved to learn. She was also stern, and rarely smiled. Still, right now Kinsley stood apart from the rest, and might be Cordelia's best shot at discovering what had happened, before the Council members noticed she was here.

"Pardon me," she said, drawing on all her training to keep her voice level. "What seems to be the trouble?"

Kinsley was tall—at least six feet—and heavily armed. Still, Cordelia was not intimidated. The woman served her, as she served all of the other skúma who'd sworn fealty to House Minneska. She lifted her chin as the guard looked down at her.

"We're sorry to have troubled you. This is none of your concern, skúma Cordelia," Kinsley said. "Simply a bit of an unfortunate incident. Your safety is in no way in question."

Cordelia drew herself up. "I am not concerned about my safety," she said, her voice cold. "Nor do I believe it is your place to determine what may or may not concern me. Who is behind those doors?"

Kinsley dropped her eyes in a gesture of deference. "It's just a boy," she said, her gaze fixed on the wooden floorboards. "And a silent one, at that. He won't speak to anyone. So you see, there is little you can do."

Cordelia stared at her, trying to discern what Kinsley wasn't saying. Surely the guard wouldn't continue to defy her in this way unless someone else had told her to do so—and the only people who would dare to set rules for Cordelia's behavior sat on the Council. Fear flooded through her, metallic on her tongue. Was whatever lay behind those doors so terrible that the Councilors had forbidden her to see it? What had happened to Dev?—for she knew it was him, as surely as she knew her own name.

She stepped closer to the guard, allowing her wolfish side to show in a way she rarely did in human form; it signified a lack of control, something that was anathema to skúma. Such a thing could mean the difference between life and death—hers, or the people around her. Still, this time she made no effort to hide the inhuman way her lips pulled back from her teeth, or the way she sniffed the air in front of Kinsley. "You," she said, the words edged with a growl, "taste like a lie."

Kinsley might be far larger than Cordelia, but she knew what that growl meant. Her eyes flicked toward the crowd of Council members who were clustered in front of the doors, confirming Cordelia's suspicions that the guard wasn't acting of her own volition. Asta stirred, prowling closer to the surface, infuriated that anyone had the gall to stand between her and a member of her pack.

"Move," Cordelia commanded Kinsley, letting the wolf's growl fill her voice. She didn't say the rest, but she didn't have to. The implications were clear enough: *Or bleed.*

Kinsley stepped aside.

Cordelia strode past, her goal the double doors that led to the Hall, telling Asta to bide—that they'd need to make it past the Council first. Her wolf growled a challenge, but Cordelia ignored it. She was in charge, not her animal half. *This is not the time for stealth or violence,* she told Asta. *This is the time for reason and charm. Let me speak.*

Inside her, the wolf settled back on its haunches. It would wait —but it wasn't happy about it. That was just fine; Cordelia wasn't happy, either.

She came to a stop in front of the Council members, all of whom had stopped their chattering and turned to regard Cordelia with identical expressions that hovered somewhere between exasperation and alarm. They must have just been in session; all of them wore their black, floor-length robes, emblazoned with crimson wolves. She scanned them quickly; the member who was missing was Councilor-in-Chief Huang. She must be inside the Hall, with Dev—assuming Dev was in there.

"Cordelia," Councilor Triesche said in greeting, her lips flattening into a thin line of disapproval. "This is no place for you."

Cordelia fought the urge to stamp her foot. *If I have ever had the power of persuasion,* she prayed to the gods, *let me have it now.*

"I smelled the blood. I heard the screaming," she said, offering her most affable smile. "I thought I could help."

"There's nothing you can do here." Councilor Triesche's eyes flicked to the double doors. "If anything, you might very well make it worse."

Inside Cordelia, Asta growled. She fought with everything she had not to let the sound trickle out of her lips; the last thing she needed was for the Councilors to think she was about to lose control of her wolf. Then they would never let her into the Hall.

"I am a skúmaskot," she said, meeting Councilor Triesche's flat gaze. "One day, I will take my seat at the table inside that Hall. Any security threats to House Minneska—any dangers to the citizens of Vik—are my business. I swore fealty to protect us all; how can I do that if you won't show me what's behind those doors?"

Councilor Rugge stepped up next to Triesche. A terrible accident had befallen him in his youth, paralyzing the left side of his face, so that only the right side moved when he spoke. Cordelia had always found it disorienting. "Child," he said, placing a heavy hand on her shoulder. "What is in that room is no threat to you."

The half of his face that could demonstrate his expression drooped with sadness. Cordelia could feel it rolling off him in waves; it had a distinct smell, blue-tinged and sour. At the scent of it, she broke.

"I know it's Dev in there," she said, her tone pleading. "Please, Councilor Rugge. Is he all right? What aren't you telling me?"

He shook his head, and inside her, Asta growled again. *Is now the time for violence, young one? He is* vox nihili, *the voice of nothing. He is the wind outside our cave, and nothing more. Go around him or through him; it matters not.*

For once, Asta's voice and hers were indistinguishable; they both wanted the same thing. Cordelia readied herself to leap, to slip past the Councilors before they could grab her. Whatever the price for such disrespect might be, she would pay it.

But before she could take a step, the double doors to the Hall opened, and Councilor-in-Chief Huang stepped out. She looked exhausted, in a way that had nothing to do with lack of sleep and everything to do with seeing something she couldn't unsee. "Cordelia," she said, her voice heavy with sorrow.

To the many-headed gods with charm; Cordelia would beg if it meant she wouldn't have to fight her way past the entire Council of Nine. "Please, Councilor Huang," she said, keeping her voice humble. "It's Dev, isn't it? Please let me see him."

Councilor Trieste gave a snort of irritation. "I told her it wasn't appropriate—" she began.

But Councilor-in-Chief Huang shook her head, her short hair shining blue-black in the flickering light of the torches that lined the walls. "Let the girl go in," she said. "He won't speak to anyone else. Perhaps he will talk to her, as they're friends. But Cordelia—"

Whatever warning Councilor Huang had meant to give was lost as Cordelia leapt past her, throwing the doors open and stepping through into the antechamber. She grasped the knob of the door that led to the Great Hall, engraved with the wolf that was the symbol of House Minneska, and flung it wide open. And then she froze.

CHAPTER THREE

Cordelia knew this room well; this was where the Council met, where she'd made the decision to take Janus as her familiar. Though she was still too young to sit in on strategy meetings, she knew which seat at the huge wooden table would be hers, when she was sixteen and of age. She'd thought about it often—what it would be like to have a voice in the decisions the Council made to take down the Commonwealths one day, to restore the Houses and the skúma to their proper seat of power.

The Hall was massive, the wooden ceiling arching high above and the white stone floor sparkling in the sunlight that streamed through the windows. It was a beautiful room, meant for grand things, and usually when Cordelia was inside it, it was filled with people. But today, she didn't see anyone at all—not even Dev.

She drew a breath through her nose, sampling the air. She couldn't see him—but she could smell him. The problem was, he smelled all wrong.

The rust-coated scent of blood, the one that she'd detected in the training room, was far stronger here. But it didn't smell fresh. It smelled...old.

The doors to the Hall snicked shut behind her and Cordelia stood still, letting Asta come forward—not to shift, but to heighten her senses. She closed her eyes, and the wolf guided her around the table and to the darkest corner, lit only by the flames of the logs that crackled in the cavernous brick fireplace.

When she opened her eyes again, there, on the floor, his arms hugging his knees, sat Dev...only, it wasn't Dev at all. His reddish-brown curls had turned the uncompromised white of freshly fallen snow—in sharp contrast to the blood that had soaked into his clothes, dyeing them a uniform shade of deep burgundy. His feet were bare and grimed with dirt. And though he must know someone had come into the room, he didn't turn from the fire. In fact, he sat inches from the hearth, as if no matter how close he got, it wouldn't be enough to keep him warm—or, Cordelia thought with a sudden chill of her own, as if he was contemplating throwing himself into the flames.

What had *happened* to him?

She drew in breath to speak—though what she might say, she had no idea—but Dev got there first.

"You didn't say goodbye," he said, without turning.

His voice was cracked, as if he'd been screaming for a very, very long time. He didn't sound like Dev. Yet he'd known it was her, even without looking. So it had to be him, appearances notwithstanding.

The speech Cordelia had rehearsed twenty-seven times, about how they couldn't be friends anymore, how her duty compelled her to set childish things aside—all of it flew out of her head, as if it had never been there at all. In that instant, she saw it for what it was—a series of pitiful excuses, covering up the fear of what would become of her when she had to lose him. And so she'd prepared to push him away first, before it could hurt her too badly, so at least the choice would be her own.

She realized now how close she must have come to losing him, after all.

Cordelia fell to her knees on the floor beside Dev. She wanted to touch him, but he seemed somehow inviolate, like a wall had come down between them—and there was so much *blood.* "Dev," she said, her tone as gentle as she could make it. "What happened to you?"

He shuddered all over but didn't speak. Instead, he stared into the fire as if the answers might be found there, for both of them.

He looked into the flames so long and so hard that Cordelia looked, too. But all she saw were sparks and shadows. Finally she said, her voice so tentative, it didn't sound like hers at all, "Where are your parents, Dev? Is that—is the blood…theirs?"

At that, he jerked back from the fireplace and turned to look at her, full on. His face was pale above the bleached white of his hair. The two seemed the only unsullied parts of his body, like he'd managed to rinse them clean after whatever had befallen the rest of him…as if he'd washed the color right out of his curls.

"In a manner of speaking," he said in that same creaky voice. "But if you mean literally—no. It's not."

Cordelia gulped. "Then…whose?"

He told her then, in fits and starts—his hands clenching his knees so tightly that the blood flaked off his pants, drifting to rest on the floor, where it settled in silent, mute contrast to the ivory stone. How they'd never made it to San Fraesco at all. How, halfway there, a band of Commonwealth exiles had come upon their camp one night, raving about evildoers and sinners whose souls must be sacrificed. How he had stepped into the woods to relieve himself before they came, returning just in time to see the exiles boil out of the trees, guns in their hands and wildness in their eyes. How they had shot first his mother and then his father while the two begged for their lives, laughing with a terrible satisfaction as they pulled the trigger.

The Commonwealth of Ashes will welcome us back as heroes, one of them had said, spitting on Dev's mother's corpse. *As warriors for the cause of righteousness. And we shall be part of the fold once more.*

Cordelia listened with a growing sense of unreality, bracketed by a horror so cold, it sank into her very bones. No wonder Dev was sitting so close to the fire. "They didn't see you?" she whispered.

Grimly, he shook his head. "No. I hid in the woods like a coward and watched them kill my parents. I…I let them die."

Cordelia wanted to shake *him*. "You're not responsible for what happened, Dev. What could you have done? If you'd gone into the campsite, they would've killed you, too."

"Maybe they should have." His voice was raw.

Her heart ached for him. "How can you say such a thing?"

"Because, Cordelia. I just—I can't—" He cleared his throat, clasping his knees even tighter—as if the gesture was holding his soul together, as well as his body. "It doesn't matter. I got away. I watched. I hid. And the next night—when they sheltered at our campsite after gorging themselves on our food—I disarmed and killed their sentry, took his gun, and shot the rest to death while they slept."

His tone was emotionless—and when his eyes met hers, there was nothing in them but a vast, yawning emptiness. Her kind, gentle Dev had vanished, all of his laughter gone—as if it had been burnt up in a fire, and the bitter ashes were all that was left. He was a stranger.

It was Cordelia's turn to shudder. "You…you killed all of them, Dev? But—how?"

"I don't know." He gave a listless, one-shouldered shrug. "Perhaps because I didn't care what happened to me…if I might die, too. It made no difference. I suppose you can do almost anything, if you have nothing to lose."

"But you did have something to lose," Cordelia said, before she could stop herself. "You had me. I know that's not much—or enough—but I worried every single day when you didn't come back. And I—by the gods, Dev, I am so sorry."

The words were pebbles, tossed into an infinite ocean of despair—but she didn't know what else she had to give him. Plump, kind Mrs. Adelman, with her scent of sugar and fried dough; soft-spoken Mr. Adelman, who always put out small, shiny gifts for the crows that visited the family's terrace…it seemed impossible that they were gone, much less that Dev had lost them in such a horrific way. Rage bubbled up inside her on their behalf—hers, and her wolf's.

He was staring at her, his eyes an illimitable blue, dark in his pale face. "I know," he said in his hoarse croak. "I...look."

His fingers moved to the collar of his shirt, undoing one button at a time. The stiff material fell away, and in the firelight, the silver of the wolf charm she had given him gleamed.

"After I killed them all," he said, "I found a stream. I knelt there and washed my hands and face over and over again, until the sun rose. And when it did—I could see my reflection in the water. All of my hair had turned white."

He lifted an unselfconscious hand to touch his curls, his fingers floating upward, like kelp in the darkness of the room. "Our horses were long gone. The bastards had eaten almost all the food. Whatever they hadn't destroyed was soaked in blood— theirs, and my parents'. I wanted to lie down and die along with them. Only two things stopped me—and one of them was you."

His hand moved to the charm again, gripping it so tightly, Cordelia was afraid he might rip it from its chain. "I knew you were here, waiting for me," he said. "Even though you hadn't said goodbye. I kept thinking of the stories I'd told you about San Fraesco—the plums and mulberries, the gold and the ships. I thought of how I'd promised to bring you a gift, and how disappointed you'd be that I couldn't."

Cordelia felt everything inside herself plummet. "Oh, Dev, no." More than anything, she wanted to wrap her arms around him...but he still seemed to be enclosed by that invisible barrier, the one that kept the world—and *her*—at bay.

"But then," he went on doggedly, as if she hadn't spoken, "I thought that I could give you a gift, after all. I could come home to you, even if I am a monster and a killer. I could tell you about the dangers that lie beyond our gates, the ones I've seen with my own eyes. And I could give you the ammunition you need to unite the Houses once and for all, to bring the Commonwealths down."

The flames rose and crackled in the fireplace as he met her

eyes dead-on. She shifted under the weight of his gaze. "You're not a monster, Dev. You're not a murderer."

"Sure I am," he said in that same indifferent tone. "I did what I had to do; that doesn't change its nature. My hands may look clean to you, but whenever I look at them, I see nothing but blood. The boy I was when I left here…that boy is dead."

"That's what you meant," she said, the realization breaking over her. "About the other thing that stopped you from lying down in the woods and dying along with them. You want revenge."

He inclined his head in the slightest of nods. "I killed them, Cordelia—but it's not like cutting down a tree. Those men—they're nothing but weeds. They'll spring right back up again, and a dozen more like them. The Commonwealth made them—made them and spit them out and set them on our trail. And they'll just keep coming." His upper lip rose in a sneer.

"I know I'm not—not the Dev who was your friend anymore. Maybe you can't stand the sight of me. But Cor." The emptiness was gone; in its place was a dark, desperate tone she'd never heard from Dev before. "You have to help me."

"I'll do anything," she vowed roughly. It was the simple truth.

"You have power here. I have none. Make them understand my parents' deaths mattered—make them *see*—" His voice broke. "I know you don't always like…what you are. But there's something about you—a certain charm—"

He caught at her sleeve when she tried to turn away. "You bewitch people, Cordelia. And not because of what you can do. Because of who you are, on the inside. The people who leap to do your bidding—do you see them doing the same for Layla or Riley? They do what Layla and Riley say because of the chain of command. But you—people *want* to do what you ask, Cor."

She bit her lip, bewildered. Could that be true? What had Gertrud said earlier—*Layla and Riley don't act this way, coasting on their charm, thinking they can bend people to their will with a smile.* Was it possible this was what she'd meant?

"I—do you think so?" she said. "Is that why you like me?"

For a moment, she saw a flash of the old Dev, a hint of his mischievous grin in the curve of his lips. "I like you because you're *you*. You're smart and fun and kind and so much more than what you let most people see. But as for the rest of it—why do you think my Imma always insisted on giving you the freshest batch of cherry puff pastries?"

The smile had faded; his voice broke on his mother's name. "Never mind my Imma. Why do you think the Council let you spend so much time with me, when you should've been training or doing a thousand other things that befit a skúma, rather than passing your free time with a baker's son?" He leaned forward, his eyes intent on her face. "You've got a way about you, Cordelia. When you speak, people listen. And if you study harder than anyone else, work harder—if you become the most powerful skúma of House Minneska—no one will be able to deny you."

Cordelia thought about what he was asking her to do: convince the Council to wage war *now*, not after they'd had time to rebuild their numbers or when the Commonwealths posed a larger threat. It seemed an insurmountable task for a twelve-year-old girl.

"What makes you think I'll have to persuade them?" she said in desperation. "Councilor-in-Chief Huang said you wouldn't talk to her—that you wouldn't speak to anyone. I could call them in here right now—maybe if you told them what you just told me, they would decide on their own—"

The cynical look he gave her was chilling. It belonged to a much older person—not Dev, who was always smiling, who always saw the best in people. "And you accuse *me* of flights of fancy," he said. "Come on, Cordelia. We both know the truth. People like you matter. If it had been a member of the Council, or a familiar, or—gods forfend—a skúma who'd been killed, they'd declare war tomorrow. But my parents and me...we're not important. Not like you are."

Uncomfortable at the turn the conversation had taken,

Cordelia shifted her weight. She and Dev had never discussed such things directly before. It occurred to her that maybe he had spoken so much about realms that only existed in his imagination because the truth was too painful to bear.

"Dev," she said at last, "I'm only twelve."

"I know." He raised his eyebrows. "But you won't be twelve forever."

Cordelia let out a long, troubled sigh. Her wolf wanted this—to fight for the Adelmans' honor, to give Dev what he needed. And so often, when it came to matters of the heart rather than the head, Asta was right. But this…it was an undertaking beyond anything Cordelia had ever dreamed.

"Please," Dev said in a quiet voice. "You said you would do anything. This is *anything*, Cordelia. The only thing. Please. For me."

Cordelia felt the weight of her destiny settling onto her shoulders, a mantle she had no choice but to bear. She had let Dev down once. She would not fail him again.

Straightening her spine, she drew a deep breath. "All right," she said. "I promise."

At her words, his jaw set, and a fierce light came into his eyes. "Swear it to me. On your honor as a skúma of House Minneska."

"I'll swear it on something that matters more to me. I will swear it on my grief for your family, and on the years of our friendship." She swallowed hard, then reached out and took his hand. He tensed, but didn't pull away. Instead, his fingers twined with hers, cold as ice against her heat; skúma's body temperatures always ran higher than the norm.

She looked down at their joined hands—light and dark, frost and fire. And then up again, straight into Dev's midnight-blue eyes. When she spoke, her voice was low, and limned with her wolf's growl. "I swore my fealty to House Minneska once," she said. "And meant it with all my heart. But now I swear it to you, Dev Adelman. I give you my teeth and my claws and my strength. I give you the power that runs in my veins and the loyalty that my words command. I give you my word that I will avenge what was done to your parents, or die trying."

Something broke in Dev then—the reserve that had held him apart from her, that had kept him together as he watched his parents die, killed their murderers, and then found his way home to Vik, blood-soaked and alone. She saw it shatter in his eyes, like ice breaking on the surface of a lake, revealing the untold depths beneath. A tear trickled down his cheek, followed quickly by another.

Her heart aching, Cordelia reached out and pulled him close. She could feel his chest heaving against her, smell the salt of his tears as they soaked her shirt, but he didn't make a sound.

She wanted to tell him that it would be all right, somehow—that she would make it so—but that would have been a lie. Instead she just held him as he cried. Far away, the double doors to the Hall opened and then thudded shut—Council members spying on them, to see if Cordelia had done what they could not. She ignored them, and soon they went away again.

At long last, Dev stilled in her arms. He pulled back, and she let him go—but instead of sliding away from her, he lifted his hand to touch her face. "You're all I have left," he whispered fiercely. "But you *are* enough."

The words struck her with the force of a blow. Her eyes on his, she reached out to touch him in a way she'd never dared to before, smoothing the damp waves back from his forehead, where they were pasted by sweat and tears. She'd always loved his chestnut curls—but there was something about his strange, bone-white hair that drew her to him: as if he'd been indelibly marked by what had happened to him, what he'd seen and what he'd done. As if, no matter what anyone said, they couldn't deny the horror of what had befallen him.

She slid her hand lower, cupping the nape of his neck. Her fingers tangled in the fine tendrils that curled there—so soft, and as silky as she'd imagined.

Dev sucked in his breath. "Cor, what are you—"

"Shhh," she told him. "Close your eyes."

She felt him tremble. But he obeyed as she tugged him closer and pressed her lips to his, sealing the promise she'd made.

She had thought their first kiss might taste like cherries and sugar. But instead, it was redolent of salt and blood, and the bitter ashes of an inferno whose flames would one day be rekindled to seek revenge.

WRATH

"A HEART OF DUST AND DREAMS"

CHAPTER ONE

I t was a beautiful day, and Cordelia Navarro, shapeshifter royalty and skúmaskot of House Minneska, had finally convinced her government to start a war.

Four years had passed since her best friend, Dev Adelman, had found his way home after killing the Commonwealth exiles who'd slaughtered his parents—covered in blood, his hair snow-white, and refusing to speak to anyone but Cordelia. What he'd told her had chilled her to the core. It had broken her heart to think about the Adelmans enduring such brutality, and shattered her further to think about Dev—only twelve years old then, just like Cordelia—visiting death on their killers in return. Cordelia was the one in training to be a warrior, not Dev, who couldn't stand to see anything suffer. He'd once rescued a butterfly with a bent wing and brought it flowers every day so it could sip their nectar, like a tiny insectoid buffet.

Dev's parents had been bakers, kind, generous people who never hesitated to feed the hungry or make Cordelia her favorite treats—puff pastries stuffed full of the cherries that hung heavy on the trees in Minneska's orchard. Motherless and raised by a succession of nannies, Cordelia had always gravitated toward Mrs. Adelman. Her shapeshifting tutor, Gertrud, had frowned on this—as well as on her friendship with Dev, who was of a far lower social class—but the Council of Nine, Minneska's ruling body, had given Cordelia tacit permission to spend as much of her free time with the Adelmans as she liked. Dev said this was because Cordelia had the gift of persuasion, charming people into doing whatever she wanted…and maybe it was true, because although it had taken four years of effort and scheming, she'd talked the Council into uniting the Houses and launching a war against the Commonwealths at long last.

The war had been a long time coming—the Commonwealths and the four Houses had an extensive, troubled history—but instigating it now had been Dev's idea. When he'd come home that awful day, he'd begged Cordelia to help him, desperate for revenge against the institution that had given rise to his parents' murderers. And although she had doubts about what a twelve-year-old girl—even a skúma like herself—could convince the Council to do, she'd agreed. She would have done anything to stop the trembling that consumed Dev's whole body and erase the vacant look from his eyes.

Four years later, both of them had changed so much. Dev had gone from being a practical joker who helped out in his parents' bakery to a grim-faced royal guard well-known for his deadly aim and his allegiance to the cause. And Cordelia, who had adored spending time with Dev in part because his stories and antics provided a distraction from her responsibilities, had devoted herself to becoming the most powerful shapeshifter in the four Houses, just like she'd promised Dev she would. She trained relentlessly, stopping only when her wolf refused to rise and her familiar, Janus, was too exhausted to continue—a state to which she had to pay close attention, since Janus was bound to her and had no choice but to do her bidding. It was her job to ensure his well-being, to make sure she didn't abuse his trust in her.

Whenever visiting dignitaries from the other Houses—Satrizona, Montyorke, and San Fraesco—spent time in Vik, Minneska's capital city and the seat of the Council, Cordelia made it her business to get to know them, planting seeds about the necessity of reclaiming the Houses' role as rulers of the Empire. She plied them with fiery ákavíti and then, when they were lost in drink, told them the tale of Dev's parents—playing up their role as martyrs and Dev's as a peasant defender of the Houses' ideals. And then she gestured to Dev himself, clad in the crimson-and-black uniform of Minneska's guards, poised at the door of whatever tavern she'd brought them to—because a skúma never went anywhere undefended, even inside the city that was their stronghold. *Look at his white hair,* she told them. *When he came home, it was the only part of his body that wasn't bathed in blood.*

Since his return from the trip to House San Fraesco that had resulted in his parents' deaths, Dev hadn't liked to be looked at much—not like before, when he was always telling stories and showing off to make Cordelia laugh. But for this, he made an exception. He and Cordelia had made a deal, and this was his end of it. He would make his outward damage visible, in return for what such a thing could do to convince the Council that the Houses should unite and bring the Commonwealths down. So Cordelia always requested him as a guard when visiting emissaries came to Vik, and he allowed himself to be her show pony.

Dev had begun his guard training soon after he'd come home. He'd stayed in the guards' quarters, since he had no other family and nowhere else to go, and they'd begun teaching him how to care for weapons and fight hand-to-hand. Now, like Cordelia, he trained daily—but where she focused on controlling Asta, the wolf that lived inside her, he worked hard to hone his body, making it just as much of a weapon as his firearm. He'd grown tall and lean, unrecognizable as the boy who'd once brought her pastries and told ridiculous jokes. Yet Cordelia still found him beautiful—though it was an acerbic, remote beauty. His facility with words hadn't diminished, but they were often laced with scorn. Even his occasional smiles were tipped with venom.

At sixteen, she had just two years left before the Council

would expect her to marry—most likely Riley, the male wolf of House Minneska who was a year older than she. Cordelia didn't love him, but skúma married for breeding and political gain, so she didn't expect to. Besides, since she was twelve years old, there'd only been room in her heart for one boy. And though Dev wasn't the same as he'd been before, she knew why this was, and still loved him on a soul-deep level she couldn't erase.

They'd kissed just once—the day Dev had come home. A relationship between the two of them would've been considered unseemly, but Cordelia wasn't sure that was what held Dev back. He didn't usually turn his scornful tongue on her...even though part of her wished he would, since at least that would be expressing *something*. Instead, he was polite to her, distant—as if he feared offending her or overstepping his bounds. For the life of her, Cordelia couldn't understand why he would feel this way. All those years ago, *she* was the one who'd kissed *him*.

Their pact to start the war was, of course, a secret—so each week they met on the bridge that had been their favorite childhood haunt. While the river roared below, Cordelia told him of her progress—which Council member she thought was bending to her will, which foreign dignitary she thought she'd persuaded to their side. Dev would listen, his head bent toward hers to make out her voice over the splash of the water and the gusts of the wind—but on the rare occasions when his fingers grazed hers, he'd pull away as if her touch had burned him. It hurt Cordelia's feelings, but she was too prideful to ask him what was wrong.

This was different, though. Today the Council had unveiled the draft of a formal declaration of war, with stipulations and a timeline. It would take months, if not years, to put their strategy into effect—there were so many moving pieces—but the confrontation they'd fought for was coming, and Cordelia couldn't wait to tell Dev about it.

There was just one problem—she couldn't find him.

It was Dev's day off, and he wasn't in the guards' quarters.

Nor was he on the bridge, in the horses' barn, or at any of the taverns that studded the City Road. As night fell, Cordelia became increasingly frustrated. Here she was, with fabulous news to tell him, and he was nowhere to be seen. Even Asta couldn't scent him.

But then, as she sat at the edge of her bed in the House of Echoes, disentangling her hair from its braid and brushing it out, the realization came to her, with the force of a physical blow.

Today was the anniversary of Dev's parents' deaths.

How could she have forgotten? She'd been so wrapped up in her good news that she hadn't even stopped to think about what day it was. Dev was somewhere, miserable and hurting, and all she'd been preoccupied with was herself.

She had to find him.

Hurriedly, Cordelia dressed, pulling on the most unobtrusive clothes she owned: dark linen pants, a black tunic, and a hooded cloak. She slid her feet into her shoes and then made her way to the window, easing it up. She'd have to climb down the trellis; there were guards stationed outside her door, and if she told them what she planned to do, they'd insist on accompanying her.

Cordelia hadn't snuck out at night like this since she was a child, meeting Dev in Vik's Shadow District on a dare. Then, they'd been young and curious about the debauchery for which the district was famous. Now, Cordelia was afraid of what she'd find—because she was sure that was where Dev had gone. She would have picked up his scent trail anywhere else; she'd canvassed the rest of the city.

Leaning out of the window to make sure no one stood beneath it, she braced herself on the sill and then swung her leg over, finding the edge of the rose-covered trellis beneath it. The climbing roses covered the side of the House of Echoes on which Cordelia's room was situated, scarlet and studded with thorns. She didn't relish the thought of encountering them—but her window was on the fifth floor, too high for even the wolf inside her to jump.

When she and Dev were children and she'd climbed down the trellis, she'd stolen gloves from the gardeners to protect her fingers, lest her nannies or Gertrud ask her why they were pricked and scratched. Tonight, she had no such protection; but she was sixteen, old enough not to have to explain every choice she made.

Bracing herself not to cry out against the pain, she clambered down the trellis, relying on her wolf's superior sense of balance and her training to prevent her from falling. The scent of the roses billowed around her, cloying, and Asta shied away in protest. Her wolf relied heavily on its sense of smell; surrounded by the roses like this, Asta was nose-blind. It made the wolf uneasy.

Cordelia herself couldn't care less about the smell; however, she was less than thrilled about the numerous thorns that stabbed her hands as she made her way to the ground. By the time she was low enough to jump, clearing the white-bloomed serviceberry bushes planted at the base of the building and landing in the grass, blood ran down her palms in thin but steady tracks. Wiping her hands on her cloak in disgust, she set out in pursuit of her prey.

Once she got to the bottom of the hill on which the House of Echoes was situated, she gave Asta free rein within her body, telling the wolf to track Dev's scent. Even in human form, Cordelia could utilize some of the wolf's superior senses; it was an advantage in a fight, as well as in everyday situations such as this.

Before, she'd only picked up old trails—but this time, she had a better sense of where he might be. Sure enough, as she approached the border between the City Road and the Shadow District, her wolf scented him at once. Without hesitation, Asta led her toward Silber Street, where the pavement was uneven and ill-kept. Here were the less-than-reputable taverns and the dens of vice, where men could buy not only wine but women. Cordelia supposed women could purchase the favors of other women and men could buy those of men here as well; it was all the same to her, a mysterious, illicit practice of the night.

She felt ill to think of Dev in the District, drowning his misery in drink and hedonism. In years past, he had been too young for such things. Instead, he had spent this day locked in his room, admitting no one, engaging in a self-imposed isolation somewhere between grief and punishment. But at sixteen, the District would surely serve him; he was a guard, and well-known for his mercenary ways. She could not imagine that anyone would refuse to provide drink to a boy who had slaughtered five grown men at the age of twelve, and then returned home to become the best sharpshooter in the guards' ranks. And if he sought something more than simple inebriation—well, Dev was a handsome boy, if terrifying. Especially in the District, some sought that edge, and thought no further than the value of their customers' coin. Sickened by the thought, she quickened her step.

By the time Cordelia had made her way past the District's vintner, suspected to infuse their wine with more than mere grapes, the streets were lit only by the occasional flickering lamp —but that was no impediment to her. She could see just fine in the dark—and besides, Asta led her unerringly onward, past the clusters of ragged drunkards in alleyways and the women who teetered down the cracked pavement in heels so high, it was a wonder they didn't fall. She followed her wolf's nose past a small wooden building from which loud music emanated and crowds spilled, wrinkling her nostrils at the smell of rotting garbage and old sweat. Beneath it all she could smell Dev's salt-and-sage scent, stronger now. He was here, and she would find him.

The trail ended in front of a brick storefront with a small brass sign that hung from a post outside the door. 'The Shining Lady,' it read. Cordelia stilled, looking the establishment over; the wooden steps were rotting and dusted with several days' worth of pollen, and the windows hadn't been washed in such a long time, she could barely see inside. But Dev's trail stopped here, and when she bent to the steps on the pretense of tying her shoe, she could smell him even more strongly. He had lingered here. She stepped to the door and sniffed the knob; he'd touched it, and recently.

Cordelia tugged the hood of her cloak tight around her face, hiding her identity as best she could. Then, steeling herself, she wrenched open the door and stepped inside.

The tavern was dark, and smelled of sawdust and hopelessness. It was also empty, save for the proprietor—a woman with a prematurely lined face and gray-streaked brown hair, wiping down the bar with an acrid, lemon-scented spray—and Dev.

The moment Cordelia saw him, she realized she needn't have worried that he was taking his pleasure in the arms of a woman—or a man. He sat alone at a corner table, a tankard of ale in his hand, clad in the casual dark clothes he wore when not on guard duty. From the way he sprawled in his chair, the looseness of his limbs, Cordelia was sure it wasn't his first drink.

"Help you?" the bartender said, her gaze flicking to Cordelia.

Cordelia drew herself up and jerked her head toward Dev. "Thank you, but there's no need," she said, endeavoring to sound businesslike rather than dismissive. "I just came for him."

The woman sniffed. "He's trouble, that one," she said. "Take him, and welcome."

Inside her, the wolf bared its teeth; Dev was hers, and speaking of him in such a way was a punishable offense. But Cordelia told her wolf to settle. The two of them had no authority here, unless she chose to expose herself for who she was, and that would certainly be more trouble than it was worth. Instead she said simply, "I intend to."

The woman sniffed again, but didn't comment. Instead, she moved on to polishing another section of the bar, her face dour.

Cinching the hood of her cloak even more tightly, Cordelia made her way over to Dev. He looked up at her, blinking indolently—and then those midnight-blue eyes of his widened. "Cor," he said, focusing on her face. "You shouldn't be here."

Cordelia fought the desire to clout him over the head. "You don't say."

He glanced behind her. "Where's your entourage?" he said, his words slightly slurred.

"I snuck out," she said, more irritated than ever.

His lips twitched in the facsimile of a smile. "The fearsome and incomparable warrior Cordelia climbed out her window? For shame. What would your public think?"

She snorted. "I don't care. And besides, I could hardly walk out my front door."

"Touché." He reached for his ale, but she slid it out of reach.

"I think you've had enough," she said. "Besides, there's something I have to tell you."

He tilted his head. "Indeed. Something you can't impart at The Shining Lady? A dreadful secret? A shameful scandal?"

"An important bit of factual information," she said, tugging on his arm. "Get up, would you?"

Dev heaved a put-upon sigh. "I will not. This is a terrible day and I fully intend to sit here, becoming increasingly inebriated, until I forget that it—and I—exist." He grabbed for the ale again and was tilting the tankard to his lips when Cordelia intercepted it. Liquid splashed over the rim, and he turned a baleful gaze on her. "Thank you so much, O Mighty One. Now I'm *wet*."

It was a good thing the tavern was so empty, because Cordelia couldn't help the growl that bubbled up in her throat. Out of the corner of her eye, she saw the bartender, who was still polishing the counter, tilt her head in their direction—and small wonder. Inside her, Asta spoke. *We need to leave this place, young one.*

Cordelia was in total agreement. The very last thing she needed was for gossip about this incident to start spreading. Gritting her teeth, she bent over the table and hissed, "As your skúma and commander, I order you to rise."

She could see the tension warring within Dev—his desire to remain here, gulping ale and obliterating himself, versus his duty to obey her. Duty won, and he got to his feet, tossing coins on the table. "As you wish," he said, sarcasm weighting his voice. He made an elaborate gesture toward the door. "After you, milady."

Cordelia would never have tolerated such an attitude from anyone else—but Dev was her oldest friend. Hood pulled tight, she spun and stalked past the bartender, who was making an elaborate production of ignoring the two of them. Behind her, Dev followed, his footsteps thudding on the creaky boards.

The air outside was fresh and sweet after the fug of the tavern, and she took a deep breath, filling her lungs. When she turned, Dev was leaning against the brick wall of the Shining Lady, looking down at her. "Where to?" he said, his tone falsely jovial. "Would you care to convey this secret of yours in an alleyway? I know a rather convenient one."

It was Cordelia's turn to sigh. "I know what today is, Dev, and I'm sorry. I miss them, too. But could you drop the act?"

He shook himself all over, like a dog shedding water. When he spoke again, some of his old sincerity rang clear in his voice. "Fine. Whatever this intrigue is, Cordelia, can it wait? I'm not myself tonight, as you can plainly see. Tomorrow I promise to be all yours again."

That was a joke. Dev hadn't been hers for years, not in the way she wanted—the way he used to be. "It can't," she said, the words clipped to hide the hurt she felt. "But I also don't intend to have this discussion standing here. Come on."

Without waiting to see if he'd follow, she turned on her heel and went back the way she'd come, winding down the narrow streets of the Shadow District. She'd passed the vintner's shop and the storefront from which the pulsing music emanated before she heard his footsteps behind her. A minute later, he'd caught up to her and materialized by her side. "This had better be good," he said.

Cordelia didn't deign to reply. Instead she led him past a couple kissing against a lamppost and a small crowd of drunken revelers. A man in the latter group called, "Join us, pretty sweetheart," to Cordelia, and Dev turned on him with such an air of menace that he shrank back into the shadows, murmuring apologies.

"You shouldn't be here," he said to Cordelia again, as they swept past the crowd. "Far less, alone. It's not safe."

"I'm not alone," Cordelia retorted. "I have you."

His only response was a snort.

A minute later, they reached the juncture of Silber Street and the City Road. With an unmistakable sense of relief, Cordelia stepped from the uneven pavement onto the cobblestones. She could defend herself, of course—but she would vastly prefer not to have to do so, or to have Dev get into a brawl on her behalf.

He followed her through the streets without another word until they reached the bottom of the hill that led to the House of Echoes. When she began to climb it, though, he caught her arm. "Where are we going?"

"Home," she said simply.

Dev's eyes narrowed. "Have you decided not to tell me this spectacular secret of yours, after all? Or..." he regarded her, head tilted. "Do you even have a secret? Or was that all a ruse, to separate me from my ale?"

He looked so annoyed, she had to laugh. "No, Dev. You're coming home. With me. So we can talk in private, and not risk being overheard."

He murmured something in which she caught the word *private* and her name, but even with her superior hearing, Cordelia couldn't make the rest of it out. Before she could ask for a clarification, though, he squared his shoulders. "Fine, then," he said, with uncharacteristic brusqueness. "Lead the way."

Keeping to the shadows so as to avoid being seen by any guards who might note their approach, they made their way up the hill, toward the looming stone edifice. They didn't speak again until Cordelia veered to the right and brought them around the building, rather than to the imposing front doors.

Side by side, they stood in the grass, in front of the serviceberry shrubs, looking up at the trellis. In the dark, Cordelia could barely make out the clinging vines of the climbing roses, but she remembered their pricking thorns well enough.

Dev cleared his throat. "That's your room up there, Cordelia." With some surprise, she realized he sounded nervous.

Had he dissolved his common sense in drink? "Yes," she agreed, her voice pitched low to avoid detection. "It is."

"When you said we were coming here, I thought you meant —" He ran a hand through his hair. "Not this," he finished, staring up at her window as if too intimidated to look at her.

Did he imagine she'd dragged him here for some kind of planned seduction? Cordelia blushed at the thought. When she spoke, her voice was a harsh whisper. "Kindly remove your mind from the gutter, Dev. I have something important to tell you, and as I mentioned, I'd prefer to share it in the most private setting possible. My room provides us with that option."

His jaw shut with a snap. She could smell the embarrassment seeping from his pores, a scent she'd always thought of as purple-tinged and vaguely reminiscent of peonies. "I'm sorry, Cor," he said, sounding humble for the first time tonight. "Truly, I meant no offense."

"Apology accepted," she said, her tone brisk. "Now, before someone catches us out here, please stop speaking and start climbing."

For once, Dev obeyed, stepping over the serviceberry bushes and beginning to scale the trellis. She heard the indrawn hiss of his breath as the thorns pricked his skin, but he was a guard, trained to persevere through discomfort. He kept climbing upward, with her close on his heels. At last he hauled himself through her open window, tripped, and hit the floor with an undignified thump. Not anticipating this, Cordelia tried to avoid him, failed, and landed directly on top of his prone body.

His hands came up automatically to steady her, and, startled, she sucked in her breath. She hadn't been this close to Dev for years, since the day he'd come back to Vik—when she'd held him as he'd cried and then kissed him to seal her promise. His shoulders were far broader now, his chest and stomach muscular from training. He smelled of ale and sweat—but also of the salt-and-sage scent that was uniquely Dev's.

She shivered, and his arms tightened around her, holding her close. "Are you all right?" he said, his lips against her ear. She could feel his breath, warm on her skin. "Did I hurt you?"

Cordelia struggled to master herself. "I believe I should be asking you that question. As you see, I landed on top of you."

He lifted a lazy hand and brushed the hair back from her face. "That's true," he mused. "I'm unharmed, Cordelia. But thank you for your concern."

With her hair out of her eyes, she could see him clearly, even in the dimness of her room, illuminated only by firelight. His pupils were dilated, and she could smell the sharp, sweet scent of desire baking off his body. He wanted her, she realized. Maybe that was why he'd been so unnerved about coming to her room.

She'd thought about kissing Dev again ever since that day four years ago. But he'd been drinking. And the last thing *she* wanted was for both of them to do something they'd regret.

Hastily, she scrambled off him, putting her clothes to rights. He regarded her for a long moment, as if he was about to speak, but seemed to think better of it. Instead, rising to his feet, he looked around.

In all the years they'd known each other, Dev had never been inside her room; it wasn't proper. He turned in a circle, taking it in: her four-poster bed, covered in a crimson comforter emblazoned with a black satin wolf; the plush white rug that covered the polished floorboards; the high ceiling, with its exposed beams; the fire, still blazing high in the hearth.

"So this is where the lovely Cordelia sleeps," he said.

Cordelia parsed his words, sorting through them for a hint of sarcasm—but there was none. At a loss for how to respond, she undid the ties that held her cloak closed and hung it on a hook by her bed. "Yes," she said at last, trying to calm the pounding of her heart. "When I'm not chasing after you."

"In all fairness, I didn't know you were looking for me. But now you have me—and it's probably a good thing, too, or I would've woken up with a gods-forsaken headache in the morning." He gave her a one-shouldered shrug. "Since you've distracted me from my annual pity party, tell me what's so important that you were willing to sneak me into your inner sanctum—not that I'm not grateful for the privilege." His lips quirked in a wicked smile that reminded her of the old Dev.

Cordelia did her best to ignore how alluring he looked, standing in her bedroom with the firelight flickering behind him —a study in contrasts, with his pale skin, white hair, and dark clothes. Dismissing the memory of how it had felt to have him hold her close, how much she'd wanted to press her lips to his, she said the only thing that really mattered. "I finally convinced the Council."

She heard his heartbeat stutter. Then his pulse picked up speed. He stared at her, shock clear on his face. "What?"

"The Council," Cordelia repeated. "I persuaded them. They're sending emissaries to the other Houses tomorrow. I can't say when it will happen—but Dev...they've agreed. They'll declare war."

Dev gaped at her. He cleared his throat, once, then again. And finally he managed, his voice hoarse, "Are you sure?"

Cordelia nodded. "I saw the drafted declaration. And there've been other attacks outside the Houses' borders. A traveling party was killed just days ago—among them, a diplomat for House Satrizona. I think that tipped the scales."

His scent deepened, settling into something Cordelia didn't recognize. It reminded her of the hot, cinnamon-spiced cider she loved to drink each fall—familiar and comforting, but with a nip that never failed to surprise her. Perplexed, she peered more closely at him—but he just stood there, looking white and shocked, like a sculpture of the boy she knew.

"Dev?" she said at last. "Are you happy? This is what you wanted—what we've been working for—"

Her words seemed to jar him from his stupor. He crossed to

her, looking down at her with an expression that resembled wonder. But still he didn't speak.

"I kept my promise," she said, her voice trembling just a little. "And it seems fitting that this is the day our dreams should come to fruition. Maybe—maybe the gods hold your parents safe in their hands, and your mother and father can see that neither of us have forgotten them…that on this day of all days, the Council should decide to rise up and avenge what was done to them."

Dev just stared at her, speechless. Inside her, Asta paced, disconcerted. *We acted to protect the pack,* her wolf murmured. *In accordance with his wishes. This is a great achievement. Why doesn't he speak?*

Cordelia didn't know. Slowly, carefully, she lifted her hand and touched his face. "Dev," she said. "Tell me what you're thinking. Please."

At her touch, his eyes refocused. Cordelia could hear his heartbeat racing, faster and faster. "I feel like I'm dreaming. Any moment now, I'll wake, my head on the table in the Shining Lady and my empty mug of ale next to me, and discover that you never came to get me at all. But if I am—then I'm not going to waste this chance."

"You're not…" she began, but once he'd begun speaking, he couldn't seem to stop.

"You are so beautiful, Cordelia." Each syllable was distinct; he didn't sound drunk anymore. Perhaps the walk or the shock of her announcement had cleared his head. "I've never stopped thinking that. I think about it every day, as I stand by your side. I dream about it at night. Like I'm probably doing right now."

Cordelia's mouth fell open. Of all the things she'd expected Dev to say, this wasn't one of them.

"You're the only good thing left in my life," he said, sadness drifting across his face like a cloud obscuring the light of the moon. "The only thing that I haven't ruined—or that someone else hasn't ruined for me. And if a dream is the only place I can say that to you, then I'll say it, and propriety be damned. I don't care if I wake up in five minutes drenched in ice water that gods-forsaken bartender dumped on my head because I couldn't stop mumbling in my sleep. You've never given up on me."

"And I won't," Cordelia said, finding her voice. "Dev, I never will."

He rubbed his chest, as if her words hurt him. "I wish I understood why. But this is a dream, and so I suppose you'll only say what I want you to—what I wish you would, in my heart."

Cordelia's own heart hurt. She reached up and took him by the shoulders. "You're not dreaming."

"Of course, that's what you would say." He gave her a rueful smile.

"You're not," she insisted.

He raised his eyebrows, their chestnut color such an odd juxtaposition against the snow-white of his hair. "If I'm not dreaming, then kiss me. But only if you want to, Cordelia. Only if you—"

Whatever he was about to say was lost as Cordelia stood on her tiptoes and pulled him down to her. She held him close, hearing his heart pound in concert with hers, bathing in that apple-cider scent, spiked now with the heady bite of desire. And then she did what she'd wanted to do since she'd fallen through the window and landed on top of him. She kissed him.

His lips were as soft as she remembered. When he parted them, he tasted like ale and disbelief and Dev—an irresistible combination. Inside her, the wolf growled, *Mine*.

She allowed herself to run her fingers over the stubble that limned his cheekbones, feeling the rough rasp of it against his skin. Her eyes closed, she deepened their kiss, letting Asta come forward enough to nip at his lower lip—just enough to tease, not enough to hurt. A low sound escaped his throat then, but he held himself still, letting her do with him what she would.

Asta wanted to scent-mark him, to claim him the way Cordelia had years ago, when she'd given him the wolf-charm meant to keep him safe. But that was too much; he hadn't given permission for such a thing, even if he'd asked for her kiss. With an effort, Cordelia made herself step away. She felt the loss of him everywhere—in fingertips and wolf-self and heart.

Dev took a deep gulp of air, as if he'd forgotten to breathe. He peered down at her, his eyes glazed, like he was indeed sleepwalking. And Cordelia waited—for him to speak, to leave, to kiss her back.

He drew another shuddering breath. And then he whispered, "Neshama sheli," his fingers brushing her cheekbone, leaving trails of heat behind.

The words were Hebrew, the language of his ancestors. Long ago, when Cordelia had heard Dev's father say it to his mother, he'd told her what it meant: *my soul.* There were so few left who spoke it now; it almost felt like a secret language between her and Dev, a form of communication only they knew.

Cordelia didn't mourn the loss of her own parents. Her mother had died giving birth to her, and though her father still lived, he had little to do with her. In their absence, she had formed a new family, made of skúma and familiars. But Dev had no one, and so for him, she'd learned the language his ancestors used to speak.

"Ani ohevet otkha," she whispered back. *I love you.*

Dev's eyes widened, and for a moment she worried that she had gone too far. She opened her mouth to apologize, to tell him that he didn't have to say it back, but there was no need. His mouth was on hers, hot and hungry, and his fingers were tangled in her hair, and then he was carrying her down, onto the crimson-and-black comforter, and for a long time, they didn't speak at all.

CHAPTER TWO

TWO YEARS LATER

It had been two years since the Council agreed to declare war —two long and difficult years, filled with beauty and brutality in equal measure. Attacks on traveling parties between the Houses had intensified, and House Satrizona in particular had vacillated, saying that perhaps they'd be better off buttressing their fortresses rather than challenging the Commonwealths. If the settlements' exiles were such a threat, they argued, what might it be like to take on the Commonwealths directly, in the heart of their power?

Scouts had reported the strengthening of the Commonwealths' Bellatorum, warriors who took life without mercy and were well-trained in the art of hand-to-hand combat. The only advantage the Houses' guards had was that the bellators didn't use guns; the Commonwealths' High Priests and Executors had outlawed them. In the Commonwealths, citizens lived and died by the Seven Deadly Sins; wrath was forbidden, and Cordelia supposed that the impersonal nature of killing someone with a firearm fell into that category.

All four of the Houses were concerned, too, that the skúma hadn't recovered sufficiently from the Twilight Massacre two hundred years before, when the High Priests led a rebellion against the ruling skúma class, decimating their numbers. In the wake of that battle, the Commonwealths were formed and the Houses shattered, reduced to shells of their former selves. Two centuries later, they were still recovering, and risking the skúma in battle seemed terribly dangerous—but the Houses would need every advantage if they were to win, and the panthers of Satrizona, the falcons of Montyorke, and the wolves of Minneska were an undeniable force to reckon with.

As for the selkies of San Fraesco, they'd compensated for their lack of effectiveness during landlocked battles by becoming master strategists. Two representatives from each House sat on the Council—they elected the Councilor-in-Chief, whose position rotated between the Houses every ten years. San Fraesco's delegates had been instrumental in forming the strategy that would succeed in demolishing the Commonwealths at last and restoring the Houses to power.

Through it all, Cordelia had used her influence to persuade the Council that war was crucial to the Houses' survival, let alone their return to dominance. Every day, the Commonwealths grew stronger; she saw little point in waiting. Her mission might have had its origins in Dev's request, but she had been pursuing it for six years, and now, at eighteen, it had become her own. She was tired of fearing Commonwealth exiles, tired of worrying that the settlements themselves might rise up and attack the Houses.

Each House was protected from discovery by mages who inherited their gifts from previous generations, much as the skúma did. Outsiders traveling through the mountain passes that surrounded Vik wouldn't be able to see the city, unless they had a mage with them—they'd feel a pervasive sense of wrongness as they gazed down into the valley where Vik was located, the need to turn and go back the way they'd come—but still, one could never be too careful. Loyalties could be bought and sold, and Cordelia was sick of seeing everyone around her as a potential security risk, of being unable to trust them.

Beyond her desire to fulfill her promise to Dev and claim her birthright, the more she learned about the lives of the Commonwealths' citizens, the more horrified she became. Her push for revolution had taken on an ideological underpinning: she wanted to set the residents of the Commonwealths free from the brainwashing that defined their existences. On top of everything else, she was sick of training for a war that hadn't yet come. So she'd wheedled and insinuated, stoked fear and brought logic to bear. And finally, her efforts had borne fruit.

The Council had sent out a series of scouting delegations to the Commonwealth of Ashes, the largest and most powerful settlement, to assess the situation and finalize their strategy of attack. What they'd discovered had surpassed their wildest hopes —a rebellion was brewing inside the Commonwealth, a resistance against its restrictions and backwards ways. The scouts had even made a contact—a scholar who offered to serve as a go-between, building support inside the Commonwealth's fence and providing them with much-needed intelligence about the settlement's logistics, including the tunnels that ran beneath its surface.

This development had energized the Council. They'd supplied the Houses' resistance movement with a name—the Brotherhood of the Wolf—as well as coded language to use with their allies. Now, the Council had agreed to send out a final scouting delegation to the Commonwealth of Ashes—and at once, Cordelia had volunteered to lead it, along with Janus, her familiar, and a complement of guards. Reluctantly, the Council had acceded to her wish—but there was just one problem. She didn't want Dev to go…and he was adamant that he accompany her.

Since that night two years ago when they'd climbed the trellis to her bedroom, the two of them had been inseparable. Everyone knew their relationship was more than that of guard and skúma, but turned a blind eye; Cordelia was expected to marry Riley in a few short months, and then she'd either take Dev as her royal consort or set him aside. There was no other option.

No one suspected the depth of Cordelia's feelings for Dev—and if they did, they didn't care. She had a responsibility to her House, regardless of her emotional attachments elsewhere, and she was expected to fulfill it. Though she and Dev had never discussed her impending marriage to Riley, she knew they had to, and soon; it was bearing down on them with the inevitable impact of a charging battalion. But first, they had to survive the war that was looming on the horizon—and before *that*, they had to resolve the epic disagreement that they'd been having ever since Cordelia declared her intent to lead the scouting party, and her refusal to let Dev join it.

When she'd first announced she intended to go—and that she wanted him to stay here—he'd looked at her in disbelief. Next he'd tried persuasion, using every tool in his considerable arsenal. Then he'd argued with her and stormed off. And since then, they'd gone around in circles.

It was their last night together; Cordelia was leaving in the morning. And though she wanted nothing more than to sleep, wrapped in his arms, Dev was *still* arguing with her.

"You don't have to go," he said, propping himself on one elbow. "The Council can just send guards, Cordelia. Why do you have to risk yourself?"

Beneath his exasperation was a plaintive note that broke Cordelia's heart. She hated herself for making him sound that way—but she wasn't doing this to him, or for herself. She was doing it because it was the right thing to do, the only way she could live with herself. What kind of leader would she be, if she didn't lead from the front lines? His battle had become hers, and now there was no turning her from it.

"You know why," she told him, tugging the covers up to her chin.

"Then take me with you. There's no need to protect me, Cordelia. What do you think you're protecting me *from?* The guards you're taking with you—Bridgette, Majun, Tia—they're fine fighters, but they have hardly any real-world experience. I'm the one who's seen what's out there. I'm the one who has those bastards' blood on my hands!"

Cordelia sighed, knotting her fingers behind her head. They had been having this exact discussion for weeks, and her patience for it had worn thin. "It's precisely because you've seen what's out there that I don't want you going, Dev. This is a scouting mission, not a guerrilla attack. I know better than anyone how much you hate the Commonwealths—and with good reason," she said, holding up a hand to forestall his retort. "But I don't want you losing sight of why we're there and charging in to lay waste to the place. I can't have you letting your desire for retaliation take precedence over our need for stealth."

He looked outraged. "You don't think I can control myself?"

She was careful not to say what was on her mind—that sometimes she felt as if he operated from a simmering pit of rage, all of his niceties a mere veneer of civilized behavior that concealed the fury beneath. "I don't want to put you in that position," she said instead. "You're the best guard we have. Stay here. Keep Minneska safe. And when we do fight—you can help to lead the charge."

He shook his head, looking more furious than ever. "You're patronizing me. Stop it."

Cordelia sat up, keeping the covers close around her body. She hated having this discussion while undressed—as if her vulnerability was being leveraged against her. "I don't mean to. But I'm not changing my mind. And I don't want to argue with you, Dev, not on our last night together. Can't you let it go?"

"You don't understand." His voice was rough. "Out there—it's brutal. Vicious. They're not like us, Cor. You think you know, but until you've seen it, you don't—you can't—"

His words faltered and caught, as if snagging on barbs. He turned away from her, and she knew he wanted to hide his face. Dev hated to show weakness, even here, with her.

She tried anyhow, putting a hand on his bare shoulder. He didn't jerk away, but he didn't turn to face her, either. "What I saw that day—it wasn't human, Cordelia," he said. "There was joy in their eyes. They were zealots. It was like they believed murdering my mother and father would grant them absolution. The thought of something like that happening to you…"

He slid out of bed, still naked, and knelt at her feet, taking her hands in his. His blue eyes were fixed on her face, dark as the sky right before the sun slipped below the horizon. "I'm begging you, Cor. Don't let me lose you too. If you insist on taking this foolish risk, let me be by your side. If we need to fight, we'll fight together. We'll fall *together*. But don't ask this of me. You can't."

Dev never begged. She couldn't recall the last time she'd seen him on his knees, unless some kind of romantic assignation was involved. But no matter how much his desperation tore at her heart, she had no intention of changing her mind. It was one thing to risk herself twice over; she couldn't do the same to him.

She shook her head, and saw his face close down, like someone had drawn the shutters for the day. His scent changed, sharpening into anger. "Fine. You value me so little, Cordelia? Insist on keeping me caged? Let's get right down to it, then. When you make it back here—assuming you ever do—why don't you ask me to be your consort." His teeth snapped shut on the last word, his jaw so tight, she could see a muscle ticking in it.

Cordelia had no idea how they had leaped from one quagmire into another—truly, the connection felt irrelevant to her—but one look at Dev, and she could see that even though they hadn't discussed this, he'd been fuming over it for some time.

She didn't need Asta to smell a trap here. Folding her arms over her breasts, she glared at him. "No."

"Ask me," he insisted. "Or were you just planning to ignore me when you married Riley? Never speak to me again? Pretend that all we have in common is a shared political agenda and a childhood love of puff pastries?"

Infuriated, Cordelia reached over the side of the bed and grabbed her nightgown, yanking it over her head. The silken material settled over her body, red as fresh blood. "Now is not the time to talk about this."

"Oh, no?" He raised a mocking eyebrow. "When should we talk about it, then? Tomorrow, when you've left me behind? A few months from now, when you stand at the altar with Riley? When you lie with him in your bridal bed, and I'm forced to pace the corridors outside your chamber, under the guise of protecting you?"

Shame heated Cordelia's cheeks at the thought. If their roles were reversed, she knew she wouldn't be able to stand idly by and watch Dev wed another, bed another. Asta would tear her rival limb from limb, and devour the remains. Unable to look at him, she closed her eyes—but he was still talking, damn him.

"What do you think about when you imagine that night, Cor?" He traced the curve of her hip, his fingers slipping over the silk of her gown. "Do you see Riley there in the bed beside you? Or do you turn your head and see my face?" His voice dropped lower, a tantalizing elixir of desire and fury. "How many times have we lain together since that first time, my love? Four hundred? Five? Do you think it will be so easy to dismiss me? Or will my ghost haunt you, even as he grips you here"—his hand tightened on her hip—"or touches you here"—his fingers slid over the flat of her belly—"or strokes you here?" They dipped lower still, and Cordelia gasped, her teeth sinking into her lower lip.

She was angry at him, true. But yet she wanted him. She loved him. That never changed. "Dev, please," she said, breathless. "Let's not talk about him anymore. Come here, and let's forget."

His hands left her, and a current of air coiled between them, sinuous and cold. She blinked her eyes open to see him staring at her from inches away, his face hard.

"Is that all you want from me, Cordelia?" he said. "My body?"

She shook her head, rage winning out. Inside her, Asta uncurled, her hackles rising. "You know it isn't."

"I think you're lying." He stood, hands balled into fists at his sides. Then he bent and pulled on his pants, each movement rough, jerky. "Go on, ask me to be your consort. At least then you'll have what you want. Me, at your beck and call, like Janus. Doing exactly what you say. Just like everyone else."

Cordelia felt cold all over. "I don't want that," she whispered.

"Sure you do." His tone was flippant, the way it had been when he'd told her about murdering the men who killed his parents, all those years ago. "I won't challenge you, then. I won't ask you hard questions. I'll worship at your feet, just like all your other sycophants—"

Cordelia leapt from the bed. She had never struck anyone, save in the heat of a feigned battle. But now her hand flashed out, with preternatural skúma speed, and cracked Dev across the cheek before he could move away. When she drew back, her handprint remained, a scarlet brand on his pale skin.

He stared at her, his expression unchanging. Horrified, she tried to apologize, even as Asta murmured that she had done the right thing; it was an alpha's job to discipline the wayward members of their pack; hierarchy was everything—

Shut up, she told Asta, misery bubbling inside her. Over the wolf's growling protests, she spoke. "Dev, I'm so sorry. I should never have done that. I lost my temper, but that's no excuse. Please forgive me."

His expression didn't soften. Instead, he looked through her, as if she wasn't there at all. "Once," he said, his gaze remote, "you left me standing on a bridge, Cordelia. I waited and waited, but you never came back. You did it because you thought you knew what was right for us, the only way forward. And because you were a coward."

The word seared through Cordelia's veins like acid. Asta spoke through her, the wolf's fury at his insubordination overriding Cordelia's guilt at striking the person she cared for most in all the world. "How dare you—"

"Growl at me all you like. You know it's true." He shrugged, meeting her eyes the way few had the courage to. "Without me, you would never have mobilized the Houses. You wouldn't be heading out on this reconnaissance mission tomorrow. You'd still be Cordelia Navarro, that lazy girl who never quite lived up to her potential." His voice rose in a nasal mockery of Gertrud's.

Heat prickled over Cordelia's body. Asta prowled just beneath the surface of her skin, and she fought to hold the wolf at bay, to speak with her human mouth and nothing more. "Think carefully before you go down this road, Dev. Don't say things you can't take back."

He snorted, rolling his eyes. "All I do is think. That, and wait for you to see things the way they really are. To see *me*. Well, I'm done waiting." He took a step closer to her, so their bodies nearly touched. She was tall, but Dev was taller; he looked down at her, and she could smell the anger rolling off of him in waves. Beneath that, she could smell something else, too—the potent tang of hurt, whetting his scent so that it stung her nostrils and brought tears to her eyes. But when he spoke, his words were calculated, cruel.

"This revolution is *mine*, even if no one knows it but the two of us. You'd be nothing without me, Cordelia. I made you what you are today." His eyes bored into hers, their blue so dark, it was nearly black. "Strike me all you want. Leave me here like a discarded plaything. Deny my place in your heart and at your side. It doesn't change the truth."

Cordelia stared at him, appalled. Long ago, when they were children, she'd thought of the two of them as fire and water. Her temper simmered and flared, quick to rise at the slightest provocation. She angered easily, and on the rare occasions she didn't get her way, everyone around her paid the price. Dev, on the other hand, had been easygoing—quick to laugh, dousing her irritation with a joke or a smile. It had been one of the reasons they'd fit so well. But when he'd come back from the Borderlands, blood staining his hands and a mission carved in his heart, that had changed. Now both of them were made of heat and flame. They burned together...but never before had she imagined that their fire would eat away at each other, razing what they had to the ground until there was nothing left.

She'd thought by loving him with all she had to offer, she could heal him. That by aligning herself with his single-minded purpose, he would be able to set aside some of the animosity that fueled his soul. It might take time, but she'd get her Dev back—the boy who invented fanciful stories about the world beyond their borders, who made her laugh when no one else could. But looking at him now, tension clear in every line of his body and his blue eyes dark as night, she knew she'd been wrong.

Dev was broken. The boy she'd known years ago would never have spoken to her this way.

"You want the truth?" she said, her gaze holding his. "I love you. I have always loved you, since we were children. But right now, I don't know who you are. And you're breaking my heart."

She swallowed hard, summoning the courage to say what she needed to next. "I don't want you to be my consort, Dev—because that would diminish you. I have no desire to control you or make you do my bidding. But can you say the same?"

His gaze flickered, sliding from hers. It was all the answer she needed.

"I think," she said, her voice soft, "that you're the one who sought to control *me*. You came home devastated and desperate, wanting revenge, and I was the only path you saw that would lead you toward your goal. You knew how much I cared for you, that I would do anything to erase your pain, no matter what it cost me. I want to make things better, Dev—to help people, to set the prisoners in the Commonwealths free. To help *you*. But you— you just want to bathe the world in blood."

He stood still, his head hanging. He had become a statue. She could barely see him breathe. But she heard the thump of his heart —stuttering and uneven, as if it was struggling to beat.

She was hurting him, and she hated it. But this had to be said.

"No matter what we do," she said in that same gentle voice, "it will never bring your parents back. They're gone, Dev. And if the revenge you got in that clearing—murdering everyone who killed them—wasn't enough, why do you think this will be? Where will it end?"

Carefully, as if of the two of them, he was the animal that might bolt, she touched the tips of her fingers to his chin, lifting his face. "I love you," she said again. "But do you love *me,* or only what I've made possible for you? Are you still capable of love—or is there only room inside you for vengeance?"

He shivered all over, as if the room was cold, though a fire blazed in her hearth. When he spoke, his voice was hoarse. "I don't know."

Cordelia cupped his cheek, fitting her fingers against the print her hand had left behind. She breathed in the scent of him—salt and sage, sweat and sorrow. And then she stepped away, feeling everything inside her shatter.

"You were right, when you told me you'd died that day alongside your parents," she said. "But unlike them—you have a choice. Your parents were kind, above all. They wouldn't want you slaughtering people in their name. You told me once you'd become a monster. Don't let that be the truth."

His arms came up, hugging himself, the way he'd clutched his knees to his chest in the Great Hall years ago. When he spoke, his voice was a whisper. "I've forgotten how to be anything else."

Looking at him standing there, Cordelia felt the anger drain out of her. All that was left was sadness—for the boy she'd lost, the one who'd lost himself. She reached down and took his hand in hers, guiding it to his throat, where the charm of the wolf she'd once given him still hung, suspended from its chain.

"Remember," she told him.

For an instant he gripped the silver figurine tight. Then pain twisted his face, and he ripped his hand from hers. "I can't."

Snatching his shirt from the floorboards, he stalked from her room without looking back.

CHAPTER THREE

Cordelia cried herself to sleep—not so much for the way Dev had stormed out, but for the realization that all along, he might simply have been using her. That the boy she loved might be no more than an empty shell, animated by grief and rage. It was the middle of the night when she finally dropped off, so exhausted that she didn't wake to the scent or sound of someone entering her room. In fact, she had no idea anyone was there until they sat down beside her and the bed gave way under their weight.

The guards were stationed outside to protect her, of course—but still, an enemy could have broken through their ranks. Her eyes opened with a start, and she drew a deep breath, scenting the air as her sight adjusted to the dimness of the room.

Dev sat beside her, his familiar scent filling her lungs and his shape no more than an outline in the dark. The evenings were still cool, and a fire burned low in the hearth, casting a dim glow on the room, as if they were both underwater.

Cordelia wanted to ask what he was doing here—if he had come back to break her heart once and for all…because if that was the case, she was fairly certain he'd already finished the job. But instead he began to speak, his words falling slow and mesmerizing into the silence of the room.

"Once upon a time," he began, threading his fingers through hers, "there was a boy who loved a girl more than anything in the world. She was stubborn and short-tempered and headstrong—but she was also beautiful and brilliant and brave. He waited each day for the moment he would see her—and even if the sun was shining, the day didn't truly seem bright until she smiled. The boy would do anything to make her smile, and when she laughed, it was the best gift he'd ever been given."

Cordelia drew a shaky breath. This was Dev's storytelling voice—the one she hadn't heard for years, not since that day on the bridge, when he told her about the mulberries and plums and sunken ships of House San Fraesco. She didn't say a word, terrified to break the spell.

"One day," Dev went on, his fingers tight on Cordelia's, "the boy was especially excited to see the girl. He'd brought her favorite pastries, still hot from the oven. His mother had pressed a box of them upon him to give to her—not just because the girl was royalty, although she was, but because his mother loved the girl, too. When his mother didn't think the boy could hear, she would talk of the girl to his father. *In another life*, she'd say, and though the boy was too young to understand what she meant, he heard the wistfulness in her tone. He recognized it, for it beat in his own chest, alongside the pound of his heart."

Cordelia was sure Dev was talking about that last day on the bridge—the day before everything changed. He rarely spoke of his parents, and then only with anger or regret—never in this nostalgic fashion, as if he could bear to remember the good things, and not the way it had all ended for them. She stayed as still as she could, listening for all she was worth. With a pang, she remembered a time when Dev's words had flowed over her in rivulets, so constant that she'd dismissed them, letting her mind wander to other things. Now each one was precious.

"The girl came to their special meeting place," he went on,

gripping her fingers tighter still. The pressure was just this side of pain, but Cordelia didn't cry out or try to pull away. She was afraid that if she did, he would stop talking. "The place was a footbridge, crossing the river that divided their city, and the boy often felt that this was fitting; while they stood on the bridge, they were between places, in the imaginary space where their friendship could exist. For she, as I've said, was royalty, and he just a poor baker's son. He watched the girl come toward him that day, the smile he loved lifting her lips when she saw the bag of treats he held in his hand—and he imagined that the smile was not for what he had brought her, but for *him*."

He paused to draw breath. Cordelia wanted to tell him that her smile *had* always been for him—that the cherry puff pastries were just a bonus—but she didn't speak, and after a moment, he went on.

"That day, the boy was excited to tell the girl about the great adventure on which he and his parents would soon embark. He knew she loved the stories he told her, and so he spun a grand tale, all about selkies and gold, mulberries and plums, and a city made of water, where you could glide through the streets on boats. The girl listened, even making up a tale of her own about plum trees that granted wishes when you ate their fruit, but he could tell something was troubling her. He didn't want to leave with this mystery between them—but he didn't know how to ask what was wrong."

With a pang, Cordelia remembered what had been bothering her that day—how she'd come to realize she felt more for Dev than simple friendship. How she'd panicked, wondering if he could ever return the favor—and if he did, how it might ruin everything. Given their current situation, this felt horribly prophetic.

The moonlight fell across his face, lighting half and keeping the rest in shadow, as if he were two different people—the twin halves of Dev, shining and dark. Loosening his grip on her hand, as if he realized he might be hurting her, he spoke again. "The boy had loved her for so long. He never imagined she could feel the same. But then she gave him a gift—a finely-made charm in the shape of a wolf, like the one that lived inside her. She said it was to keep him safe while he traveled, and so he wouldn't forget her. And before the boy could think better of it, he told her the truth: that such a thing would never be possible. If he'd had the words, he would've told her that long ago, his love for her had been etched on his heart."

He lifted his free hand, brushing her hair back from her face. His expression matched his touch—tender, gentle—and Cordelia realized how long it had been since she'd seen him look that way. She'd forgotten that he could.

"When the boy said that to the girl," Dev went on, "he saw a look in her eyes that he'd never seen before—one that spoke to the desire that lived in his soul. And so he found the courage to ask her a question. If such plum trees as they'd spoken of were real, he asked, what would she wish for?"

Cordelia felt tears cloud her eyes. She remembered the panic she'd felt then—as if the worst thing that could happen was for her to tell Dev what she felt. As if her honesty would be their destruction.

"The girl ran away rather than answer him," Dev said, tucking a wayward strand of hair behind her ear. His fingertips were calloused from hours of training, their roughness at odds with his delicate touch. "The boy thought surely she would come back. He waited for hours and hours. But she never did."

Guilt scythed through Cordelia at the thought of Dev sitting on the bridge, alone, waiting for an answer that would never come. She wanted to tell him she was sorry. But before she could speak, he went on.

"The boy did indeed go on his journey, and terrible things befell him. By the end of it, he had lost his parents at the hands of fanatics, and shed their blood as his vengeance. Steeped in misery, he found his way home. At night, he slept clutching the wolf charm she'd given him in his fist. He was empty, save for his love for the girl—a miniature sun, burning bright in his chest. She was all he had left. He would find his way back to her."

He gave Cordelia a sad smile. "When he got home, he wanted to tell his story—but all his words left him until the girl stood by his side. He reached down into himself for the love he'd always borne her—the bright light that had guided him home—but instead, all he found was darkness. He couldn't make her smile anymore. He didn't recognize himself—but the girl seemed to see him, and cared for him anyway. She promised to help him seek revenge, and for a moment, he felt a little less alone."

Cordelia couldn't help it—she had to say something. "You aren't alone, Dev. You never were. Even that day—when those terrible things happened—I was with you. In your heart. And what I wished…it was for a world where we could be together."

"You've always seen the best in me. Even now." He traced the shape of her lips, as if he was memorizing them. When he spoke again, his voice was husky. "No matter what I say or do, somewhere inside me, there's still that little boy who loves you more than anything in the world, Cordelia. And somewhere inside *him* is that light, burning like the sun."

He bent his head and pressed his lips to hers. Their first kiss had tasted like blood and ash; this one tasted like goodbye.

"You told me to remember," Dev whispered. "And I will never forget, neshama sheli. Not anything that has passed between us, whatever comes."

He wrapped his arms around her, holding her close. They sat like that for a long time, as the fire burned to embers and the sun began to rise. In its light, she could see the silvered tracks of tears on his cheeks, and knew they were mirrored on her own.

Cordelia clung to this moment, memorizing every bit of it. They had said and done terrible things to each other, but in the circle of his arms, she felt that all fall away. Later, she would gather her supplies and marshal her team. Later, she would don the armor that she wore as the skúmaskot Cordelia, royal member of House Minneska and shapeshifting warrior. But now, as she held Dev tight and felt him hold her in return, she was content to be a girl in the arms of the boy she loved.

But morning came, and as if the rising sun had shattered the spell, Dev slipped from her arms. He stood, looking down at her. Cordelia expected him to bid her farewell—but instead he said, breaking the fragile silence that had settled between them, "I have something for you."

Cordelia blinked, surprised. The old Dev had loved to give and receive presents—but he hadn't given her a gift since those cherry puff pastries on the bridge six years ago. "Really?"

His lips rose in a crooked smile. "You look so shocked. I did promise you a present once, Cor—and I seem to recall I never delivered."

Was he *joking* about the events that had led him to return to Vik empty-handed? "That was hardly your fault," she managed.

"Still. Close your eyes," he said with the wicked grin she hadn't seen in forever.

Her heart pounding, Cordelia obeyed. She heard fabric shifting, as if he'd reached into his pocket. A moment later, he said, "Okay, you can open them now."

When she looked, Dev was standing in front of her, a hopeful expression on his face and something coiled in his hand. She peered more closely at it; the fine links of a gold chain shimmered in the morning light. At their center lay a small golden charm—a snake swallowing its own tail.

Dev's free hand rose, and he touched a finger to the silver wolf that hung around his throat. "Once, long ago, this charm led me back to you," he told Cordelia. "I give you this symbol now, in hopes that it will do the same."

Cordelia stared at the necklace, dumbfounded. Guards made a steady salary, but it was hardly extravagant; they received room and board as part of the job, and the compensation reflected their lack of expenses. A gift like this must have cost as much as Dev made in several months of work.

"I had the goldsmith make it for you before I knew you'd be

leaving," he said, his eyes on hers. "I'd wanted to give you something for a while, but I had to save up for it—and then it took him time to get it right. I wanted it to be special. Do you like it?"

Cordelia didn't trust her voice. "It's beautiful," she managed at last, echoing what he'd said to her years ago, when she'd given him the wolf charm. "I'll wear it with pride."

A huge smile broke across his face, like the sun making its way from behind the clouds. "May I?" he said, gesturing toward her.

"Of course," she said, and he bent to fasten it around her neck.

"It's an ouroboros," he said as his deft fingers closed the clasp. "The symbol for eternity and perpetual return. It means a story that never ends. We are connected always, you and I. And no matter how far you travel, or what choices you make—wherever our paths lead us—we will always be a part of each other."

Tears welled in Cordelia's eyes. "But Riley—"

Dev drew back, shaking his head. "I owe you an apology, Cordelia. I should never have said the things I did. This revolution—it's ours, together. Without you, it would be nothing more than the wishful thinking of a bitter boy. I spoke from anger; I insulted and belittled you, and I beg your pardon."

"I forgive you," Cordelia said. Her hands trembled, and she clenched them to hide it. "If you'll forgive me for striking you."

"I deserved it, and more." Straightening, he gave her a small shrug. "There's no excuse for how I behaved. It's just—the thought of you going into danger without me...and knowing you'll come home only to marry another man...it tore me apart. But in the end, none of that matters."

She sat up, the covers falling away. The charm settled into place at the base of her throat, cold against her skin. "How so?" she said, fighting to keep her voice level.

He ran a hand through his hair—which, she couldn't help but notice, was already tousled beyond bearing. Whenever Dev was troubled, he tended to muss his hair; clearly, he'd had much on his mind since he left her.

"Since we argued earlier, I've done nothing but walk and think," he said, confirming her suspicions. "I've walked for hours, wondering if you were right...if there's no room inside me for anything but vengeance."

Bracing herself, she looked up at him. "And?"

He gave her a small, sad smile. "Ani ohev otach, Cordelia," he said. "With all that I am, all that I have—I do love you. You're the only girl I've ever loved. You'll always be the only one."

The tears overspilled, coursing down her cheeks. Gently, he wiped them away. "Be safe," he said with devastating simplicity. "Come back to me. And when you do—I will try to be worthy of your return."

He turned before she could reply and strode from her room, shutting the door behind him. Touching her fingertips to the gift he'd given her—the one that meant their story would go on forever—Cordelia slid from her bed and began to prepare for war.

LUST

"THE HEART OF HIDDEN THINGS"

CHAPTER ONE

Miriam Larsen woke, panting, from a nightmare of books aflame to see her dorm-mate staring down at her, lips pressed into a thin, suspicious line.

"What were you dreaming about?" There was a note of accusation in Genevieve's pinched voice, undergirded by a hint of vicious curiosity. "Something you need to confess to the Priests?"

Genevieve Johannsen had the cot next to Miriam's in the girls' dormitory, and the two had known each other since they were children. In the Commonwealth of Ashes, where they lived, citizens lived and died by the rules of the Seven Deadly Sins: pride, greed, lust, envy, gluttony, wrath, and sloth. Friendship wasn't permitted—attachment was seen as the first step on the road toward chaos—but of course, there were people one felt an affinity for, and people one did not. Miriam had grown up in the Nursery with Genevieve and had never been able to stand her. The two rarely spoke beyond necessities, and Miriam had no intention of confiding in the other girl about her dream—the one that violated every oath she'd sworn.

Miriam was a scholar. It was her responsibility to tend the Commonwealth's store of books, to peruse their moral content for lessons that could help citizens better understand the thorny path that led to virtuousness and the slippery slope toward sin. Fire was a scholar's worst enemy, and she lived in fear that she'd somehow make a mistake that would lead to the Library's destruction. Apparently, that terror had bled into her subconscious—but there was no way she would admit to dreaming about such a thing. To Genevieve, that would be one dangerous step away from the act itself.

"Nothing," she told the other girl now, pushing her blankets back and sitting up.

"Really?" Genevieve's feathery blond eyebrows knitted, and her thin lips pursed tight. "Because you look quite guilty. Also, if you don't get up now, you'll be late for catechism."

Genevieve was quick to find fault, a natural Informer. Miriam knew at the slightest whiff of wrongdoing, the girl would go running to the High Priests. And failure to protect the books for which Miriam was responsible would be considered a slothful sin of the highest order. It was no wonder she had nightmares about destroying the Library; if she did, she'd surely find herself kneeling on the stones of Clockverk Square, a bellator's blade pressed to her throat and one of the Priests standing over her, carrying out the Executor's sentence of death.

The Executor ruled the Commonwealth; what he said was law. He commanded the blades of the Bellatorum Lucis—the warriors of light. These were the Commonwealth's enforcers, sworn to protect citizens from the corruption that stained their souls. All her life, Miriam had found them terrifying. She was determined never to give them any reason to notice her—and not drawing a potential Informer's attention to her was the first step.

"I'm fine," she said, sliding off her cot and ignoring Genevieve's judgmental sniff. She went about her business— taking her allotted three-minute shower, dressing in the green tunic that marked her as a scholar, filing into Clockverk Square for catechism under the watchful eyes of the crimson-robed Priests, eating breakfast with her fellow citizens—but all the while, she could feel Genevieve's eyes on her, assessing, judging. As she left the dining hall, she trembled under the weight of the Priests' stares, half-expecting them to drag her away.

She was relieved when she and Genevieve went their separate ways—Genevieve to her work in the dairy, and Miriam to the Library—but she couldn't shake the worry that the other girl had seen or heard something untoward. What if Miriam had talked in her sleep, and Genevieve had heard her say something about setting the Library aflame? What would happen to her then?

Miriam was still preoccupied by this an hour later, as she stood on a ladder, straining to reach the Library's highest shelf. Aric, the scholar assigned to work alongside her, was taller—but he was busy sorting through a box of moldering books, so the task fell to Miriam.

She'd never fallen from one of the Library's ladders before. Half her focus was on her work; the other half was on Genevieve, which was the only explanation she had for what happened next. One moment she was reaching for *Paradise Lost*, and the next she was falling, the ladder going in one direction and her body in the other. She grabbed for the shelf to steady herself, missed, and crashed to the ground in a hail of books.

Dante's *Divine Comedy* struck her in the solar plexus, tumbling into her lap. She looked up, stunned—in time for a volume so massive it could only be *The History of the Commonwealth: A Compendium* to smack into her forehead. The world grayed and blurred at the edges, narrowing to a single, wavering point. And then, all at once, it went dark.

She woke to see a medic kneeling over her, no doubt summoned by Aric. The Commonwealth was relatively small—no more than ten thousand people—so the medic was familiar, though she'd never spoken with him before. His name, Miriam recalled through the fog in her head, was Kennett Gundarson.

They were the same age. Miriam had been Chosen to be a scholar the same day he'd been Chosen to be a medic—almost a year earlier, when they'd both turned seventeen—but she'd never spoken to him. Why would she? In the Commonwealth, boys were an irrelevance. Children were conceived in test tubes and carried by surrogates—then raised in the Nursery by Caretakers, with no knowledge of who their biological parents had been. Residents of the Commonwealth considered their fellow citizens only in light of the services they could provide—a seamstress to sew their clothes; a butcher to slaughter their beasts; an Instruktor to teach their children—not in terms of their significance on a personal level.

Friendship was forbidden. Romantic love—and of course, lust—was punishable by death or exile to the Borderlands that surrounded the Commonwealth, filled with brutal hordes bent on citizens' destruction. Sometimes, the Priests would have the bellators deliver particularly egregious sinners to the Borderlands, sedating the Bastarour who roamed the forest that ringed the edge of the Commonwealth and the electric fence. On other occasions, the Priests released the sinners into the forest, where they were at the mercy of the Bastarour—genetically-modified beasts trained to rend their prey limb from limb. If, by some miracle, the sinners managed to evade the Bastarour, they'd come smack up against the fence, which would fry them where they stood.

The Commonwealth's citizens never got to see what happened to sinners who were exiled to the Borderlands or condemned to the forest; they just knew such unfortunates never returned. By contrast, Miriam had witnessed a man and woman executed for fornication the year she turned fifteen. They'd been beheaded side by side, holding hands in one last futile gesture of rebellion. The horror of it was with her still.

Just the same, as Kennett knelt over her, Miriam couldn't help but notice how gentle his touch felt on her forehead, blotting away the blood. His eyes were as green as the pines in the woods that surrounded the City, and his hair as black as the night sky, just before the first stars came out.

Miriam closed her eyes, horrified. Poetry belonged in the pages of the books she studied—to be analyzed for its moral content, not appreciated as an art form. It certainly had no place in her mind as she lay on the floor, looking up at Kennett. What if he noticed? What would he think of her then?

"Miriam," he said. "How do you feel?"

She must have been delirious from the blow. That was her only excuse. Because when she blinked and looked up at him, she didn't give him a sensible answer. *My head hurts, but I'll be fine*, she could have said. Or, *Thank you for your attention; I'm sorry to have required your services.*

But instead, she blurted, "'I did not die, and yet I lost life's breath.'" It was a line from *The Divine Comedy*, which had quite literally knocked the air out of her body.

The moment the words left Miriam's lips, she felt like a fool. Most citizens of the Commonwealth didn't read much; they learned their lessons at the hands of the Instruktors, and then went on to pursue whatever their Chosen career might be. Those selected as medics studied science and mathematics, not literature. Miriam expected this one to dismiss her words as evidence of possible brain damage, and, dragging herself up to her elbows, prepared to explain.

But the boy with the gentle hands looked down at her, a small smile lifting his lips, and replied, "'There, pride, avarice, and envy are the tongues men know and heed, a Babel of despair.'"

He had quoted *The Divine Comedy* back to her. Miriam stared up at him, stunned.

"You'll need stitches," he said. "Here." And, with a minimum of fuss, proceeded to numb her skin and sew her wound closed while she lay on the Library floor.

"Watch for signs of concussion," he said in a professional tone as she sat up. "Headache, dizziness, and nausea. One of the Caretakers should probably check on you each hour through the night. And also—wait. What are you doing?"

Though Miriam was indeed dizzy, she'd gotten to her feet, *The Divine Comedy* in her hand, and was making her way back to the ladder. She wasn't badly injured, and there could be no excuse for leaving the books scattered on the floor.

"Reshelving," she said as she stepped onto the bottom rung of the ladder.

Kennett was free to leave. But instead, he lingered, standing at the base of the ladder to hand Miriam the books. His forwardness unnerved her. What if he'd noticed how she'd looked at him before, and his continued presence was a test of her virtuous behavior? What if—Architect forbid—he was an Informer?

She eyed him carefully, but there was nothing on his face but a resolve that matched her own. "If you're going to be so stubborn," he said, "then the least I can do is to stay here and keep an eye on you, in case you need further medical assistance."

Miriam could've pointed out that Aric was perfectly able to pass the books to her, as well as to call for a medic again, should one be needed. But then Kennett would've gone away, and to her bewilderment, she didn't want him to leave.

"You like to read?" she said despite herself as he slipped a copy of Machiavelli's *The Prince* into her hand, careful not to let their fingers touch. She'd often felt that curiosity should be the eighth Deadly Sin—certainly it was hers.

"I do. Though I don't have much time for it. I come here on Idle Day sometimes."

Aric, who had gone back to sorting through the box of volumes that had fallen victim to moisture, snorted. "You do," he confirmed. "And you don't always put the books back where you ought to, either."

To her amusement, Kennett flushed and ducked his head. "When I was here reading last week, I lost track of time and was almost late for evening catechism. I didn't get a chance to finish the book and shoved it back on the shelf haphazardly." He bit his lip. "I'm truly sorry. It won't happen again."

Miriam's curiosity got the better of her. "What were you reading?"

There was only one book left on the floor; he bent to lift it, smiling up into her eyes. Something about that smile made her feel as if he'd pushed her off a cliff and then stood there, watching her plummet. How could a simple lift of his lips make her so dizzy? Surely it had to be the blow to her head.

"Milton's *Areopagitica*," he said, pressing the volume in question into her hand. "'For books are not absolutely dead things, but do contain a potency of life in them to be as active as that soul was whose progeny they are.'"

Miriam took the book from him, momentarily speechless. If her soul possessed a language of romance—not that such things were allowed here—he had just spoken it.

"You read philosophy?" she said, finding her voice. She glanced down at Aric, who—thank the Architect—was still focused on his box of books. The last thing she needed was for him to look up and realize Miriam was behaving in such a peculiar fashion. All it would take was one misplaced glance, a single word spoken out of turn, and she could find herself face-to-face with the Bellatorum's Lead Interrogator.

The Library was Miriam's life; she was one of just twenty-three scholars chosen to safeguard the Commonwealth's history and the knowledge their citizens needed to carry out their work—a coveted position. She'd never wanted to be anything else. The careers that the Executor Chose for them were a lifetime assignment; should they sin badly enough to lose their appointments, they were relegated to a life amongst the natural-born, carrying out the Commonwealth's most menial duties. If Miriam lost her position, she would have nothing...and that was *after* she'd endured whatever punishments the Priests had in mind.

The Priests' punishments were creative in the extreme—the only art form permitted in the Commonwealth, where creativity for its own sake was seen as the first step down the road to dissolution—and cruel. Fear flashed through her body for the second time that morning at the thought of what they might devise for her...but Aric merely grunted, hefting the box of books in his arms and winding his way back into the stacks, toward the restricted section of the Library. She watched him go, then turned her attention back to Kennett, who shrugged.

"I prefer to read books about science—or medicine. If I'm to be a medic, I want to be the best one I can be—to truly help people," he said. "But I've read all the science and medical books the general section of the Library has to offer, and so I figured I might as well keep going and work my way through the other tomes. Though I'll be honest—they don't come as easily to me as the rest."

Despite Miriam's anxiety, a strange thrill moved through her. Kennett Gundarson wasn't prolonging his time in the Library because he was an Informer, bound to report to the Priests. He was still here because he loved books, like she did—because he wanted to *learn.*

Miriam understood hungering for knowledge, feeling as if what you wanted to know was just out of reach. Even as a scholar, the information she was allowed to access came in bits and pieces, based on what the Priests and then the Senior Scholars believed was appropriate for her experience and rank. It was the same for any occupation in the Commonwealth—they were allowed just enough information to perform their tasks well, and no more. Anything else could lead to undue pride in one's work and envy of others' prowess.

Still, when Miriam read the classic volumes that comprised the bulk of the Library's holdings, she found herself taking more from them than she knew she was meant to. Turning the pages, she often thought not of the frailty of the human soul, but of the fantastical quests that the characters took—adventures of a kind she would never get to experience. As a scholar, she was not meant to *imagine,* but rather to analyze—but sometimes she couldn't help herself. She found herself craving to know what the volumes in the restricted stacks held, even though she wouldn't be allowed to access them until she was a senior scholar.

She wondered if the restricted books would broaden her

world, giving her insight into what lay beyond the Commonwealth's electric fence. They'd always been told the Borderlands contained no more than ruins through which hordes of vicious sinners prowled, searching for victims—but Miriam harbored a sinful desire to see for herself...and, barring that, to *know.*

This curiosity was a terrible flaw, one she did her best to hide. But it was part of her, nonetheless—and she saw the echo of it in Kennett Gundarson's eyes.

This was no good. She needed him to leave, now. She needed to never see him again. She needed—

"You need to come back in a week for me to check on those stitches," he said. "Ask for me at the Infirmary." There was that smile again.

Miriam wanted to demur, but on what grounds? "Fine," she said and gave him a curt nod.

Gathering up his medical kit, Kennett nodded at Aric, who'd reemerged from the stacks, and left the Library. Miriam turned to slide *Areopagitica* back into place, appalled. What was happening to her?

She knew one thing—she shouldn't go to the Infirmary to see Kennett, not even if she ripped out all of her stitches and was gushing blood. Being in his presence somehow brought out the worst in her.

She had to go, though; to do otherwise would be to arouse suspicion, since Kennett had doubtless entered medical orders into his log under her name. If her supervisors followed up—after all, she'd been injured in the course of her duties as a scholar—and she'd failed to obey Kennett's instructions, the senior scholars would want to know why. They might interview her, and Aric too —he'd been present when Kennett stitched her forehead. And under such pressure, who knew what her fellow librarian might say?

So she would go to see Kennett—but she would be on her

guard. For as she clung to the ladder with one hand and reached up, finally managing to retrieve *Paradise Lost* with the other, she knew in her heart how easy it would be to fall.

CHAPTER TWO

By the time Miriam went to the Infirmary, she'd convinced herself the events of the previous week had been an aberration—the unfortunate result of head trauma. She'd even brought Kennett a small token of appreciation—a copy of *Areopagitica*, checked out for him with her scholar's privileges, so he could take his time perusing it and not have to cram all of his reading into Idle Day.

The side benefit of this was that should she choose to spend her Idle Days in the Library, Kennett wouldn't be there. He could read the book on his own and return it via the drop slot when he was finished. She wouldn't have to risk running into him and dealing with the bewildering feelings he evoked in her—unless, of course, she fell off the ladder again.

She hadn't seen Kennett since the previous week—but she'd dreamed about him, terrible nightmares in which Aric had dumped his box of books onto the wooden floor of the Library and gone racing to the Priests to tell them she'd engaged in inappropriate banter with the medic who'd come to stitch her wound. She dreamed of the bellators dragging her down to the dungeons, of sitting filthy and starving in a cell as she waited to hear what her punishment would be. And then she woke to see

Genevieve asleep next to her, her body turned to face Miriam's as if waiting to blink her eyes open and catch her in the act of subconscious sedition.

The Priests encouraged them to confess their sins—to Inform on themselves—but Miriam hadn't felt the need to do such a thing. They were only dreams; her behavior toward Kennett hadn't crossed any lines. Still, to say it hadn't been a restful week was an understatement.

The Infirmary was crowded with patients and medics, the hum of complaints and diagnoses filling the air. It smelled of antiseptics and bleach, an astringent scent that stung Miriam's lungs when she inhaled. She had to wait to see Kennett and spent the time sitting in an uncomfortable molded chair, paging through Plato's *The Republic*—which she'd read many times before, but always had something new to offer.

Miriam actually found herself looking forward to seeing Kennett in this simple, controlled environment. It was an excellent opportunity for her to perceive him as a fellow citizen, not as some kind of absurd composite of leaves and sky who shared her thirst for knowledge. She would laugh at herself, banish her nightmares, and be more careful on the upper rungs of the Library's ladders forevermore.

But when they called her number and sent her back to his station, she was disturbed to find that those clear green eyes of his, blazing with intelligence, were as distracting as they'd been before—as was the wide smile with which he greeted her. She settled onto the wooden examination table, wishing she was somewhere—anywhere—else.

"So," Kennett said, oblivious to her discomfort. "How goes it? Any more painful literary encounters?"

Miriam shook her head. "No, thanks for asking." Rummaging in her bag, she pulled out *Areopagitica*. "I checked it out for you with my privileges," she said, her tone as neutral as she could manage. This wasn't forbidden; a scholar could do such a thing for a citizen, as long as they kept careful track of their lending history and ensured the books were returned in a timely fashion. "So you can actually finish it."

Kennett glanced down at the book. His arched eyebrows rose, those green eyes widening. "You climbed that ladder again—against medic's orders—to bring me *Areopagitica?*"

Miriam narrowed her own eyes at him. "It's my job," she said stiffly. "You expressed curiosity about this book; as a scholar, it's my responsibility to provide intellectual resources to fellow citizens as appropriate. Rather than criticizing me for fulfilling my duties, you might thank me."

That infuriating grin widened—as if he found her amusing. "Thank you, Miriam," he said, taking the book from her. She felt his fingers brush hers—accidentally, of course—and had to suppress the shiver that radiated out from the place where they'd touched.

Kennett set the book on the counter behind him and moved in to examine her stitches. He brushed her hair back from her face, his touch light but sure. "These look fine. They'll dissolve on their own in another week or so."

His eyes were still fixed on her, with more intensity than seemed warranted. She fidgeted on the table, glad she was only here for her head injury and not a physical exam; if she'd come for the latter, he would surely be able to hear her heart pounding. "What is it?" she said, her voice harsher than she intended. "Why are you staring at me that way?"

He took a step back, dropping his gaze. "I apologize. I was actually wondering if you might be willing to tutor me. As I've told you, I find the philosophical books I've read difficult to interpret—but I've found there's an element to healing beyond the merely scientific. If I had a more nuanced understanding of the working of my patients' minds, then perhaps I'd be better at my job."

"You want me to tutor you?" By the Architect, of course he did. It was true that information was given to all of them on a utilitarian basis—piecemeal, based on what they needed to do their jobs. It made her think better of Kennett, somehow, that he was interested in seeking more—but did he have to seek it with her?

"There are twenty-three scholars available for such a task," she said, hoping she sounded dispassionate rather than desperate. "Why me?"

He gave a one-shouldered shrug. "I don't know any other scholars personally. When you brought me *Areopagitica*, I thought you might be willing, since you have such great commitment to your work. But if it isn't possible, I understand."

This was *not* how their encounter was supposed to go. Miriam been trying to get rid of him by handing him the book, not encouraging him to seek her out. But if she refused, how would that look?

"All right," she told him, getting down from the table. She tried not to look directly at him; what if her expression gave her peculiar feelings away? "Meet me at the Library on Idle Day at one o'clock sharp. We'll start with *The Odyssey*."

CHAPTER THREE

On Idle Day, Miriam secured her favorite table in the Library—near the front windows, where the waning autumn sunlight found its way inside—and pulled a copy of *The Odyssey* off the shelf in preparation for her discussion with Kennett.

The book had always been one of Miriam's favorites, because of Odysseus's epic quest. She'd always identified more with Odysseus than Penelope—she was enthralled by the battles he fought with mythical creatures and gods, his shipwreck and narrow escapes. She loved how Odysseus used his mind rather than brute strength to find his way out of difficult situations, and fantasized that if she were ever in such trouble, she would do the same.

Of course, she wasn't supposed to imagine herself having adventures like Odysseus, but rather to consider the sins that had inspired Homer to compose such a poem—the wrath that led to the Trojan War; the lust that caused Calypso to trap Odysseus on her island; the greed of the men who opened the bag containing Odysseus's treasure; the gluttony that spurred the men to feast on the cattle of the Sungod Helios despite dire warnings not to do so. Still, Miriam couldn't help but imagine herself in Odysseus' shoes—and she contented herself with the thought that if she never spoke of this to anyone, then surely her imaginings did no harm.

The sunlight struck Kennett's face as he walked toward her, his hair gleaming blue-black and his eyes lighter than usual—fresh-cut grass rather than pine needles...and *why was she still thinking of him this way?* Heaving a sigh, she got to her feet and greeted him in a whisper, heedful of Senior Scholar Joseph seated two tables over. The senior scholar was in conversation with Aric, who never failed to seize an opportunity to claw his way upward in the ranks.

Aric's groveling attitude aggravated Miriam. They were meant to earn their positions on merit alone, not by jockeying for advantage. She wouldn't stoop to his level—but when she considered the idea of him getting promoted while she spent her days reshelving books, she had to suppress a verboten twinge of envy.

No wonder Aric had known Kennett hadn't restored *Areopagitica* to its rightful place. He must live in here, taking every opportunity to cozy up to the senior scholars. Miriam herself usually chose to spend her lone free day outside when the weather was fine—and sometimes even when it wasn't—preferring the fresh air, however cold or damp, to the confines of the room where she spent six days a week.

Miriam loved her library, but sometimes she needed to escape.

Through Kennett's eyes, though, she saw the Library as she had the first time she'd set foot in it—a magical box filled with books, whose pages, once cracked, could transport her to the corners of the universe she would never be privileged to see.

Sitting down on the chair next to Miriam, Kennett gave her a bright smile. "All right," he said in a stage whisper. "Where do we start?"

"With Telemachus," she said briskly, opening *The Odyssey* to its first page and doing her best to ignore how her pulse quickened at his proximity. He wanted a tutor; that was what he would get, her vulnerability to sinning be damned. "As you may recall, the goddess Athena appears to him in disguise..."

This was the beginning of their conversation, which would continue on every Idle Day for the next two months and beyond. *The Odyssey* was a lengthy tome, after all, and there were many thorny moral questions to discuss. They studied one book each week, gradually making their way through the epic poem. Kennett hung on Miriam's every word, listening to her analysis of the text and posing questions of his own. She came to live for Idle Days, for their conversations and the questions he provoked in her. Her mind felt as if it were coming alive bit by bit, and despite her initial reluctance at tutoring him, she hoarded textual interpretations in between their meetings, eager to share her opinions with him and ask his own.

Miriam worried about this, even though none of it was strictly forbidden. Was it wrong to look forward to their conversations this way? Nothing they talked about was inappropriate; anyone else in the Library could overhear anything they said, and frequently did. Still, Miriam found herself as captivated by him as she'd been the first time they met. Once, eager to underline their respective points with backup from the text, they'd reached for the book at the same time, and their hands had brushed. In the instant before Kennett drew back, whispering apologies, Miriam was swept by the same all-consuming shiver that had rippled through her when she'd handed him *Areopagitica*.

What might such a thing mean? Did he feel it too? If so, he gave no sign.

Whatever it meant, it couldn't be good. Miriam had to hide it from him—and anyone else—at all costs.

Over the weeks that they'd studied together, Miriam had sometimes felt as if his gaze lingered on her longer than necessary —but surely it was her imagination? There was no way he saw her as anything other than a scholar and a tutor, which was as it should be. She was the sinner, the one who stupidly—and sinfully —wanted more. She'd prayed to the Architect for this desire to go, but it wouldn't leave her. Every time she saw him, it was worse—and her nightmares of imprisonment had returned, even more virulent than before.

All Miriam had ever wanted was to be good at her job. Now here Kennett was, destroying everything. And yet, at the thought of their sessions together ending, a sick feeling curdled her stomach.

The fall passed this way, dying slowly into winter. On the eighth week of their Idle Day tutoring sessions, they'd just finished discussing Calypso's sinful behavior toward Odysseus when Kennett glanced up at her.

"Do you want to take a walk?" he said.

"A what?" Miriam gaped at him. In the two months they'd met to study, they'd never once left the confines of the Library.

"A walk, Miri." He raised an eyebrow. "As a medical professional, I'm recommending it. We've spent an awful lot of time sitting. And, you know, cardiovascular activity is important for overall health."

It occurred to Miriam that he was *teasing* her—not a typical occurrence in the Commonwealth. "Very funny," she said, her voice dry. "And what did you call me?"

He had the good grace to blush, ducking his head as he'd done that first day in the Library when Aric had given him a hard time about misshelving books. "Miri?" he said, making it a question.

Her name was Miriam. No one had ever called her anything else. Nicknames weren't illicit in the Commonwealth—just pointless. But she found she liked the sound of 'Miri' in Kennett's mouth—like she was someone else with him, a braver, freer version of herself. A girl who might actually go on a quest, like Odysseus.

"I'm sorry," he said, pushing his chair back from the table as if he thought she might ask him to leave. "Did I offend you? I think of you that way sometimes—like a sort of shorthand—"

"I'm not offended," Miriam told him, doing her best to suppress the frisson of excitement that swept through her at the idea that he thought of her when they weren't together. Maybe someday soon she'd get over this, like the bout of influenza she'd had last autumn. Until then, she'd have to pretend it didn't exist. "And yes, fine. We can continue our discussion outside. But first, reshelve *The Odyssey*. Properly, of course."

"So bossy," he said, giving her that impossible smile of his. But he did as she said.

Miriam found herself watching him as he lifted the book from the table and strolled to the shelves, stretching to put *The Odyssey* back where it belonged—and dropped her eyes, horrified, a hot blush heating her cheeks. She had no business noticing the lean, long line of his back as he slid the book into place, or the way his dark hair fell into his eyes and he brushed it back again. This could only end in disaster.

As he made his way back to their table, she stood hurriedly, her eyes on the ground. He stopped in front of her, clearing his throat. "Your face is all red, Miri," he said, pitching his voice low so as not to disturb the smattering of other citizens in the Library. "Are you feeling all right? Do you have a fever?"

He lifted his hand, as if to press it to her forehead, and she leapt backward, nearly tripping over her chair. "I'm fine. It's just hot in here. Can we go?"

"Of course," he said, dropping his hand to his side—but she caught the hint of puzzlement in his eyes. "After you."

Miriam strode toward the door, more embarrassed than ever. What had he made of her peculiar behavior? With any luck, he'd think she hadn't wanted him to touch her forehead because it was improper—not because she nursed a secret, sinful desire to feel his fingers on her skin.

Outside, the frigid air cooled her burning cheeks; it was December, a week before the celebration of the Architect's Arrival that marked the turn of the new year. This ceremony constituted the Commonwealth's only festivities. Everyone would gather in Clockverk Square and the surrounding streets, even the Executor and the Priests. There would be a bonfire, and spiced hot chocolate, and chanting. It was the one time of year all of them came together for celebration.

Kennett led the way through the Square, which was crowded with people enjoying the fresh air during Idle Day. They passed Genevieve, who glared at them both. It was her default expression; still, Miriam felt a twinge of uneasiness at the sight.

She reassured herself for the thousandth time that she and Kennett were doing nothing wrong. They were simply a tutor and a student, taking a walk during which they would discuss the finer points of *The Odyssey*. Still, she couldn't shake the suspicion there was something amiss—something Kennett wasn't telling her. Otherwise, why choose to leave the Library now, after two months of studying inside?

Kennett leading the way, they stepped off the cobblestones of the Square and onto the path that led to the outskirts of the City and the vineyards, where the Priests grew the grapes for their ceremonial wine. That warning sense flared again, stronger this time.

"Where are we going?" she asked Kennett, her skepticism clear in her voice.

"For a walk." He spun to face her, lifting his hands—the picture of innocence. "I'm not spiriting you away to the Borderlands, Miri, I promise—just going for a stroll. How do you expect to exercise if you won't venture off the streets of the City?"

He set a brisk pace, and she struggled to keep up, ignoring his ridiculous comment about the Borderlands. Though gluttony was a sin and they ate no more than their allotted rations each day, poring over books day in and day out hadn't done much for her physical condition. She was sufficiently winded that, as they went up one hill and down another, she didn't waste her breath on conversation—at least, not until they came to a stop in the vineyards.

Miriam looked around at the bare arbors and the skeletal remnants of the vines. "You want to talk about *The Odyssey* here?"

A shifty look crossed his face, and the alarm bells inside her clanged at a fever pitch.

"Or—you don't want to talk about *The Odyssey* at all." She fisted her hands on her hips. "What are we really doing here, Kennett?"

He looked left, then right, as if assuring himself that they were alone. "I have a question to ask you, Miri," he said, lowering his voice. "And before you say no—hear me out."

"A question you couldn't ask me in the Library?" To the nine hells and back again with this mess. Miriam knew she should turn around and walk right back the way they'd come, but curiosity held her in place. What could Kennett possibly have to ask her that was so important, he needed to keep the conversation a secret?

He scuffed his regulation brown leather shoes in the dirt, his voice pitched just above a whisper. Even though they were alone in the vineyard, one never knew who might be listening. "You know how much being a good medic matters to me. I do the most I can for my patients, but I know there must be more. I can feel it. There's so much I don't know." Raising his head, he met her eyes. "I get so frustrated sometimes, Miri. It's not a matter of pride. I just...I want to be able to heal them, and it troubles me so much when I can't. It's my calling, the way being a scholar is yours."

He was sincere—she could feel it. Still, she didn't understand why he was telling her this. "Your concern for your patients is admirable, Kennett. But what does any of this have to do with me?"

His gaze held Miriam's, and she fought not to look away. "I know the Library has a restricted section. There have to be more medical books in there—there must be."

"You want me to get you into the *restricted stacks?*" Her voice squeaked. "I don't have a key. I'd have to get one from a senior scholar. And even then, you'd need permission from the Priests to enter. I'd have to fill out the paperwork—"

"You misunderstand. I don't want a single book, like you get with a formal request. I want to see all of them, so I can decide for myself what I need to learn." There was a quiet insistence to his voice she'd never heard before. "People's *lives* are at stake, and information's given to us in dribs and drabs—just enough to do our jobs. I'm a good medic, but I could be so much better. I just need to know more."

She backed away from him, shaking her head. "I can't, Kennett. No matter how noble your cause. If we got caught, I'd lose my job."

"We won't get caught." His voice was honeyed, convincing. "I've thought about this a lot. We can go during the celebration on the eve of the Architect's Arrival. It's dark, and the streets will be crowded. No one will notice we're missing."

It would be the best chance they'd have—but still, how could she justify taking such a risk? Miriam shook her head again, feeling vaguely regretful when she saw the disappointment in his eyes—but not regretful enough to change her mind. "I'm sorry, Kennett. I can't."

But he didn't give up. "I have a young patient—Annalise—in my care who's sick with a fever she can't shake. I've tried everything, but she's getting worse and worse. What if there's something in those stacks that could save her life?"

Miriam froze, her foot catching on a root that protruded from the soil and almost dumping her onto the ground. Kennett caught her by the arm, then let go, as if the act had scorched his fingertips. "Please, Miri," he said, his eyes fixed on hers. "There's no time for the paperwork. And I can't just let her die."

Miriam didn't know what to do. On the one hand, doing as he asked would be violating the letter of her oath—and though she didn't know what the punishment would be, she was sure it would be swift...and terrible. That was one of the worst parts of the Priests' punishments—how, each time, they devised them to fit the sinner and the sin, unerringly coming up with what would devastate you the most. No two punishments were the same—and somehow, not knowing what to expect made it all the more terrifying. Covet your neighbor's promotion to supervisor, and you might find yourself laboring from sunup to sundown alongside the natural-born, your body caked in mud, so everyone who saw you knew you were as base and low as the earth from which your ancestors crawled. Show pride in your work as a carpenter, and you might wind up chained in the Commonwealth's dungeons while a bellator smashed your fingers with a hammer—the tool of your trade.

Miriam could only imagine what punishments they'd devise for her. Maybe somehow they could make her forget all the knowledge she'd ever gained. It made her quake to think of facing the consequences of violating the oath she'd sworn on Choosing Day, when she'd promised to uphold the duties of a Commonwealth scholar.

On the other hand, her life was dedicated to the pursuit of knowledge. If she refused Kennett now, was her oath just empty words?

Giving Kennett access to the stacks would be upholding the spirit of her promise, if not the letter—wouldn't it? If there was knowledge in the restricted section that could save the life of a child, how could she stand in his way?

It was sinful to care for this child, as she suspected Kennett might. But perhaps his feelings went no further than a medic's sworn duty. And Miriam imagined he could no sooner let a patient die if he had the power to save them than she could willfully set the Library's books aflame—no matter what her nightmares held.

In all the books they'd been reading together, the hero took a risk and made a difference. What if this was her chance?

Kennett stood still, those clear green eyes scanning her face. "Please, Miri," he said again. "Please help me."

Miriam drew a deep breath. And then she leapt. "All right," she told him. "I will."

CHAPTER FOUR

his was how they found themselves alone in the Library, while the celebration carried on outside. It was pitch black —they didn't dare turn on a light and risk discovery. The only windows were at the front of the building, nowhere near the shelving units, since sunlight could damage the books—but that was danger enough.

It was a terrible risk—but Miriam told herself this was her quest, the only one she would ever have. And it was for the sake of knowledge, which couldn't be a terrible thing. All Kennett wanted was to be the best medic he could, to save a child's life. The Priests would never let him explore the restricted section on his own. As a scholar, she was performing the ultimate service. And then there was the rest of it—her own insatiable curiosity to know what these hidden stacks held.

"Miri?" he said from beside her, his voice a breath. "I can't see anything."

Miriam couldn't, either. But she didn't need to. She knew the Library the way she thought she'd known her own heart, before she'd tumbled from the ladder and woken to see Kennett kneeling over her. She knew its scent of ink and paper, the peculiar stillness that always seemed to hover in the air.

"Here," she said, reaching out in the darkness. It wasn't a sin if it had a purpose, was it? Not if he needed her, to find his way?

Her fingers brushed his, and he jerked backward in surprise. "You want me to take your hand?" There was a curious note in his voice—not the revulsion she'd feared, but something unfamiliar she couldn't interpret.

"How else will you know where to go?" she whispered, her voice brisk. "Otherwise you'll wind up blundering into shelves and knocking things over. You'll make a bunch of noise, and where will we be then?"

Slowly, without another word, he slid his fingers between her own. He must've been keeping his hands in his pockets; his touch was warm, enveloping the iciness of her skin. A strange, electric current seemed to prickle between them, but she didn't pull away.

"You're freezing, Miri." Ever the medic, he rubbed her fingers, trying to warm her. If he felt any hint of that odd current, he gave no sign.

"It's cold outside," she said, doing her best to keep her voice steady. "Come on."

Their fingers linked, she led him to the back of the stacks, moving between the shelves by memory. They reached the door that led to the restricted section, and Miriam fumbled in her pocket for the key she'd stolen. She'd never done such a thing before, never stepped outside the rules that governed all their lives. She felt terrified—but also excited, as if she was part of something larger than herself…as if her life had finally begun.

It was a challenge to make the key fit in the dark, but finally she succeeded. The door swung open with a creak that made Miriam wince, and then they were inside.

Kennett shut it behind them and turned the lock, plunging them into blackness. Then he pulled his hand from hers. She heard him fumbling in his coat pocket a moment before she heard the scritch of a match, and the wavering light of a candle pierced the darkness of the stacks.

Miriam sucked in a breath, horrified. It was as if her

nightmares had come to life. "You brought *fire* into the Library? Are you crazy?"

"How else are we going to see?" he hissed back. "It's not like we can turn on a light. I couldn't do it out there because of the windows. But in here, there are none."

He had a point. Still, she couldn't help but imagine all of these precious books going up in flames—all of that knowledge lost forever. "Be careful," she warned, and beside her, she heard the ghost of a laugh.

"I think it's a little too late for that."

Kennett had a way of making her smile in the most troubling of circumstances. She couldn't decide if it was one of his best qualities or a dire flaw.

By the light of Kennett's candle, they made their way down the aisles one by one, holding the flame close enough to the spines to see their titles. Miriam thrilled at what the candlelight revealed —books about art and dreams and music. A whole world at her fingertips, if she was brave enough to read. And before they left, she swore to herself, she would.

Kennett rounded the next corner—and then stopped so short, she ran into his back. "Look, Miri." He sounded awed. "Here they are. And there's so *many*."

He held the candle higher so she could see, moving it along the shelves. He was right—these were all medical books. Studies of human anatomy and physiology, disease processes, the mind itself. They had taken a risk—and thus far, at least, it had paid off.

"Hold this, would you?" He thrust the candle at her and grabbed the first book at hand. Opening it, he gave a low growl of frustration. "By the Sins. I can't see a thing."

"Here," she said, stepping close to him and holding the candle over the page. He smelled of winter and the spiced chocolate he'd drunk in the Square, before they'd made their escape. Those baffling feelings of wanting to touch him, to brush that dark hair back from his eyes, surged through her. And yet she didn't back away.

She told herself he needed the candle to see—which was the truth. But the deeper truth, the one she was reluctant to acknowledge even to herself, was that if this was the only chance she'd get to be this close to Kennett, she didn't want to give it up.

"This is incredible," he said, turning the pages. "I suspected—but I had no idea—" He glanced up from the book, his eyes bright. "Thank you, Miri. Thank you for risking so much to bring me here. I'll find something here to help Annalise. I know I will."

"You're welcome," Miriam told him, striving to keep her tone dispassionate—though the fervent gratitude in his voice moved her. "I suppose in a way, this could be considered an extension of my duty."

Kennett bit his lip. "Don't do that, Miri. Please."

His statement confused Miriam. "Don't do what?"

"It's just the two of us here. Don't hide behind your job. Admit it—you're curious, like I am. You're driven by what drives me—to *know*."

Miriam felt as if he'd stripped her of her skin. How had he seen so much? What if all of this had been a trick, to root out her deepest vulnerabilities?

"I'm supposed to want to know." Her voice shook.

He was silent for a moment, during which the candle flickered and went out. But he didn't light it again. Instead, there was a slight current of air between them. Then, gently, carefully, his palm came to rest against her face. "Don't be frightened. I'm not threatening you. I'm trying to say—you don't see yourself clearly. You're more than just a scholar. You're brilliant. And brave." He sucked in a breath. "And beautiful." The last word was a rasp, torn from his throat.

Miriam stood still, mesmerized by the feel of his palm against her skin, the words that had just left his lips. Was she dreaming? Surely this couldn't be real.

Then Kennett snatched his hand away. She felt a sudden coldness where it had been, and stupidly wanted it back again. "By the Architect, Miri," he said, sounding as stunned as she felt, "I'm sorry. I shouldn't have done that—I don't know what—"

He stammered on, apologizing, assuring Miriam such a thing would never happen again—but she was only half-listening. Yes, such a touch was a sin—and she was a sinner for wanting it. But if she was truly brave, as he'd said, as she'd always wanted to be—if this was the only quest she would ever have—then perhaps she owed it to herself to experience it to its fullest. When would she ever get another chance?

"Miri." Kennett sounded desperate. "Please, say you'll forgive me. If you need to confess this to the Priests, I understand. What you must think of me . . ." He sank to his knees, as if his legs had given out. "By the Sins, I don't want to think about you like this. I know how incredibly wrong it is." His voice was a gravelly scrape. "I told myself it was only about the books, the knowledge I needed to help my patients. But I knew better. And now..."

Her mind whirled, snatching possibilities out of the air and then discarding them. She thought about the two of them, alone here; the enormity of the sin that might lie before them—and to her shock, found the notion didn't trouble her nearly as much as it should. She wanted this one night, this miracle of an evening, with Kennett and these mysterious, strange books. No one would know; no one would find out. It would be their secret.

She was tired of living in terror. This one night, she wanted to be brave. She wanted to take what she craved—what was freely given—without worrying about the consequences.

"We should go," Kennett said, sounding more miserable than ever.

Miriam found her voice. "But your books—"

"To the nine hells with the books," he said fiercely, rising to his feet—but she stood with him, threading her fingers through his to make him stay.

This was a moment Miriam would never have again. She wouldn't let her fears make her give it up. Kennett had as much to lose as she did; he would never betray her.

"'I have been and still am a seeker,'" she told him, her voice a whisper, "'but I have ceased to question stars and books; I have begun to listen to the teaching my blood whispers to me.'" It was a quote from Herman Hesse's *Damian*.

Kennett froze, his fingers stilling in hers. Miriam swore she could feel his pulse stop. Then it resumed again, this time at a frantic pace. "What are you saying, Miri?"

"I don't want to leave." Her voice shook, but it came. "And if you've sinned, then so have I—because I've thought about you, too."

The book fell to the floor. One hand still in hers, he braced himself on the shelf behind Miriam with the other, as if to keep from falling. They stood for a long minute, listening to each other breathe. And finally he whispered, his words stones that tumbled into the dark, "'Smooth the descent, and easy is the way.'"

He didn't say the first line of the verse, from Virgil's *Aeneid,* but he didn't have to. Miriam knew it well: *The gates of hell are open night and day.*

There in the blackness of the Library, the spines of the books pressing against her own and Kennett's chocolate-scented breath warm on her skin, Miriam felt a certainty that had nothing to do with the things they had been taught—the sanctity of virtue and the boorishness of sin. She lifted her hands to his face, feeling the roughness of his stubble rasp against her palms—then slid them lower, learning his body the way she'd learned the words of so many books…with utmost attention to detail and a singular focus that committed them to memory.

His breath caught in his throat as her fingertips traced the abacus of his ribs. "Miri, what are you doing?"

Miriam had no idea. But she did know that being here, with him, like this, was exactly what she wanted, despite the risk.

"'The more a thing is perfect,'" she quoted Dante, her hands drifting across the flat plane of his stomach, hearing him gasp into the dark, "'the more it feels pleasure and pain.'"

He pressed his face to hers, and only then did she realize he was crying. "I'm not perfect, Miri. A perfect boy wouldn't want you like this. Wouldn't risk your life. I'm selfish. How can you not see that?" His voice turned bitter, like he had a mouthful of ash and was spitting it out with every word.

Miriam shook her head, and felt his fingers tangle in her hair, his grip desperate, as if he feared that at any moment, she would be ripped away. "These past two months have been the best of my life, Kennett. I don't want to lose that—or you. We can go back to how it was; no one has to know. Let us have this—just for tonight."

He exhaled, a slow, broken breath—the sound of surrender. "This is a doomed venture, Miri. I know it. And yet—all I want is to be here, with you, in the dark. I know—I *know*—it's a grievous sin. And yet, I can't bring myself to care."

Miriam realized then that the death grip he had on her hair had little to do with thinking she would vanish. He'd wrapped his fingers in her hair to keep from touching her—because he didn't trust himself.

But Miriam trusted him. She knew he would never hurt her— would sacrifice himself before he let her come to harm—and not just because he'd sworn an oath to heal. She wasn't sure how she'd come by this conviction; it was bone-deep, nothing like the intellectual knowledge she'd gleaned from her books. But it was strong, and true, and real.

"I'm sorry, Miri." He lowered his face to her shoulder. His tears wet her skin. "I promised to do no harm, and look what I'm doing to you."

His grief tore at Miriam, as if something was ripping loose, deep in her chest. She felt it go—the last mooring that tethered her to who she'd been, fraying and finally giving way. She was a tiny boat, adrift in the unfathomable sea of herself. And what she was comprised of, it turned out, was a bottomless pit of rage—not at Kennett, but *for* him.

She didn't care if wrath was forbidden in the Commonwealth. She wanted to get her hands on a bellator's sverd and skewer everyone who had ever made the boy in her arms despise himself this way.

"Kennett," she said, struggling to keep her voice level, "I've spent my life inside books. I've read of love and hate, of civilizations that have crumbled to dust because of men's wickedness. I know what evil looks like, and you're not it."

He lifted his head from her shoulder. Miriam couldn't see him, but she didn't have to. She knew every line of his face, every expression that coursed through those deep green eyes. "You're so certain." His voice was a whisper; his fingertips skimmed her cheek, drifting over her skin.

Miriam lifted her hand to wipe away his tears. "You can believe me," she said, willing him to listen. "For I am a scholar, and we do not lie."

Kennett's hands were still in her hair. Slowly, carefully, he closed the tiny distance between them. She felt the length of his body against hers, felt him tremble. He lowered his head, his lips ghosting over her temple, her eyelids, her cheeks. "Miri, be sure." His voice was a breath in the darkness. "There is no going back from this."

But Miriam didn't want to go back. She wanted only to go forward, with him—no matter how short their path.

His lips were a centimeter from hers. And yet still he held back, waiting.

Like every child growing up in the Commonwealth, she and Kennett had watched vids from before the Fall, showing them the ramifications of the Deadly Sins. They'd seen the perils of dating, a sinful practice which often ended in a lustful kiss and the mysterious *more* that was punishable by death. And in the pages of the books they'd studied together, they'd read of characters sinning. They were meant to study such things, to learn how easy it was to commit acts of sin and how important it was to cling to the virtues, since a single choice could strip them away.

Miriam had, as she told Kennett, lived her life in those books, rarely looking up. There had been so little worth fixing her eyes on. But he was different. Even invisible in the darkness of the Library, he shone—the brightest, most beautiful thing she had ever seen. He was the candle that illuminated the endless gloom of her days—a tedium she had mistaken for comfort and safety. And Miriam knew she would rather live a week by the light of that flame than be condemned to a lifetime of the dark.

She stood on her toes and touched her lips to his, tasting chocolate and the salt of his tears. "I am absolutely sure."

He didn't ask again. Instead he kissed her back, his hands leaving her hair at last, roving over her body with a reverence that made Miriam wonder if he wanted to memorize her, too. He lifted her, and she felt the spines of the volumes on the shelf bite into her back as their clothes fell away. It seemed fitting that the books were their witnesses—filled with words, but mute. They would never betray Miriam's secrets.

She had been wrong to think Kennett was a candle. He was a fire, blazing bright—and she threw herself into it, wanting only to be consumed. Together, they burned.

What they were doing was forbidden. They had no map, no instruction manual. None of her books could show them the way. But they found it, somehow, together.

After, in the stolen minutes they had left to themselves, Kennett held Miriam close. She half-expected words of love; but it was both too soon and too late to speak of such things. Instead, his palm still flat against her heart and their bodies slick with sweat, Kennett whispered into her hair, "Alea iacta est." Latin, for *the die is cast*—the words Julius Caesar had uttered when he crossed the Rubicon.

That was the first time. But it wouldn't be the last.

CHAPTER FIVE

Miriam would never regret loving Kennett. But she had no illusions about what would happen if anyone found out there was more between them than Idle Day study sessions and lively debates about the finer points of ancient philosophy.

She'd thought what happened between them would only occur once—but she'd known nothing of such things. Instead of quenching the thirst she felt for him, their sin had only made her want him more—and he felt the same.

In public, they ignored each other—not overly difficult, since other than mealtimes and ceremonies, they were rarely in the same room. They stole their time together, snatching it from the jaws of their daily lives under the ever-vigilant eyes of the Priests and the Informers. Never again did they risk the confines of the Library—though the information Kennett found that night had indeed saved Annalise's life. Instead, they met in the woods despite the cold, in the vineyards, in the shadows of the trees that edged the rocks of Black Falls.

Miriam knew what she and Kennett were doing was beyond wrong. But she craved him, the way she'd only craved knowledge before. When she wasn't with him, she longed to hear his voice, to feel his touch on her skin.

She told herself they were already damned. The Architect had judged them from the moment they committed their sins—maybe even from the first second sinning had crossed their minds. Kennett was right; there was no going back. And what choice did they have? It wasn't as if they could leave. Even if they were willing to take their chances with the hordes in the Borderlands, the only way out was through the forest, where the Bastarour roamed—which was no way out at all. They were stuck here, chained to their fate—and although both of them knew they inched closer to discovery with every clandestine meeting, they couldn't seem to stop.

The first time Miriam missed her monthly courses, she figured it was a fluke. After all, she wasn't always regular. By the second time, though, she began to worry. The food in the dining hall smelled peculiar to her; in the three minutes allotted to her to shower each day, her body felt different to her somehow, more rounded. Very quietly, she began to panic.

She said nothing to Kennett, hoping she was mistaken. But the next time they were together, he cupped one of her breasts in his hand, his touch not that of a lover but of the medic who had stitched up her forehead that very first day. "Miri," he said, and in his voice she heard both an extraordinary joy and a foreboding horror.

She burst into tears, which was as much answer as he needed. He held her to him, stroking her back, trying to soothe her. But both of them knew the truth: by giving life to the child that now grew within her body, they had signed their own death warrants.

"We'll hide it," Kennett said when they drew apart. "As long as we can."

It was February. Miriam knew from watching the surrogates who bore the Commonwealth's children that the process took approximately nine months. As a medic, Kennett knew this even better than she—though only midwives delivered the Commonwealth's babies, so male medics would not be exposed to the impurity of the process. "But it'll be the summer," she said, wiping the tears from her eyes.

She didn't have to say more. All of their clothes were standardized, to prevent the sin of taking pride in their appearance. The uniforms librarians wore in the summer months were modest but light. She knew what the surrogates looked like when they were bearing heavily. There was no way she and Kennett could hide a full-term pregnancy.

"We'll figure something out. I promise." He took her hand in his. Despite his efforts to stay strong for her, his green eyes were filled with tears. "By the Architect, Miri, I am so very sorry."

"Will you stop apologizing? This is *not* your fault," she told him. "We made our choices together. And I would rather die alongside you than live in a world where you didn't exist."

"You're not going to die." He pulled her to him again, his voice rough. "We have a little time," he said against her hair. "We're smart, the two of us. You're the most brilliant person I know. We'll think of something."

He stroked her hair as she tried to imagine what that might be. She wracked her mind, as she had every moment since she'd suspected she was pregnant, but could think of no solution.

And then she felt Kennett suck in a breath, as if something had occurred to him.

"What?" she asked him, but he shook his head, his arms still tight around her.

"Tell me." She pulled back, looking up into his face.

"There are herbs," he said, sounding hesitant. "It would be dangerous—but I could get them for you…if that's what you want."

Herbs—to get rid of the child, he meant. Miriam knew she should consider this. Her life would be forfeit anyhow, if they were found out; what was a little danger? But before her conscious mind could make a decision, her mouth spoke for her. "If I pay for this with my life, then so be it. But the child is innocent. I'll not condemn it, too."

She drew a deep breath, then said the rest of it: "Don't worry. I won't betray you, Kennett."

His eyebrows drew down, as if in puzzlement. "What do you—"

"If they find me out, I will never speak your name," she said, tugging her shirt to rights. "I don't care what they do to me."

Kennett's jaw dropped. "By the Architect, Miri, do you think I care about any of that? All I care about is *you*. And if you think I would let you go through this sin-infested mess alone, then you are insane." He folded his arms across his chest, staring her down. "You are *not* to protect me from this, Miri, do you understand? We started this together, and we will finish it the same way—no matter how we end. Promise me."

Miriam knew she could be stubborn—and normally, Kennett was the one to give. He was far more likely to compromise in most scenarios…but apparently, not this one. His eyes fixed on Miriam's, refusing to let her drop her gaze. And finally she said, the words emerging on a sigh, "I promise."

His arms came around her again—but then one of his hands dropped to her stomach, his palm curving around the baby growing within. "In another world," he said, sounding immeasurably sad, "this would be cause for celebration. I wish that was the world in which we lived."

Miriam laced her fingers through his, holding their baby together, and for a moment, imagined that world—where she could bear Kennett's child and watch it grow, where they could be a family, together. "I know," she said, leaning against him, listening to the steady beat of his heart. "I wish so, too."

Miriam's eighteenth birthday came and went. They didn't celebrate such things in the Commonwealth, other than a means of marking the time. Miriam personally measured the months in smaller increments, based on the changes in her body, the way her stomach grew. She felt as if she were a ticking clock, the hands moving ever closer toward an inevitable end.

Soon, she felt the child stirring within her. At night she would lie with her hand pressed to her belly, marveling at the jab of a knee or an elbow. Kennett smuggled her some of the special vitamins meant for the surrogates, and she took them daily, wanting to give their child every advantage.

She named their child Lucien, which meant 'bringing light' in Latin. She'd always thought of Kennett as the flame that lit her darkness, and resolved to think of their baby the same way. If she managed to carry him to term, he—she had decided it was a boy, for no other reason than a feeling she had—would be relegated to being one of the natural-born, fated to do menial tasks. But at least he would be alive.

Miriam hated the idea of leaving Lucien, but what choice did she have? Their best-case scenario was that somehow she and Kennett would escape detection until he was born, and they'd be able to smuggle him into the Nursery among the other newborns, his parents unknown. She'd never heard of doing such a thing, but it seemed the only path open to them. Even that seemed a dicey proposition—surely the Executor would demand the midwives check each woman of childbearing age for signs of a recent birth, and then it would be all over for them.

It made Miriam furious to think of Lucien subjected to the indignities of the natural-born. She imagined a little boy with Kennett's beautiful eyes and her olive skin, her thirst for knowledge and Kennett's gentle heart, forced to scrub toilets and dig ditches for his entire life, and felt a forbidden wave of wrath break over her.

All along, she'd thought her worst sin was the overt pride she took in her work. How wrong she'd been.

Was this the only way people lived, in all the world? Was there no other way?

The months passed, and the clock of herself ticked. She and Kennett hardly dared to meet, terrified to draw any unnecessary attention to themselves. The last thing Miriam wanted was to give anyone a reason for their glances to linger on her.

But as her belly grew, she could feel time slipping away, like sands through an hourglass. One night, as she climbed into bed, Genevieve said, her voice laden with suspicion, "You've put on quite a bit of weight, haven't you, Miriam?"

Miriam's heart pounded unevenly, but she lifted her chin. "I don't know what you mean," she told Genevieve. "Perhaps you should visit the medics and have your eyesight checked."

"My eyesight is fine." Genevieve slid beneath the blankets of her cot, her gaze fixed on Miriam's midsection, as if she could see through the coverlet and the fabric of Miriam's shift to what lay beneath. And Miriam knew then that her time had run out.

When she and Kennett met again, in the vineyards at dusk the following evening, she told him what Genevieve had said. He ran a hand through his dark hair, his face grim. In the fading light, his broad shoulders blocking out the last bit of the sun as it sank below the line of the arbors and beneath the horizon, he looked like a boy made of light and shadows—as if Miriam had conjured him from the deepest desires of her heart. But when she blinked, he was still there—flesh and blood, pain clear in the depths of his sea-glass eyes.

"Miriam," he said, "no matter what happens, remember I love you."

Despite all they'd been through, they'd never spoken these words to each other before. Perhaps it was ridiculous, given that she was bearing Kennett's child—but there were few words more forbidden to utter. It was as if Kennett had been saving them up for her like some kind of treasure, a precious gem for her to carry next to her heart.

"I love you, too," she told him, and watched his face light with joy.

He lifted a calloused hand to cup her chin and bent his head, his mouth finding hers. The kiss was bittersweet, flavored with the tears she hadn't known were streaking her cheeks and the unmistakable taste of farewell.

They were still standing that way when the worst found them: Priest Traasen, in his blood-red robes that swept the ground as he walked, and the two bellators that accompanied him, clad all in black and studded with weapons. Miriam recognized one of them by his bright red hair—Kilían Bryndísarson, who she knew had had the cot next to Kennett when they were both seventh-formers, before the Choosing. The other one was Efraím Stinar, five years into his training and already one of the Thirty, the Bellatorum's elite corps whose services were reserved for the most egregious of infractions. Next to them was Genevieve, her pug-nosed face set in a vicious mask of vindication.

"You see," she said to the Priest, pointing at Miriam—specifically, at her belly, which there was no longer any point in trying to hide. "I told the truth."

The Priest's eyes swept over Miriam and Kennett, contempt clear in every line of his face. Then his voice rang out through the vineyards, righteous and resonant. "Miriam Larsen. Kennett Gundarson. I find you guilty of the sins of lust and fornication. You will be sentenced to execution in Clockverk Square. As you have sinned, so will you die—together."

Miriam felt a tremor run through Kennett and into her. Still, he squared his shoulders, and she straightened her spine. They had agreed to meet this fate with dignity. She had just a single question—the only one that really mattered.

"What about the child?"

The Priest drew himself up, regarding her with disgust. "You will be confined to the hospital until the child is born, and your fellow sinner held in the dungeons, to contemplate the fate that awaits you both. Then your bastard spawn will join the ranks of the natural-born, and the two of you will face the bellators' blades."

His lip curled, as if the air surrounding Miriam and Kennett had gone rancid. "Bellators, remove the boy from my sight. I'll escort the girl to the hospital myself. She's no threat to me."

The bellators strode forward, their faces expressionless. They crushed fallen grapes as they went, the tart, sweet scent of happier times filling the air. Neither of them drew their weapons; they didn't have to. There was nowhere for Miriam and Kennett to run.

She clung to Kennett—for what did it matter now?—and felt his arms tighten around her. He'd worried they were a cage—but they were a cradle, a place of refuge. They had always felt that way to her.

He held her close, the child alive and moving between them. The person they had made, together—the physical manifestation of their love and their sins.

"I am a medic." His voice was a shattered whisper. "But I have no idea how to heal a broken heart."

Those were the last words he said to Miriam, before they took him away.

CHAPTER SIX

The pain of childbirth was nothing compared to the ache in Miriam's heart—from losing Kennett, and from the knowledge that she would soon lose her son.

She saw her Lucien only once, just after he was born—when the midwife pulled him from her body and took him to the scale in the corner of her hospital room to be weighed. She wasn't meant to see him, but she struggled to her elbows nonetheless and strained to look. Hungrily, she drank him in: the olive skin and high cheekbones so like her own, the shock of black hair and lucent green eyes that marked him as Kennett's. He was beautiful, perfect. Hers, if only for that moment.

When he started to wail, the need to comfort him was visceral. Miriam hated the clinical way the midwife prodded and poked him. She wanted to tear the woman's hands from him, to hold him close. But she knew better than to move.

"Can I hold him?" she said, her voice cracked from screaming. "Just once?"

The midwife glared at her in silence, swaddling Lucien in a blanket. She swept Miriam's baby up, still wailing, and took him away without a word.

Miriam knew she would never be allowed to see him again.

Still, that didn't stop her from pleading when Efraím Stinar entered her room hours later, doing the bellators' regular sweep to ensure she hadn't leapt out the window—which, in her current state, was a laughable proposition.

"Please," Miriam said, hating how pitiful she sounded. "Please let me see him one more time."

Bellator Stinar paused, his hand on the doorknob. "I couldn't do that even if I wanted to—which I most certainly do not."

Something about the gleeful tone of his voice alarmed her. "What do you mean?"

"Your bastard son is dead." He bared his teeth at her in a snarl. "And tomorrow at sunrise, you will be too—by my hand."

Miriam felt her heart thud to a stop—not at his casual mention of her execution, which was hardly a surprise, but at what he'd said about her beautiful Lucien. She'd heard her baby cry—loud and healthy, if gut-wrenching, like Kennett had told her he would. What could have happened to him?

"How?" She choked out the word.

Bellator Stinar took pleasure in her misery; she could see it in the expression of satisfaction that lit his eyes. "That's none of your concern, girl," he said. "But perhaps the Architect sensed the evil in his soul and snuffed it out before your bastard could bring a blight upon the world." That malicious shark's grin lifting his lips, he turned his back on her.

Miriam thought of the single, shining moment when she'd been allowed to see Lucien. When those wide, green eyes had looked into hers, she hadn't seen corruption. She'd seen pure, perfect innocence.

She refused to believe the Architect had taken Lucien because of her sins. Perhaps something invisible in his body had been broken. She wished more than anything that she could ask Kennett if such a thing were possible, but of course she could not. She was marooned with her grief, which was so monstrous, it threatened to devour her whole.

In the Commonwealth, citizens didn't cry often, save in the

case of children who'd skinned a knee or broken an arm. Crying implied that you'd lost something that mattered to you, and they were never allowed to possess anything worth having. But as the door shut behind Efraím Stinar with a click, leaving Miriam in darkness, she felt the first hot tear trickle down her cheek. And alone in the dark, she wept for the loss of her child—and for everything that might have been.

"G&ETT; UP." T&HEE; VOICE WAS HARSH—AND VAGUELY FAMILIAR.

Miriam blinked and opened her eyes, which felt swollen from crying. Through the thin white curtains, she could see that it was still pitch-black outside. Surely it wasn't time yet. "Who's there?" she asked, her voice hoarse.

"Bellator Bryndísarson."

So it was time, after all. With difficulty, Miriam struggled upward. The place between her legs ached and throbbed. "All right," she said, her voice dull. Lucien was dead, and soon she and Kennett would be too. All that remained was to see it through. "I won't fight you."

"You'd better not." There was an odd hint in his voice—was it *amusement?* "I've come to help you escape."

Obviously she was still asleep—or perhaps hallucinating. Could enough grief and terror do that to a person? She fell back down on the bed with a thump, shutting her eyes again.

"Get up." A large, strong hand shook her by the shoulder. "We don't have much time."

Even her hallucinations were demanding. She opened her eyes again, squinting into the darkness of her room. Sure enough, Kilían Bryndísarson was crouching by her bedside, his hair a flash of copper in the shadows and a blade in the hand that wasn't gripping her shoulder. "Is this some kind of trick?"

He tugged her to a sitting position, and Miriam had to bite her lip to suppress a hiss of pain. "Kennett said you wouldn't trust me

—although what you think you've got to lose, I can't imagine—so he made me memorize something for you." Hooking a hand beneath her elbow, he pulled Miriam to her feet. "'But to return, and view the cheerful skies, In this the task and mighty labor lies.'"

Miriam's heart, which had been lodged behind her ribs like a lump of ice ever since Bellator Stinar told her Lucien was dead, gave a painful thump. That night in the Library, before they'd kissed for the first time, Kennett had whispered a line from the Aeneid to her: *Smooth the descent, and easy is the way.* This was the second half of the quote—about how hard it was to find your way back from Hell.

Hard—but not impossible.

"Do you believe me now?" He gave her upper arm a shake. "I mean you no harm. Quite the contrary. But we've got to go."

Setting her feet, Miriam looked up into his shadowed eyes. "Why would you help us?"

A pained expression flickered across Kilían's face before it returned to its usual inscrutability. "Because if we were allowed such things, Kennett would be my friend." His lips flattened into a grim line. "Now, move."

Outside Miriam's hospital room, the two bellators assigned to guard her sat, slumped and unconscious, in the chairs that flanked her door. "What did you do to them?"

"You can thank Kennett. There are unanticipated advantages to having a medic's knowledge of drugs and herbs." He stared dispassionately down at his fellow warriors. "They went to sleep like babes in the nursery. And Kennett swore that when they woke up, they'd have no memory of anything beyond the moment they took their places for their shift."

She had a moment of fierce pride in Kennett, and allowed herself the privilege—they were well beyond the point where such things mattered. "What a pity," she said, her tone short, and saw Kilían's eyes widen.

"You'll have to move fast," he said, looking her up and down. "Can you do that?"

"I can do anything I need to do," Miriam told him, and it was the truth. If this was their one chance, she wouldn't waste it.

Kilían didn't ask again. Silently, he led her down a back stairwell, then out into the dark and toward Marketour Square. They ducked into an alleyway, and he paused at a metal door set into the concrete, pulled a keyring from his belt, and undid the lock. The door swung open, revealing a steep staircase that led into blackness.

The thought of forcing her weakened body down those stairs was overwhelming. But waiting for her at the bottom was Kennett and—somehow—freedom, so Miriam made herself step through the trapdoor and onto the steps. They were metallic and slippery with moisture, and she hung onto the railing with all of her strength, imagining that she was climbing down a ladder in the Library. She had done that a hundred times; this would be no different. She wasn't descending into the pit of Hell. This was just a staircase, and it would have a bottom. All she had to do was keep climbing down.

The door clattered shut above her, and then the steps creaked as they took Kilían's weight. Oddly, his presence reassured her. She took a renewed grip on the railing and willed herself to climb faster. And finally she took one last step and felt not metal under her feet but the firm grit of concrete.

She stood to the side, and then Kilían was on the ground beside her, unclipping something from his belt. A moment later, the thin glow of a flashlight pierced the dark.

"Come on," he said, and turned without another word, heading into the gloom beyond the weak beam of his light.

They walked through what had to be some kind of tunnel system for what felt like forever. The damp air clogged Miriam's lungs, and she felt the blood dripping between her legs, which trembled with the effort of holding her upright—but she refused to slow down, even when it meant she had to hold onto the wall to keep from falling.

Kilían cleared his throat. "Are you all right?" His voice was gruff, as if he was unaccustomed to asking such things. Most likely he was; bellators dealt in death and pain, not comfort.

"I'm fine." Miriam kept her voice clipped, so as not to reveal the extent of her exhaustion. "Keep going."

A low, grudging chuckle emerged from the dark. "Kennett said you were tough. All right; I'll take you at your word. It's not too much longer now."

He hadn't lied. In a few minutes, the tunnel narrowed, then dead-ended at a door. Kilían pulled the keyring off his belt again and fit one into the lock, which swung wide with a groan, revealing a small room filled with—of all things—books.

But for once, Miriam hardly had eyes for them. Because in the middle of the room, one eye blackened and a deep purple bruise on his cheek, was—

"Kennett!" She threw her arms around him, and felt his come tight around her in return, holding her close. He smelled of dirt and blood and hunger—but the thump of his heart beneath her ear was as strong and steady as it had always been.

He set Miriam away from him and laid a palm against her cheek, gazing down at her with wonder, as if he could hardly believe she was real—and a deep, abiding sadness. "Miri, I heard about the baby. I'm so sorry."

"There you go, apologizing again." She sniffed, trying to hold back the tears.

"I wish I could've been there." His eyes shone, glassy with tears of his own. "Maybe I could have saved him."

"It's not your—"

Kilían cleared his throat. "About the infant—I have reason to believe Bellator Stinar might be mistaken."

Miriam's eyes grew wide, and she felt her pulse quicken, threatening to choke her. Into the fissure that had cracked her heart ever since she'd heard those horrible words—*Your bastard son is dead*—flowed a thin river of hope. "What are you saying?"

The bellator met her eyes. "Efraím told you what he knew to be true," he said, his voice expressionless. "But I have reason to believe otherwise."

"Our baby is *alive?*" She was torn between wanting to leap for joy and claw his face to ribbons for not telling her sooner. "By the nine hells, what are we doing down here, then? We have to go back. Kennett, we have to find him, take him with us—"

But Kilían was shaking his head. "There's no way. I don't know where they've taken the child, and tracking him down would take more time than we have." He shifted his weight, and the weapons on his belt clinked against each other. "The sun will be rising in an hour, and you need to be well clear of here by then."

"To the Sins with the sun! You got Kennett out, and me too. Surely we can rescue Lucien. I'm not leaving him behind." Her voice broke. "I can't. Kennett, tell him."

"Miri." Kennett took her hand, and when she looked up at him, the tears had overflowed, streaking his cheeks. "This is wonderful news. But Kilían's right—how are we supposed to find him in time? If we go back, we'll all die—together."

She lunged for the door, heedless of the way her abused body protested. "You leave, then. I have to go back—I have to find him—"

Her hand closed on the knob, and then Kennett's arms were around her, restraining her.

"I'm sorry, Miri. I really am. But his best chance at life—and ours—is for us to go."

Miriam kicked and struggled, but Kennett held her fast. "I'm so sorry," he said again and again, and for once she didn't tell him not to apologize. She hated both him and Kilían with a bright, fiery intensity that threatened to tear her apart. All she could think of was her Lucien, lost and crying, subjected to who knew what fate, as she and Kennett abandoned him to save their own skins.

"Let me go!" she said, fighting against Kennett's grip, but he wouldn't loosen it.

"I can't, Miri." Tears choked his voice. "I wish I could. Seeing you this way—leaving him behind—it kills me. If I thought we had the slightest chance, I'd go back for him in a heartbeat."

"So you're not even going to try?" She struggled harder.

His voice broke. "Please don't hate me. I can't lose you, too."

Miriam wanted to ask if he didn't care about losing Lucien—if she was all that mattered to him—but she knew the answer. Of course he cared. She knew him too well to suspect anything else. He was stopping her from going back because he'd brought himself to accept what she couldn't bear to—that their only chance at salvation was to leave their son behind.

Misery churned in her stomach. It surged upward, into her chest, her throat—and then she was sobbing, harsh, animal noises that tore themselves from her body. Her grief was so great, it seemed to inhabit her—like an invasive force she was helpless to resist.

At last she wore herself out and collapsed, limp, against Kennett's chest. The anger was gone, replaced with a weary sadness...lit by a gleaming hint of joy. Lucien was alive—but she would never see him again.

Kennett stroked her hair. "It's the right choice," he said, sounding as exhausted as she felt. "The only one."

"It might be the only choice." She forced the words out. "But that doesn't mean it's right."

"Miriam." Kilían had never said her name before; it sounded unfamiliar coming from his lips, stilted. "I'll look after the infant."

"What?" She lifted her head, eyeing him incredulously. Bellators didn't look after anyone but themselves.

"You have my word. I'll do all I can to make sure he comes to no harm."

She stared at him, looking for a twitch or a sidelong glance that would indicate he was lying. But his eyes were steady, clear and blue, with nothing in their depths save sincerity.

It was a peculiar promise, from a suspect source. But it was all she had.

She drew herself up and stepped back from Kennett. "Swear it, on your honor as a bellator." Her voice was hoarse from sobbing, but the words came clearly, laden with conviction.

Kilían held her gaze. When he spoke, his tone was solemn, his face grave. "On my honor as a bellator and the strength of my sverd, I do so swear."

Next to Miriam, she heard Kennett suck in a surprised breath. A bellator could swear no higher oath. They valued nothing more than their honor and their sverds—the razor-sharp blades they wore strapped to their backs. It would have to be good enough.

"All right," she said, lifting her chin. "All right, I'll go."

Kilían inclined his head, as if acknowledging what had passed between them. Then he turned to Kennett. "You remember what I told you?"

Taking her hand, Kennett nodded. "Go through the tunnels beyond there." He pointed to a small door Miriam hadn't noticed before, set in the opposite wall of the room. "Follow the sketches of the wolf's face; they'll lead us where we need to go. We'll come out on the other side of the electric fence. Someone will meet us there and help us get away."

"That's it." Kilían nodded. "And remember, they'll ask you for proof that you've come from the Brotherhood. When they say, 'Speak of the wolf, and he will come,'" you'll reply—"

"A wolf does not bite a wolf." Kennett's voice was clear and sure.

The Brotherhood? It had to be some kind of resistance movement. Which could only mean one thing: Kilían Bryndísarson, loyal bellator, was a traitor to the Commonwealth. He'd brought the two of them to a hidden room full of books—which Miriam wished desperately she could explore; their content had to be incendiary for them to be concealed this way—and was facilitating their escape, for no other reason than that he considered Kennett to be his friend.

Then again, Kennett could lead a person to take incredible risks. Who knew that better than Miriam?

"I have to get back," Kilían said, his voice rough—not from indifference, but as if it concealed some deep, forbidden emotion. "May the blessings of the Architect be with you both. Stand strong."

"Thank you, Kilían. For our lives. And for your promise to our son." Kennett's voice was as rough as his. And then, to Miriam's amazement, he let go of her hand and embraced the bellator, heedless of the deadly weapons that hung from his hips.

Shock spread across Kilían's face—followed by a grief so profound it mirrored Miriam's own, and a strange, aching hunger. Then his face went blank. Slowly, he lifted his arms and returned Kennett's embrace. "Don't waste it," he said, his voice a croak— and then he disengaged himself, slipped through the door to the tunnels, and vanished back the way they'd come.

Kennett and Miriam stared at each other—for once, wordless. And then she crossed to the small door that led to the unknown and yanked it open. Together, they stepped through, taking their first steps on the road toward freedom.

But as the door that led to the tunnels thudded shut behind them, as Kennett pulled a flashlight from his pocket and shone the beam on the moldering walls, looking for the face of the wolf, Miriam couldn't help but look back. And she swore an oath of her own.

Somehow, someway, someday—she would come back for their son. She didn't care how long it took, or what she had to sacrifice. She would see her Lucien again.

"Miri." Kennett's voice was a whisper. "Look."

Miriam followed the beam of the flashlight. There, on the uneven wall of the tunnel, was the sketch of the wolf, just as Kilían had promised. Beyond it was darkness—but at the end, if the bellator could be believed, someone was waiting to welcome them. Miriam and Kennett just had to be brave enough to look.

She had always wanted to know what lay beyond the Commonwealth's boundaries—though she had never intended to find out this way, at such a terrible cost. At long last, she had her quest—at the expense of a broken heart.

But Miriam made up her mind that whatever happened, her story would not be a tragedy. It couldn't be—because she had the boy she loved by her side, and a promise she'd sworn to keep.

With one last glance at the world that had raised and tricked and trapped her—the one that still held Lucien prisoner—she plucked the flashlight from Kennett's hand and led the way toward the light.

This story originally appeared in an earlier form as "Smooth the Descent" in UNBOUND: STORIES OF TRANSFORMATION, LOVE, AND MONSTERS, published by Five Points Press.

ENVY

"A HEART OF FROST AND FIRE"

CHAPTER ONE

In the Commonwealth, friendship was not allowed. Still, Kilían Bryndísarson had never been able to deny the pull he felt toward Kennett Gundarson.

It had begun when they were twelve years old—earlier than that, if Kilían was brutally honest with himself. That day, Kilían and his fellow Nurserymates had been running an obstacle course in the woods that surrounded the City, with the Mothers judging them. If any of them failed to complete it in the allotted time, all of them would have to run it again. Discipline was vital to life in the Commonwealth, and the Mothers instilled it at every turn.

Kilían was a fast runner; he almost always came in first in the challenges the Mothers set for them. The only one who came close to matching his speed was Kennett, and despite the fact that pride in one's accomplishments and envy of another's skills were forbidden, whenever they ran these courses, Kilían always tried as hard as he could to beat him. The Priests were always watching; the Mothers said so. At the age of twelve, Kilían already knew he wanted to be a bellator, and excelling at physical challenges was an excellent way to get the Priests' attention.

Mother Truelson blew the whistle, and Kilían broke from the crowd of his white-clad Nurserymates and bolted from the starting line, Kennett hot on his heels. He darted into the woods, heading for the canvas tunnel that signaled the course's first obstacle. Dropping to his belly, he wriggled through the tunnel, then came out the other side and sprinted for the clearing where the climbing wall stood. This was where he lost Kennett; the other boy could give him a run for his money on flat ground, but Kilían was by far the better climber. He glanced down when he reached the top; sure enough, Kennett was only a quarter of the way up, the sun gleaming on his dark hair, picking out its blue-black highlights. Bizarrely, Kilían thought of the pictures of seals he'd seen in books from before the Fall—of the animals' wet, shining obsidian skin, of their grace underwater. Then he turned away and vaulted over the wall, landing hard on the packed earth, and the image vanished.

Panting, he took off for the wooden balance beams, walking sure-footed along one and then another. As he leapt off the second one, executing a perfect shoulder roll, and came up onto his feet, he heard the sound of Kennett's feet hitting the ground beneath the climbing wall. The familiar thrill surged through him—the adrenaline-soaked sense of being at once the hunter and the prey. He sucked in a deep breath, inhaling the pungent scent of pine trees and leaf mold, and took off around the next curve, following the orange flags that the Mothers had staked in the dirt.

There were certain elements of the obstacle course that never changed—the climbing wall, the beams—and others that altered each time. These were the challenges, the ones Kilían loved best. Rounding the corner into a thicker part of the woods, he jumped over a log that the Mothers had positioned across the path and grinned as the finish line came into view—an orange ribbon strung between two trees. He took off for it at a full-out sprint— and his foot caught on something, sending him flying through the air. He landed in a heap of fallen leaves with a grunt, a sharp pain shooting through his ankle as he fell. Above him, the blue sky spun.

From where he lay, he could see the orange ribbon of the

finish line fluttering in the breeze that stirred the trees and swept his sweat-drenched hair back from his face. Still struggling to catch his breath, he planted his palms in the dry, crumbling leaves and tried to push himself to his feet—but as soon as he put weight on his injured ankle, it gave way, sending him back down again. His pants had torn when he fell, and blood trickled from his knee, soaking the white fabric and dripping into the leaves.

By the Sins, what had he tripped over? Shoving himself to his elbows, he craned his head and saw a vine strung across the path, tied between two low scrub-bushes. His face flushed with mortification. What kind of bellator would he be if he couldn't even recognize a simple camouflage trap when he saw one? He wasn't worthy of the title. Self-disgust settled in his stomach, acrid and shifting.

To make his humiliation complete, Kennett chose this moment to round the bend. Kilían prayed to the Architect that he'd be foiled by the vine, too—but no. Kennett glanced down at the ground at the last moment and then leapt over it, his lanky limbs coiling as he launched himself into the air and then unfolding as he landed on the other side. It occurred to Kilían that there was something oddly beautiful about the way Kennett moved. He was always competing against the other boy; he'd never had the chance to watch him before.

By all the Virtues, what was *wrong* with him, thinking about Kennett—about anyone—like this? In the Commonwealth, attraction of any kind was forbidden; children were the product of artificial insemination, and lust—one of the Seven Deadly Sins— was punishable by death. Kilían's face burned scarlet, and he was grateful that the other boy was fixated on the course rather than his surroundings.

Naturally, this was the moment that Kennett's eyes found him. Kilían thought grimly that if his bright-red face wasn't obvious enough, his red hair might as well be a flag announcing his presence. If he ever managed to become a bellator, he'd have to disguise it during any training exercises that involved concealment.

Kennett's eyes settled on Kilían's flaming face, then flicked toward the finish line. Kilían knew what he must be thinking: he'd beaten Kennett at the past four races. With his opponent sprawled in a pile of leaves, clutching his ankle, Kennett's victory was assured.

Resigned, he waited for Kennett to run the last ten yards, to seize the victory that was rightfully his. But instead, the other boy's eyes fixed on Kilían, and he slowed, then stopped.

Kilían didn't understand.

Retracing his steps, Kennett knelt in front of the spot where Kilían lay. Without a word, he bent and tugged Kilían upright. His eyes scanned Kilían from head to toe, and Kilían felt an unaccustomed sense of warmth course through his body.

"You're bleeding," Kennett said.

Confusion made Kilían's tone snappish—but not wrathful. Never that. "I know."

Matter-of-factly, Kennett reached out, wiping the blood from Kilían's knee with his sleeve. Together, they regarded the abrasion that remained.

"It's not bad. Just a scrape," Kennett said at last. "You can still finish."

Kilían shook his head. "My ankle," he said, wrapping his fingers tighter around it.

Kennett looked back toward the trees, where they could both hear the sound of the slower students making their way through the course. Kilían couldn't understand what he was doing—didn't he want to win? Why wouldn't he just leave and go on to the finish line? But instead, Kennett braced himself and, before Kilían could protest, the other boy hauled him to his feet.

"Come on," Kennett said, putting an arm around Kilían's waist. "I'll help you. We'll finish together."

Hesitantly, Kilían put his arm around Kennett's shoulders. This kind of touch—in the name of practicality—wasn't forbidden...but then why did Kilían feel that sense of warmth again, the one that had suffused him when Kennett touched his knee? This time it washed over him in wave after wave. His body tingled wherever it pressed against Kennett's, and when he took a deep breath, trying to steady himself, Kennett's scent flooded his nostrils—pine needles and dirt and sweat.

"Come on," Kennett said impatiently, tugging him forward. "We can still win."

It was true—the sound of the other students crashing through the brush was louder now, but still far enough away that he and Kennett would beat them to the finish line, even moving slowly. He took a tentative step forward, then another. His ankle wouldn't bear his weight without complaint—but Kennett's grip on his waist was firm, and he let himself lean on the other boy as they limped forward, around the final bend.

"Lean on me, Kilían. We can do this," Kennett whispered as they went. "Remember, 'the race is not to the swift or the battle to the strong.'" These were the words that the Mothers read to them each night, along with the parables of the sins that had led to the Empire's Fall.

Kilían bit his lip so hard it bled, trying hard not to let his reaction show. To contradict the Mothers when they spoke of such things was heresy—but he believed these words to be lies. Perhaps they held true for the Commonwealth's citizens at large, but certainly not for the bellators whose ranks he aspired to join. "There are many kinds of strength," he whispered back.

It was a simple statement—but when Kennett's hand tightened on his waist, he imagined that perhaps the other boy was reveling in the sensation of this unexpected intimacy, just as he was. For the ninety seconds it took for them to reach the finish line, he let himself imagine things that were beyond verboten: lying in the meadow beyond the vineyards with Kennett, his head on the other boy's chest, looking up at the clouds that drifted across the sky; pressing a kiss to Kennett's lips under the watchful eye of the sickle moon.

Something was terribly wrong with him. Kissing was forbidden, let alone kissing another boy. Not that it mattered who you kissed, he supposed; getting caught doing it only ended one way: on your knees in Clockverk Square, with your neck bared for a bellator's sverd.

Kilían had always expected to be the one wielding the blade. He had no plans to find himself on the receiving end.

It didn't matter, he told himself, shaking his head to clear it as they limped across the finish line together and Mother Truelson came forward to exclaim over what had become of his ankle, which had now swelled to a puffy mess three times its normal size. It made no difference how he felt about Kennett; he could never, ever act on it. In fact, he would never think about it again. That would be best.

Kilían was determined—it was a quality for which the Mothers had praised him over the years. Once he made up his mind to do something—or not to do it, for that matter—he always accomplished it. There had never been a goal he'd set for himself that he'd failed to achieve.

But as Mother Truelson peeled Kennett away from him, he felt the loss of the other boy's touch keenly—as if a gift he'd never expected to receive had been stolen from him. He glanced over his shoulder as the Mother led him to the sidelines and saw Kennett standing there—his dark hair gleaming in the light that filtered through the trees, his green eyes bright under the arches of his eyebrows—and felt a spear of something he could only label as desire stab through him, as sharp as he imagined the bellators' blades to be. And he knew then that he was lying to himself if he believed he could never dwell on how it had felt to have Kennett's hands on him again—that gentle, assessing touch; that firm, insistent grip.

It would be his secret, he decided as Mother Truelson eased him onto a rock and pushed up his pant leg, poking and prodding at the bruised flesh of his ankle. And the keeping of it—however painful—would hurt no one but himself.

CHAPTER TWO

SIX YEARS LATER

I t was the Eve of the Architect's Arrival, and fat flakes of snow fell on the Commonwealth of Ashes, blanketing the citizens gathered in Clockverk Square, washing them clean. The snow dusted the crimson robes of the High Priests where they gathered on the raised dais. It spangled the dark hair of the Executor, the Commonwealth's leader, like tiny stars.

Newly-minted, eighteen-year-old bellator Kilían Bryndísarson stood at the edge of the Square, one hand resting on the dagur in his weapons belt, scanning the crowd for signs of trouble—which, in the Commonwealth, meant evidence of sin. Here, citizens lived and died by the tenets of the Seven Deadly Sins—pride, greed, lust, envy, gluttony, wrath, and sloth. It was the Executor's job to ensure no sin went unpunished; the Priests' job to determine the nature of those punishments; and Kilían's job, as a bellator, to carry them out. He was an enforcer, a warrior, and—when the time called for it—an executioner.

He had never wanted to be anything else.

Here in the Commonwealth, you were either a fat, compliant sheep or one of the watchful dogs guarding the flock. And Kilían was no one's sheep.

His eyes flicked over the mass of citizens in the Square,

indulging in the lone annual celebration that the Commonwealth permitted its citizens. They were grouped according to activity, as they ought to be—queued up to receive tiny cups of spiced hot chocolate, aligned in the space below the dais to chant the prayer that recognized the significance of the Architect's arrival. No one was touching, beyond the unavoidable brush that such a crowd necessitated; there were no raised voices or overly joyful celebrants. No one attempted to wrangle an extra cup of hot chocolate—this would be unpardonable evidence of gluttony. Nor did they worm their way too close to the prized group selected to recite the Prayer of Arrival, in proximity to the Executor and the Priests; this might be seen as evidence of envy of the others' positions. They did exactly what they should, following the rules like the compliant sheep he knew them to be. And though Kilían would never have admitted it to anyone else, he was beginning to get the tiniest bit bored.

His eyes swept the crowd once more—and stalled at its edge. There, stepping off the stones of the Square onto the darkness of the path that led to the Education Center, the Library, and the Rookery, was Kennett Gundarson—with a strange girl in tow.

It had been six years since that morning in the woods. At their Choosing a year before, Kilían had become a bellator, as he'd hoped, and Kennett had been named a medic, fulfilling the promise of the healing touch Kilían had felt when the other boy had tended to his bleeding knee. Still, no matter how much time had passed and how hard he tried, Kilían had never stopped feeling the way he always did when he saw Kennett—as if a spark that usually lay dormant in his chest had flared to life. He'd hoarded every moment he'd gotten to spend with Kennett as they grew up—collaborating on projects under the watchful eye of the Instruktors, training alongside him during their mandatory physical fitness sessions, eating next to him in the dining hall.

When the Mothers assigned Kennett the cot next to his during their seventh-form year, Kilían couldn't decide whether he'd been cursed or blessed by the Architect. He'd lie awake at night, long after the Mothers had declared lights out, listening to the even sound of Kennett's breathing—like a wave, crashing on the shore and then retreating again. Sometimes, when he felt particularly daring, he'd turn on his side, open his eyelids a crack, and watch Kennett sleep by the moonlight that streamed through the dormitory's windows. He'd imagine what it would be like to slip onto the cot next to him, to run his hands through Kennett's sleek dark hair, to feel the heat of Kennett's body against his own.

Kennett would never be his; Kilían knew that. But in the Commonwealth, no one could be anyone's. In the Nursery, they even had communal toys, since attachment was the first step on the path toward sin. He'd long since reconciled himself to the fact that his feelings for Kennett were his cross to bear—and at least he'd never have to witness the other boy belonging to someone else, the way Kilían wished Kennett belonged to him.

But now here was Kennett, slipping off the path that led away from Clockverk Square, a girl right behind him.

A forbidden wave of envy broke over him, soaking him in sweat despite the cold. Gripping the hilt of his dagur, he wove his way through the crowd, seeking to follow them. He told himself that he was only doing his duty, that whatever Kennett and this girl were up to was clearly against the rules. Citizens were meant to be in the Square right now, not slinking off somewhere—and a boy was never, ever meant to be alone with a girl, unsupervised and alone in the dark. Such activities could only lead to sins of the most grievous kind.

All of this was true enough. But what he could barely admit— even to himself—was that he had no intention of punishing Kennett, no matter what he found him doing. The girl, on the other hand…

Kilían faded into the shadows, his black clothes blending effortlessly into the darkness beyond the lamps of the Square. His footsteps were silent on the packed earth of the path as he tracked Kennett and his companion. Bellators were trained to hone all of their senses and make themselves unobtrusive when the situation called for it; Kennett and the girl wouldn't know he was there unless Kilían wanted them to.

The two of them weren't touching; they walked side by side, setting a fast pace, but other than the fact that they weren't supposed to be doing—well, whatever it was they *were* doing— Kilían couldn't figure out what they were up to. He glided along behind them, flattening himself against the rough stone of the Education Center when the girl paused, glancing behind her as if she sensed someone in pursuit.

The moonlight fell full on her face, illuminating her olive skin and high cheekbones. Other than the boys he'd grown up with, Kilían was most familiar with the citizens who'd been brought to him for interrogation—in his first year as an apprentice, he'd already shown an aptitude for prying citizens' secrets out of them. This girl had never found her way to his chambers. Still, he knew her somehow.

As she spun back around, ducking under the archway that led to the Library with Kennett right behind her, he rifled through the mental files he maintained on the citizens of the Commonwealth —and then he had it. This girl had been part of their Choosing ceremony; Miriam was her name. She'd been Chosen to be a scholar—which explained why the Library was a place of interest to her. It did *not* explain why she was heading toward it during the celebration for the Eve of the Architect's arrival, much less with Kennett in tow.

Kilían crept closer still, until he was standing on the other side of the archway. If he'd wanted to, he could've reached out and touched Kennett's back. He imagined himself yanking Kennett into the shadows with him, demanding to know what he was doing with this girl, who had clearly led him astray. But if he confronted Kennett with the girl as a witness, he'd be compelled to follow through on dragging both of them before the Priests— and that was a risk he wasn't willing to take.

Cursing the girl to the nine hells and back again, Kilían watched as she pulled a key from the pocket of her green scholar's tunic. She hesitated before sliding it into the Library's lock, tilting her head to the side, and Kennett spoke, his voice hushed.

"What is it, Miri?" he said.

At the sound of his voice—soft and gentle, everything that Kilían was not—that virtueless spike of envy stabbed through Kilían again, followed by with a white-hot anger so intense, it scalded his throat. Kennett had a *nickname* for her? Such things weren't done in the Commonwealth; they intimated a sense of closeness that was irrelevant at best and verboten at worst. What was the relationship between the two of them? Surely they were not—

"I thought I heard someone," the girl said, her voice pitched as low as Kennett's own.

Despite his training, Kilían's heart picked up speed as he shrank back into the shadows. The girl was a scholar, made for sedentary pursuits. There was no way she should've been able to sense the presence of a bellator who didn't want to make himself known, even an apprentice like Kilían. Were her instincts unusually strong—or had he betrayed himself in some way?

"You're just nervous," Kennett said, his tone reassuring. "There's no one here but us."

"I suppose you're right," the girl said, and she slid the key into the lock. The door to the Library swung open, and the two of them disappeared inside.

As soon as the door shut behind them, Kilían stepped into the archway. He couldn't hear them; the door was solid wood and the building's façade, like all those in the Commonwealth, was made of stone. Nor could he see them; though there were windows at the front of the Library, they weren't foolish enough to turn on the lights.

By the nine hells, what could they be doing?

He could jimmy the lock of the Library and follow them inside, catching the two of them in the act. The High Priests sat on the dais in Clockverk Square, along with the Executor himself, and the Square was full of citizens. Dragging Kennett and the girl into the Square for punishment now would be damning for them —and a boon for Kilían. He was only an apprentice, but he had his eye on becoming one of the Thirty, the Bellatorum's elite group of skilled warriors. A discovery like this, during the Commonwealth's highest-profile ceremony, would be a tremendous coup. He would gain the attention of Lead Bellator Sondheim, not to mention the Executor and the Priests. Everyone who mattered would know what he was capable of.

But depending on what he caught them doing, it might spell Kennett's doom.

He thought about Kennett's low voice, saying, *What is it, Miri?* Was it possible that Kennett felt for the girl what Kilían felt for him—and had acted on it? If that were the case, and Kilían interrupted them mid-sin, it would mean Kennett's death.

He should go in. It was his duty as a bellator. He should see this through to its natural conclusion—and in so doing, perhaps he could rid himself of the sinful feelings he felt for Kennett once and for all. Such feelings, even when kept secret, were a terrible weakness. They were preventing him from fulfilling his calling. He'd sworn an oath to protect the Commonwealth from threats such as this; the Executor had told them often enough the commission of a single sin might set off an avalanche that could send them all hurtling into the abyss.

Kilían drew a deep breath. Perhaps they had left the door open. If that was the case, he would go in. They would have brought his justice on themselves.

He lifted his hand and set it on the knob, rattling it. It was locked.

By the Sins. Was this a test of his fealty—a trap? He stilled, attuning himself to his surroundings, glancing back the way he'd come and upward, toward the roofs of the Library and Education Center...but he saw no one, and all he heard was the steady pounding of his heart. The wind blew, gusting down the passageway between the buildings, bringing with it the bite of winter and the scent of coming snow—but no hint of other human beings.

Kilían was alone.

He drew another deep breath, then a third, imagining the look of surprise on Kennett's face when he barged through the door, blade in hand. How hurt Kennett might be, even as he accepted this fate as his due.

He had no business caring for Kennett's feelings; they were extraneous, an impediment to his duty. It was drilled into every citizen, the catechism they recited each morning: *With attachment comes tenderness. With tenderness comes love. With love comes loss. With loss comes hate. With hate comes chaos. Out of chaos comes order.* But he couldn't help it.

His fingers tightened on the doorknob. It would be easy to open it, either with the finesse of the tip of one of his blades in the lock, or the brute force of a shoulder against the jamb. It would be the work of a moment.

He couldn't do it. To condemn Kennett would mean damning the best part of himself, the one flight of fancy he'd allowed himself in years of deprivation and asceticism.

Traitor, he thought, but the word didn't frighten him the way it should. Whatever Kennett and the girl were doing in the Library, he was complicit in it now. And a small, wicked piece of himself savored this connection to the boy he loved—even if Kennett didn't know it existed.

Breath hissing through his teeth, Kilían stepped back from the door and turned away, heading back the way he'd come.

CHAPTER THREE

Kilían had thought he'd known what torture was: being sprayed with ice-cold water and then electrocuted, the voltage cranked up again and again, so he could understand what his interrogation subjects felt, the better to extract information from them; having his Bellatorum mentor shove slivers of wood under his nails and then try to force him to confess a secret; being collared and then slammed face-first into a wall repeatedly, the lead bellator's hand fisted around the leather ring that encircled his neck as he catalogued Kilían's faults. He'd taken all of these stoically, as befitted a bellator, but inside he'd been furious and humiliated. It had taken every bit of his strength not to fight back, to make Mentor Falk and Lead Bellator Sondheim pay. And when all was said and done, he'd thought he understood what it meant to take a person to the breaking point, and then push them over the edge.

How wrong he'd been.

Over the months since he'd watched Kennett and the girl sneak into the Library, he'd made it his business to find out what they were up to. As a bellator, he had more freedom than most. After dark, he had free range of the Commonwealth—and he used it, seeking out all the places where he thought two people wishing to evade detection might hide. It didn't take him long to come upon Kennett and the girl again.

They met in the vineyards, where the grapes were grown for the wine used in the Priests' ceremonies. In the meadow where Kilían had imagined lying with Kennett so long ago, looking up at the clouds. In the woods where Kennett had helped Kilían to the finish line. Even at the edge of Black Falls, the place where the Bellatorum's older, useless fighters leapt from the cliffs, giving themselves an honorable, warriors' death. And in all these places, they lay together, committing the Commonwealth's most grievous sins.

Kilían stood in the shadows, watching as Kennett brushed back the girl's hair, his touch tender. His heart splintered into a thousand ice-cold shards as Kennett bent to kiss her, whispering how beautiful she was, how lucky he felt to be able to touch her this way, no matter the cost. The first time he saw Kennett's usual gentleness sharpen into ferocity as their bodies melded together, becoming a single being, indistinguishable from the dark, he nearly fell to his knees.

To watch them like this, doing nothing to put an end to it, was traitorous—he knew that well enough. But he couldn't seem to stop.

Standing in the shadows, he imagined it was him Kennett embraced, him to whom Kennett whispered such things. And the knowledge that it would never be—worse, that even if Kilían did nothing to report the two of them, someone would catch them in the act, and then Kennett would be executed for his sins —it was a thousand times worse than the electroshock or the slivers of wood or the collar. He would endure any of those again, and gladly, if it meant he didn't have to watch Kennett and the girl together. If it meant Kennett wouldn't be sentenced to death.

He knew the girl's name—how could he not, with all the endearments Kennett whispered to her; *Miri this, Miri that*—but he couldn't bring himself to think it. To do so made her real.

And more than anything else, he wanted all of this—wanted *her*—to go away.

He could have arranged for something unfortunate to befall her. Wanted to, with an intensity so great it was almost painful. But such a thing would've hurt Kennett, and that was the one thing he couldn't bring himself to do...even if, should anyone find out Kilían had known about this all the time and done nothing, it would be him on his knees in the Square right next to Kennett and the girl.

Still, watching the two of them sin together, he couldn't help but wonder if dying alongside Kennett would hurt less than this.

He had to do *something*. He couldn't go on this way. But what could he do that wouldn't destroy him and Kennett both?

As he deliberated, trying to find a solution, the decision was taken out of his hands.

He was sparring in the training room, trying his blade against Efraím Stinar—five years his senior, Stinar was the best of the younger bellators, and thus an excellent outlet for Kilían's frustration—when High Priest Traasen walked in, Lead Bellator Sondheim at his side.

As was appropriate, Kilían and Stinar snapped to attention, blades sheathed, backs straight, and hands at their sides. The High Priest came to stand in front of them, his red robes sweeping the floor, and Kilían had to fight to keep his heartbeat steady. Was it possible that Bellator Sondheim and the Priest had discovered his perfidy, and were here to haul him away? It took all of his training to steel his face to blankness, determined to betray nothing.

"Bellator Stinar. Apprentice Bryndísarson," Bellator Sondheim said, his face settling into its usual stern lines. "Your assistance is needed for a most unfortunate task."

As the senior bellator—and because the Architect forbid he

ever appear to be anything but perfectly compliant—Stinar spoke first. "I live only to serve, sir."

Kilían had never liked Efraím Stinar—not that such things mattered. He admired the senior bellator's skills, but something about the man himself rubbed him the wrong way. Maybe it was Stinar's coldness, the way he never seemed to feel anything, even the emotions that were permitted in the Commonwealth. He was relentless and single-minded: excellent traits in a bellator, but exhausting qualities in a human being.

But in the Bellatorum, the chain of command was everything. Kilían knew what he was supposed to say, and so he said it, the words clipped and his chin raised: "As do I, sir."

"Good," Priest Traasen said. His voice was high-pitched and nasal, and the small, smug smile that lifted his lips sent an icy centipede skittering down Kilían's spine.

Please, he thought, a desperate prayer sent to the Architect. *Please don't let this be about Kennett and the girl. I'll do anything. Just don't let me lose him.*

It was a sinful prayer, and Kilían knew it. Perhaps that was the problem. Or perhaps the issue was that Kennett had never been his to begin with. Because when he and Stinar followed the Priest out of the training facility, they found a girl with a nose like a pug dog's waiting for them on the paving stones, the expression on her face mirroring the Priest's. She led them unerringly through the City and to the vineyards, Kilían's heart sinking further with each step. And when finally they reached the arbors, thick with vines and hanging heavy with burgundy grapes, there stood Kennett and the girl in each other's arms, her face streaked with tears and his lips on hers.

Kilían felt his heart thud. It was a painful feeling, as if the organ was threatening to stop beating altogether. He fought the urge to rub his chest. Instead he stood straight, his sverd at his back and his weapons belt strapped around his hips, his right hand resting on the hilt of his dagur. A staticky sound roared in his head, so that he barely heard the pug-nosed girl when she spoke.

"You see," she said to Priest Traasen, pointing at Miriam's midsection. "I told the truth."

Every time Kilían had come upon Kennett and the girl together, it had been too dark to make them out clearly—though he'd certainly seen enough. But now, in the fading light of dusk, he saw what he hadn't been able to perceive before: Miriam's belly was swollen, round. And Kennett's hand rested on it, as if to protect whatever lay within.

A small, shocked sound escaped Kilían's throat, as if someone had punched him in the stomach. The girl was carrying Kennett's child.

He didn't think it would've hurt more if Stinar had stabbed him.

The Priest's self-satisfied smile widened. Then he spoke, his nasal voice booming through the fruit-laden arbor. "Miriam Larsen. Kennett Gundarson. I find you guilty of the sins of lust and fornication. You will be sentenced to execution in Clockverk Square. As you have sinned, so will you die—together."

Kilían had been wrong—again. He wished Stinar *would* stab him. Anything would be better than this.

He willed Kennett to show courage—and he did, squaring his shoulders. Beside him, Miriam—Kilían forced himself to think of her by name; denying her existence would do him no good now—stood straight. "What about the child?" she said.

The Priest eyed her, looking more contemptuous than ever. "You will be confined to the hospital until the child is born, and your fellow sinner held in the dungeons, to contemplate the fate that awaits you both," he said, wiping a hand across his mouth. "Then your bastard spawn will join the ranks of the natural-born, and the two of you will face the bellators' blades."

Nausea roiled in Kilían's stomach. What if the Priests decreed that *he* kill Kennett? There was no use pretending he could do it. He knew himself well enough to understand he'd rather cut off his own arm than wield his blade in service to such a thing.

He'd fail at his duty in front of the entire Commonwealth, his sinful feelings for Kennett laid bare. And then he'd be executed by his brethren.

The static in his head ratcheted up to a fever pitch. His vision swam.

Through the buzzing that filled his ears, he heard Priest Traasen speak again. "Bellators, remove the boy from my sight. I'll escort the girl to the hospital myself. She's no threat to me."

Kilían wanted to laugh. Not a threat? She'd destroyed everything Kilían held dear. Rage bloomed in his belly, fierce and hungry, as he strode toward the two of them, obeying the Priest's orders. Beneath his boots, he felt the grapes that had tumbled from the arbors give way, perfuming the air with a sweet-sour tang. He wished he could crush Miriam as easily—but then what would happen to Kennett's child, doomed to live out its life as a cursed natural-born, carrying out the Commonwealth's most menial tasks? It would be a miserable life, that was for certain. But at least the child would live.

The girl clung to Kennett, as if he could protect her from what was about to happen, even as Kilían took hold of his left bicep and Stinar grasped his right. He felt Kennett tense beneath his grip, his skin as warm as Kilían remembered, but he didn't fight to pull away. Instead, he spoke to Miriam, his voice barely louder than a breath.

"I am a medic," he told her. "But I have no idea how to heal a broken heart."

This, Kilían thought as he and Stinar dragged Kennett away from the girl who carried his child, was a sins-forsaken shame. Because where Kilían's heart should be was nothing but a morass of splinters that caused him pain with every breath.

He could feel Kennett's eyes on him, and stubbornly refused to return the favor. If he looked at Kennett, surely everything he was feeling would be clear on his face. Instead, he stared straight ahead, his fingers tight on Kennett's upper arm. If this was the last time he ever got to touch Kennett, he wanted to remember it.

In the gathering dusk, they marched Kennett through the City and down to the dungeons, ignoring the curious looks and whispers of passers-by. Stinar pulled a ring of keys from his belt, opened a cell door, and shoved Kennett through. Then he slammed it shut and strode off without a word, leaving Kilían standing there.

They regarded each other through the bars in silence. And then Kennett spoke. "Kilían—" he said, and it sounded like an entreaty.

"Don't." The word was rough, as if it had been torn from Kilían's throat. It had been years since he'd heard Kennett say his name. Hearing it now, from the wrong side of prison bars, with a death sentence hanging over Kennett's head—Kilían thought it might break him. "I can't help you," he said, willing Kennett to understand.

The sentence came from a wellspring of desperation—by the Architect, how he wished there was something he could do—but it came out all wrong, as if he thought Kennett deserved to die. Still, Kennett didn't wince. Instead, he stepped closer to the bars.

Most people were frightened of Kilían; bellators were intimidating to begin with, and even as an apprentice, Kilían had already gained a reputation as a merciless interrogator. But Kennett didn't tremble or cower as if the bellator was something to fear. His green eyes wide and guileless, he looked at Kilían with an open, pleading expression—as if he thought the bellator was his only hope.

"I know you can't help me," he said, wrapping one hand around the bars. "I would never expect you to. But Miri—Kilían, please—"

Kilían was the one studded with weapons and free; Kennett stood, bruised and powerless, in a cell. But hearing the misery in Kennett's voice, he felt as if he were the helpless one.

He would've given Kennett anything he asked for. It was just

Kilían's luck that the one thing Kennett wanted was for him to save the life of the girl he despised.

Still, if it was within his power, he would've made it happen. But he couldn't fight the entire Commonwealth singlehandedly. He was just one bellator, and an apprentice at that.

"Kennett," he said, and heard his own voice break. "There's nothing I can do."

He expected Kennett's shoulders to slump, for the other boy to turn away. But instead, his eyes lit with a brilliant fervor. "Come here," he said.

Kilían knew he should refuse. But as if those words had compelled him, he stepped closer, until he was right in front of the bars, his face an inch from Kennett's. He could smell the other boy —the faint scent of the crushed grapes from the vineyards, the acrid scent of fear.

"What?" He bit out the word, trying to seem indifferent—as if this proximity to Kennett didn't threaten to bring him to his knees.

Kennett brought his other hand up, as if to grip the bars—but instead, he reached through them, fastening his fingers on Kilían's sleeve. Kilían stiffened—touching a bellator was forbidden—but he didn't pull away. They were the same height; he looked into Kennett's green eyes, which had always reminded him of the pool of water at the base of Black Falls—depthless, yet filled with light. "What?" he said again, more gently this time.

Kennett bit his lip. And then he mouthed silently, *Do you want to help us?*

A moment ticked by, then two. Kilían thought about his career as a bellator, which had only just begun. Of the oath he'd sworn, and what it would cost him to break it.

And then he thought about what it would cost him to lose Kennett. How the best part of him would die alongside the other boy in the Square.

In the end, it was no contest at all.

CHAPTER FOUR

I t was one thing for Kilían to promise Kennett that he would try to save Miriam. It was another thing entirely for him to figure out how to bring such a plan to fruition.

He'd been thinking of little else since Kennett made the request of him, and still had no idea of how it might be accomplished. The Commonwealth was a series of concentric circles: the City, flanked by its vineyards and fields; then the woods where the bellators trained and citizens occasionally participated in activities like the obstacle course; then a sprawling tangle of grass and low-lying shrubs that separated the woods from the forest, where the Bastarour roamed, genetically modified beasts with a taste for human flesh; and then the electric fence, which surrounded the Commonwealth in its entirety. On the other side of the fence were the Borderlands, inhabited by vicious hordes who lived by no moral code at all—sinners who were jealous of the security the Commonwealth citizens endured, and took great pleasure from rending exiled citizens limb from limb. Rumor had it they were cannibals, starved and craving the flesh of citizens raised on a steady diet of nutritious meals.

From time to time, sinners were exiled to the Borderlands, but such individuals were simply set free at the edge of the forest, with nothing but their wits to sustain them. In his lifetime, Kilían had never heard of any of them surviving the Bastarour. If they managed that much, they'd have to figure out a way to open or scale the electric fence, which was live at all times and required a code to deactivate. And then, on the other side of the fence, they'd have to confront the wastes and the savages.

Even if Kilían could retrieve the girl from the hospital, where she was imprisoned in a separate wing under armed guard, what in the nine hells would he do with her? Was he meant to shepherd an untrained citizen through the forest, singlehandedly defeat the Bastarour, magically deactivate the fence, and then let her loose in the Borderlands, only to have her be devoured by the hordes? Or did Kennett mean for Kilían to go with her into the Outside—to defend her against whatever came?

The Architect help him, he considered it. Life in a world where Kennett didn't exist would be empty for him, meaningless. Maybe it would be better to have his last, seditious act take place in service to what Kennett would have wanted of him.

What *he* wanted, more than anything else, was to figure out a way to save Kennett. To the nine hells with the girl. But the dungeons were closely guarded, and Kennett was inside a locked cell. It was possible Kilían would be able to find a way to work himself into the guard rotation, but even if that was the case, he wouldn't be guarding Kennett alone. And even if he somehow got Kennett out, he'd face the same dilemma: the forest, the Bastarour, the fence, the hordes. Not to mention, he was sure Kennett wouldn't leave without Miriam.

It was a sins-forsaken mess.

As he stood on the training ground at attention with the other bellators, his hands linked behind his back and his spine straight, he turned the dilemma over and over in his mind. But he could think of no solution.

Lead Bellator Sondheim stalked up and down the ranks of his black-clad warriors, scrutinizing them for weakness and insufficiency, and Kilían schooled his face to blankness, terrified that somehow he'd reveal the conflict that raged within him. He was Kennett's and Miriam's only hope, as feeble as that hope was. If he fell, they would have nothing.

Sondheim came to a stop and pulled his dagur from his belt, twirling the weapon between his fingers. The blade flashed silver in the light of the rising sun. "Bellators," he said, and the ranks—Kilían among them—answered promptly, "Sir."

"As you are aware," Sondheim said, "we have a double execution on our roster: Kennett Gundarson and Miriam Larsen, a medic and a scholar who have committed the most egregious of sins. It is our honor and our privilege to carry out the edict of the Priests in putting them to death."

Next to Kilían, Efraím Stinar's eyebrow twitched infinitesimally, betraying his distaste. Kilían wanted to slide his blade between the senior bellator's ribs. But instead, he faced front, his legs set slightly apart and his head held high, the picture of an attentive soldier, as Sondheim paused in front of David Lunde, a bellator known for his facility with a sverd. Lunde's throwing arm could use practice, but for close-up bladework, there were few better.

"Bellator Lunde, you'll execute the girl," Sondheim said. "And as for the boy…" He resumed his pacing, his gaze roving over the assembled bellators as he went, and Kilían held his breath.

Please, he prayed. *Please, anything but this.*

But as usual, the Architect laughed in the face of his prayers, because Sondheim's sharpened gaze settled on his face. "Apprentice Bryndísarson. You've not had the pleasure of executing a sinner yet. Let this be your first opportunity."

Bile rose in Kilían's throat, and for an alarming second, he thought he might actually vomit. "Me, sir?" he said, swallowing it back down again.

"You know him, no?" Bellator Sondheim's lips rose in a mirthless smile.

"Yes," Kilían admitted, "but I don't understand—"

"Well, then perhaps it'll be welcome for him to see a friendly face at the end. Consider it a kindness." Sondheim clapped him on the back, hard enough to make him stagger. "That's an order, Apprentice Bryndísarson. Is there a problem?"

Sondheim was watching him closely, those hawklike eyes of his narrowed. Feeling sicker than ever, Kilían straightened his spine and smoothed his face to blankness. "No, sir. It would be my honor."

"Excellent." Bellator Sondheim lifted his hand and stepped away. "They'll be executed the dawn after the girl bears her brat. The midwife assigned to her tells me she likely has about three weeks to go. That should give you time to prepare yourself. Use it wisely."

KILÍAN THOUGHT HE MIGHT NEVER SLEEP AGAIN. HIS HEAD POUNDED, his heart ached, and his mind whirred, going over and over what had happened on the training grounds that morning.

Few decisions that Bellator Sondheim made were a coincidence. Had he chosen Kilían to execute Kennett because he suspected that Kilían harbored sinful feelings for him? Would Kilían be forced to decapitate Kennett, only to find another bellator's blade at his throat?

It didn't matter, anyhow. He couldn't take Kennett's life. He'd sacrifice his own first.

But what was he to do? *Three weeks*, Sondheim had said. And what if she dropped the brat early? He had to figure out a plan now—but he had no idea what such a thing could be.

Exhausted and heartsick, he prowled the grounds of the Commonwealth all night, ending up at last in the damp tunnels that ran beneath the City, providing bellators with underground access to the buildings in the event of emergency. One branch led to the prison cells, and Kilían felt the pull of Kennett's presence, like a magnet drawing him onward—but he couldn't take the chance. Every time he stood in front of Kennett, he risked giving himself away. Instead, he walked in the opposite direction, one he'd never taken before, as it ran smack into a dead-end. That seemed fitting, Kilían told himself as he made his way down the narrow passageway. It was the perfect metaphor for his situation.

He made his way without the aid of a flashlight, trailing the tips of his fingers along the dripping walls of the tunnels to orient himself. After all, it wasn't as if he was actually looking for something. But he found it, nonetheless.

He heard them before he saw them: a male and a female voice, speaking low, as if they were afraid of being overheard. The sound was coming from where he estimated the end of the tunnel to be, about fifty feet in front of him.

"Speak of the wolf, and she will come," one voice—the female's—said.

And on its heels came an answer, one that made no sense to Kilían, but which was clearly the accepted response: "A wolf does not bite a wolf."

Kilían didn't recognize either of the voices, but that meant little; the Commonwealth held ten thousand citizens. He could hardly be expected to know all of them, except when his business required it.

Still, something about this exchange struck him as unusual. Who would be meeting at night, in secret, in the tunnels beneath the city—speaking in code, no less—unless they had something to hide? He stilled, flattening himself against the wall of the tunnel, and listened for all he was worth.

"You've taken a huge chance, coming here," the male voice said. "What possessed you?"

The female laughed. "And you think we're safe, out there in the woods?"

Kilían froze, pulse skipping. Had this female come from the Borderlands? He'd never heard of such a thing.

"There's danger, and then there's idiocy." The man sounded aggravated. "Of all people, Cordelia, surely you know the difference."

"And I have the tools to defend myself." Amusement threaded the woman's voice. "Better than most."

"You think your claws and incisors are going to protect you from a battalion of armed bellators?" The man snorted. "Not even you are proof against a poisoned blade."

The woman named Cordelia laughed. "Do you see any bellators here, Joseph? Really, perhaps spending so much time with your books has made you soft."

Joseph. Books. Kilían flipped through the mental roster he kept of the Commonwealth's citizens, searching for a match—and then he had it: Senior Scholar Joseph, a white-bearded man in his fifties who Kilían had seen the last time he'd done a routine patrol of the Library. He hadn't taken much notice of Joseph, distracted by the sight of Kennett and Miriam sitting at one of the tables, their heads bent together as they examined the contents of a book. But now he did as he'd been trained, erasing everything else from the memory other than the person in question. Kennett and Miriam vanished. The shelves winked out of existence. All that remained was Scholar Joseph, sitting at a desk next to Aric, a suck-up who'd been in Kilían's seventh-form dorm. Joseph had seemed dutiful enough, the picture of a dedicated academic. But now—

"It's the perfect disguise." Joseph's aggravation was gone, buried under self-deprecation. "Who would suspect mild-mannered, obedient Scholar Joseph of sedition?"

Kilían's mouth tasted of metal. Joseph was a traitor—a rebel of some kind. And this Cordelia had come from the Outside—he was sure of it. The talk of claws and incisors bewildered Kilían—it must be another kind of code, phrases that only meant something to the two of them.

He cared little for their talk of rebellion, astonishing though it was. Cordelia had gotten in somehow, and clearly she didn't intend to stay, which meant one thing: She could get out again. And if she could, so could Kennett and Miriam.

He drew a deep breath of the moldering air and pushed off the tunnel wall, striding in the direction of the voices. In a minute, his fingertips grazed solid wood: a door. He slid them lower, and found a knob. Bracing himself, he yanked it open.

He was standing in a small room, lined with books and lit by a single wavering lantern, mounted on the wall. In front of him stood Scholar Joseph and a tall, lithe girl close to his age, her chestnut hair woven into a single braid and her amber eyes wide and shocked. She bared her teeth, and he could have sworn she growled at him. It was not a human sound.

Kilían shut the door behind him and stood with his back to it. "Greetings," he said, his voice as neutral as he could make it.

"Bellator." Her voice held the hint of that growl, and her odd eyes didn't fall from his own.

Scholar Joseph, on the other hand, looked terrified. He'd flattened himself against one of the shelves as if he wished the books would open up and suck him inside. Seeing this, Kilían couldn't help but smile; it was nice to feel like himself again, like the warrior he'd spent his life yearning to be rather than some lovesick, trapped boy.

"Bellator Bryndísarson," the scholar said, his voice trembling, "I swear this isn't—"

"Don't waste your breath." Kilían's hand dropped to his dagur, his fingers playing idly with the handle. "I mean you no harm, as long as you cooperate."

"What do you want here?" The girl's eyes ran over him insolently, from toe to head, as if she was assessing his potential as a threat and finding him wanting. Under other circumstances, Kilían would have taken this as an invitation to show her exactly how much of a threat he could be. But this time, he just smiled.

"I want what you want. Safe passage."

"You want to leave the Commonwealth?" Her eyes narrowed. He could have sworn they were a lighter color than they'd been a minute before.

"Not me. Two others. Tell me how, and I'll let you live—and say nothing of what I've heard here tonight."

"Let me live?" The girl's upper lip curled. "What makes you think you have that kind of power?"

"Cordelia." Scholar Joseph sounded steadier now. "I know this man. He may be young, but he's one of the best among the bellators' ranks. His interrogation skills are unparalleled, and as for the rest of it, look at him." He gestured at Kilían, indicating his weapons belt, the sverd strapped to his back, and his general, hair-trigger self. "You made a mistake by not bringing your familiar with you tonight, illness or no. In close quarters like this, victory against a bellator is far from assured. He offers us a bargain. Why not listen to what he has to say?"

Kilían inclined his head toward Scholar Joseph, acknowledging both the compliment and the reasonable nature of his suggestion—but he didn't take his eyes off Cordelia. He didn't know what Joseph meant by a familiar—more code, perhaps?— but it was clear that between the two of them, she was the dangerous one. He didn't quite comprehend how, but just because you didn't understand the nature of a weapon, that was no reason to underestimate it.

"Start talking," Kilían suggested, drawing his dagur from his belt. "My patience is wearing thin."

THIRTY MINUTES LATER, KILÍAN STOOD ON THE OTHER SIDE OF THE wooden door again, his mind reeling and his worldview upside down. He had learned several disturbing—and helpful—things. And most important of all, he knew how he could use them to save Kennett.

He now knew that a resistance against the restrictive world of the Commonwealth existed, called the Brotherhood of the Wolf. Select citizens, including Scholar Joseph—he'd refused to name the others, and Kilían hadn't pressed him; right now, such information was irrelevant—belonged to it. Cordelia did indeed come from the Borderlands. She was one of the resistance's ringleaders, and others were camped outside the Commonwealth even now. If she was to be believed, the Borderlands were inhabited not by cannibalistic hordes, but rather by human beings simply trying to survive—and to systematically take down the Commonwealth of Ashes, as well as the other, lesser Commonwealths scattered across the Empire.

Most important of all, built into the wall of the room where he'd found Joseph and Cordelia was a door that led to another set of tunnels, one that burrowed underneath the forest and the fence and emptied into the Borderlands. According to Cordelia and Joseph, the Bellatorum's Thirty used it to patrol the land beyond the fence. This was how Cordelia had come in—and it was how Kilían could lead Kennett and Miriam out, as well.

He'd brokered a deal with the scholar and the stranger. He would say nothing about what he'd overheard, about his knowledge of the resistance, as long as they accepted Kennett and Miriam into their ranks. In return, Scholar Joseph would keep his mouth shut about Kilían's intentions.

"If you don't," Kilían had said, the tip of his blade beneath the scholar's chin, "I will find you before the bellators take me down. And your life will be the price."

Joseph had blinked repeatedly, afraid to nod lest he skewer himself on Kilían's blade, and Kilían had known the scholar believed him.

"We'll shelter them," Cordelia had said, sounding skeptical. "But how exactly do you plan to extract them from custody and get them to us?"

"That," Kilían had said with more confidence than he felt, "is my business. I'll hold up my end of the deal, if you do the same. Do we have a bargain?"

They'd shaken on it, the strength in the girl's grip taking Kilían by surprise. There was something unusual about her, no doubt about it. But he had no time to figure out what that might be. Dawn was nearing, and she'd vanished into the tunnels that would take her back to the Outside. Scholar Joseph had found his way back to his bed. And here stood Kilían, alone in the tunnels.

There was a long, twisted path between Kilían's current situation and his goal. Kennett was still in the dungeons; Miriam was still imprisoned. Both of them were still scheduled for execution—one of them at his hand. Complicating matters further, he had no idea exactly when Miriam would give birth, or how she would care for a child on the Outside if need be. But despite all the obstacles in his way, for the first time, he felt a spark of something that he thought had deserted him a long time ago.

Hope.

CHAPTER FIVE

Kilían managed to work himself into Kennett's guard rotation two days later, mainly through a stroke of luck. The bellator assigned to guard Kennett came down with a sudden high fever, and while bellators were generally encouraged to push through physical infirmity, fevers implied a contagion that might spread through the enclosed cells of the dungeon like wildfire. So, Bellator Skye was consigned to the infirmary, and Kilían, who'd happened to walk into the training room when Sondheim pulled Skye off duty, took his place.

It was the night shift, but when Kilían made his way down the narrow corridor that held the cells, his heart picking up speed at the thought of seeing Kennett again, he found the other boy wide awake, sitting on the bare metal cot that was the cell's sole piece of furniture. He shot to his feet when he saw Kilían, his thin face brightening.

Kilían rubbed his chest, trying to make the uncomfortable, searing sensation he always felt when he saw Kennett—as if someone had lit him on fire from within—go away. There were only a few prisoners in the dungeon, but the last thing he wanted was to betray the fact that a relationship existed between himself and Kennett beyond guard and convicted sinner. The other bellator assigned to this shift was on a bathroom break, but the Commonwealth's prisoners didn't hesitate to Inform on each other—or on anyone else, for that matter—if they thought it could buy them clemency.

Kennett stepped forward, his mouth opening as if to speak, and Kilían held up a palm to forestall him. "Sinner Gundarson," he said, keeping his voice brusque, "is there something you require?"

Kennett didn't move back, and Kilían feared he might give everything away—honestly, the boy hadn't an ounce of guile—but then he held up his left arm. "I fear I've cut myself on the edge of the cot," he said. "I might need antibiotics. Can you take a look?"

"You're the medic," Kilían said, loud enough for anyone who might be listening to hear. "But I'll look, if you insist."

Obligingly, Kennett approached the bars. Even in the dim light, Kilían could see that someone had blackened his eye. Fury surged through him at the sight, but he held it in check.

"How is Miriam?" Kennett mouthed, so no one could overhear. "The baby?"

It had been too much to hope that the light that had illuminated Kennett's face had been for Kilían's sake. No, it was only that Kennett hoped Kilían might be able to bring him news of the girl and his child. Disappointment swirled in Kilían's stomach, mixed with a bitter swill of resignation. But he said, making a show of examining Kennett's arm, "As far as I can tell, all is as it should be. I'm far from an expert in such things."

The tense set of Kennett's shoulders relaxed a fraction. "No news, then?" he said, aloud this time. "I've been asking, but no one will tell me anything, no matter how I plead."

"The two of you have sinned," Kilían said, infusing his voice with disgust, even though it hurt him to talk to Kennett this way. "There is no reason anyone should share any information with you about your fellow sinner—or your bastard spawn."

Kennett winced, as if Kilían had struck him. Surely he understood that the bellator was playing a role—that this was what was necessary? "Of course," he said, his eyes lowering to the floor of the cell, stained with the blood of its previous occupant. "I meant no disrespect."

Drawing a deep breath, Kilían channeled the version of himself that terrified subjects in the interrogation chamber, making them piss themselves before confessing every sin they'd ever considered committing. "Eyes on me, prisoner," he snapped. "Before I give you a second black eye to match the first."

Kennett's head came up, eyes wide with shock, and Kilían reached out, fisting the material of Kennett's filthy shirt and pulling him forward, so that his body smacked into the bars. He leaned down, his lips an inch from Kennett's. "I've found a way out," he breathed, so quietly that he could barely hear it himself. "For both of you."

If Kilían had thought Kennett's eyes were wide before, that was nothing to them now. His eyebrows rose, too, their black arches disappearing beneath the fall of his hair. "How?" he mouthed.

Kilían shook his head; it was too complicated to explain, and any information that Kennett had was intelligence that someone could beat—or interrogate—out of him. Instead, with his free hand, he reached into the pocket of his gear and yanked out a piece of paper. He plastered it against the bars, so Kennett could read the words printed on it: *I need an injectable drug that will incapacitate instantly and induce memory loss. And I need it now.*

Kennett tilted his head, as if considering. And then he gestured for a writing implement.

Fishing in his pocket again, Kilían handed him a pen. His brow wrinkling, Kennett took the paper, ironed it out against the wall, and wrote. Then he handed both back to Kilían.

Mnemosyne, the paper read in Kennett's uneven scrawl. *In the lockbox behind the medics' station on the hospital ward. One full syringe=3 hours' unconsciousness, plus memory loss predating the time of injection.*

Kilían stared at the note for a long moment, memorizing the

information. Then he wrote, *Tomorrow night. Be ready,* and held the paper up, between his body and the bars, for Kennett to see.

"Clean yourself up, prisoner," he said, crumpling it into a ball. "And stop wasting my time."

Releasing his grip on Kennett so abruptly that the other boy staggered backward, he strode off down the corridor, his hand on his dagur and his heart thumping so hard, it threatened to batter its way through his chest.

GETTING HIS HANDS ON THE MNEMOSYNE IN THE MORNING WASN'T AS difficult as Kilían had anticipated it might be. A simple matter of misdirection and triggering an alarm that drew the medics' attention, and he was behind their station, jimmying the lockbox, extracting the Mnemosyne, and replacing it with the saline-filled syringes he'd liberated earlier in the day, while doing a routine sweep of the Infirmary. By the time the alarm had been deactivated, he was out from behind the station and long gone.

What he hadn't anticipated was that while he was in the dungeons with Kennett the night before, Miriam had gone into labor. By the time he swiped the Mnemosyne from the medics' lockbox, her execution was already scheduled for the following dawn—along with Kennett's. And when he paid a clandestine visit to the hospital ward to assess how many guards they had on Miriam's door, he found none other than Bellator Stinar himself there, striding into her room.

Concealed in a supply closet that shared a wall with Miriam's chamber, he could hear the rumble of Stinar's voice—though he hadn't anticipated what the senior bellator had to say.

"Your bastard son is dead," Stinar told her.

Even through the wall, Kilían could hear the condescension in his voice—and Miriam's gasp of horror. "How?" She sounded on the verge of tears.

Stinar said something indistinct, and then, "Perhaps the

Architect sensed the evil in his soul and snuffed it out before your bastard could bring a blight upon the world."

Kilían sucked in a breath before he could stop himself. Even for Stinar, that was cold.

The door to Miriam's room snicked shut and Kilían heard the sound of Stinar's footsteps, making their way back down the hall. He stood still, taking in what he'd heard. After everything, had the infant truly not survived—or was this just cruelty on Stinar's part, a trick to make the girl suffer as much as possible before she met her end?

He knew he shouldn't care about such things. In the Commonwealth, children were borne by artificially inseminated surrogates, then raised in a communal Nursery by the Mothers. The notion of parenthood, of belonging to a family unit, was nonexistent; the only vocabulary Kilían had for such things came from the vids of the time before the Fall. He had no context within which to value the idea of family. But this was Kennett's child—a piece of him that might remain behind, even living the shameful existence of the natural-born. If this was the only part of Kennett that Kilían would have left, he wanted to know the truth about the infant's fate.

Pressing his ear to the door, he listened hard; no one stirred in the hall outside his closet. He cracked the door ever so slightly, and saw nothing but an empty hallway; the two guards who flanked Miriam's doorway were just around the corner. This closet was at the top of the back stairwell; he'd chosen it for its ease of access. Silently, he eased the door open the rest of the way, slipped into the stairwell, and began to make his way down the steps.

But before he'd reached the first landing, he heard voices below him. To his shock, he realized one of them was the Executor's, who rarely traveled anywhere without a full complement of guards.

"You'll do as you're told, Midwife Annika," the Executor said. "Give me the infant."

"Of course, sir." The midwife's voice was subdued but obedient. "If I may ask, though—why are we to say that the child is dead? Is it defective in some way, beyond its nature as a natural-born?"

"You may *not* ask." The Executor's tone was steel. "As for what you are to say, you'll say what you're told, and won't question it. The girl will be led to understand that her infant has died, which is perhaps a mercy before she faces the blade in the morning. Am I clear?"

"Yes, sir." Kilían heard a rustling sound—perhaps the blankets in which the child was swaddled? "I'll make sure the other midwives understand, sir."

There was silence, cut briefly by an infant's shrill wail—but it retreated as the Executor carried the child further down the steps. Kilían barely had enough time to escape to a higher landing before the midwife's heels came clacking upward. She was muttering to herself: *not right, poor little lamb, bad enough to be a natural-born without all this.* Under normal circumstances, Kilían would've hauled her off for interrogation; contradicting the Executor's word was heresy. But these circumstances were far from normal, and he could only stand there, listening to her stream of complaints as she yanked open the door that led from the stairwell back to the ward where Miriam lay.

So Kennett's child lived. This was, he decided, a good thing— but he wouldn't tell Kennett about it, or the girl, either. They'd likely want to retrieve the baby, and the child was in the grasp of the Executor now. Such a thing would mean signing their death warrants—and likely, Kilían's along with it.

He had all the pieces he needed: Knowledge of Miriam's location and the nature of her guard; five syringes of Mnemosyne, four for necessity and one for luck; the cooperation of Cordelia and her band of rebels. The only thing left was to wait for night to fall.

CHAPTER SIX

Kilían used the first two syringes of Mnemosyne on Bellators Traalf and Unger, who were assigned to guard the dungeons that night. A vague sense of guilt pervaded him as he strode up to Traalf, asked him how many prisoners the dungeons currently held, and—as the man opened his mouth to reply—stabbed him in the arm with the needle. Kennett had been right; almost immediately, he could feel the bellator's body start to slump as the drug took effect. He eased Traalf to the floor and went in pursuit of the second guard.

He found Unger in the supply room that adjoined the cells, taking inventory of the new handcuffs that the Commonwealth's metalsmiths had forged. It was easy enough to engage him in conversation about their craftsmanship, and then—when Unger held one up to demonstrate its superiority—use his grip on the cuff to tug the other bellator forward and slam the plunger down.

Attacking his fellow warriors felt terribly unnatural, especially because they'd never suspected his defection; the Bellatorum was a vicious pack, but a pack nonetheless, fiercely loyal and quick to root out the weakest link. As a gifted interrogator, Kilían had earned his rank as a top apprentice. No one would possibly suspect he'd betray them.

He dropped Unger to the ground and went back for Traalf, dragging him into the supply room next to his comrade. Then, liberating the key ring from Traalf's belt and shutting the door behind him, he went to retrieve Kennett.

He moved down the shadowed corridor that held the cells without a sound, the keys clutched tight in his fist to keep them from jingling. The other prisoners were asleep, their faces turned toward the wall; but Kennett stood at the bars, waiting for him. A fresh bruise marred his cheek, but his face lit with a bright, expectant smile.

Kilían felt his heart lurch, the way it always did when he saw Kennett. What would it be like when the other boy was gone? Would he merely feel nothing at all?

Banishing the thought from his mind, he tried one key after another until he found the one that fit the lock to Kennett's cell. Then he took Kennett by the arm—plausible deniability was everything; if anyone saw him, he could always say he was escorting a prisoner—and led him from his cell, fixing Kennett fiercely with his eyes to warn the other boy not to say a word. Pausing briefly to return the key ring to Traalf's belt, he took Kennett's arm once more and pulled him through the archway that separated the dungeons from the rest of the underground.

There was an exterior entrance to the tunnels that would be far more efficient for Kilían to use when he retrieved Miriam, but in this case, it was faster to stay underground. Relying on his ability to make his way in the dark, honed in countless nighttime training missions with the Bellatorum, Kilían guided Kennett down the tunnels until, at last, they reached the room with the wooden door.

It was locked, as Kilían had known it would be; but he had secured the key from Scholar Joseph earlier that day, so he wouldn't have to waste time picking the lock in the dark. He unlocked it, stepped inside, and pulled Kennett in behind him, locking the door at once to prevent further incursions. Stepping to the side, he lit the lantern mounted to one of the walls; the space was windowless, and there was no gap beneath the door. No one would be able to see it burning.

The room smelled of mustiness and mold, just as it had before. In the wavering light of the lantern, he and Kennett stared at each other. The other boy's face was white and set, but it softened as he looked at Kilían.

"Thank you," he said, reaching out a hand to touch the bellator's sleeve.

"Don't thank me yet." Kilían stepped backward, disengaging himself. To have Kennett right next to him, like this—yet totally inaccessible—it was too much.

For an instant, Kennett looked as if he wanted to apologize. Touching a bellator wasn't done—they were above such casual gestures, inviolate—and for once, Kilían was grateful for such a tradition. With luck, Kennett would take his rejection as an extension of the natural order of things, rather than what it was: a desperate effort to exercise restraint.

The apologetic look faded from Kennett's face, replaced with misery. He ran the offending hand through his hair, mussing it even further. "The guard—Traalf—he told me Miriam had the baby. And that it was a boy. But Traalf said the baby—that he—" Kennett's voice broke, and Kilían understood: Traalf had been instructed to pass on the same message that Stinar had—that the infant was dead.

Watching Kennett suffer needlessly was like a slow, awful kind of death. But telling him the truth would be even worse.

Still, despite the fact that he lied for a living—concealing and twisting information lay at the heart of being a skilled interrogator —Kilían couldn't bring himself to lie to Kennett. Instead, he simply gave a curt nod. "Miriam lives," he said, avoiding the subject of the infant. "I heard her voice. She's fine, and soon you'll be with her again."

Using Kennett's feelings for the girl as a means of keeping the truth from him burned like acid in Kilían's mouth—but it worked. Though Kennett's eyes were glassy with unshed tears, he gave a sharp nod, seeming to master himself again. "This place—Kilían, where are we?"

Drawing a deep breath, Kilían gave a quick rundown of everything he'd learned that night with Scholar Joseph and the woman Cordelia. As he spoke, Kennett's eyes got wider and wider, the same way they had that night in his cell. Kilían had to look away; their pull was too strong. He wanted more than anything to tell Kennett how he felt; when would he ever get another chance? But Kennett loved Miri, not him. He would *never* love Kilían; after tonight, Kilían would probably never even see him again. Confessing such a thing would be pointless and selfish. And besides, they had no time.

He cleared his throat. "The Brotherhood is waiting for you. You'll go through the tunnels on the other side of that door, and they'll be there, on the other side, in the woods. They'll take you to safety. But first, you'll need to prove who you are. You'll say, 'Speak of the wolf, and she will come.' And in exchange, they'll respond, 'A wolf will not bite a wolf.'"

Kenneth paled, his gaze skittering away. "I'm not a wolf, Kilían." His voice was low, ashamed. "Not even a little bit. What if I can't do this?"

With his hair falling into his eyes and his shoulders hunched, Kennett looked as vulnerable as Kilían had ever seen him. And Kilían couldn't help it—his control slipped. He felt it go, and some part of him welcomed the loss.

Reaching out, he took Kennett by the shoulders, his fingers digging in. This close, he could see the way the bruise on Kennett's cheek faded from midnight blue to a brilliant purple. He wanted more than anything to run his fingers over it, to offer comfort. But such things were not permitted. Instead, he gave Kennett the only thing he could—his word.

"Don't worry," he said, his eyes fixed on Kennett's. "You may not be a wolf, but I am. And I will protect you. As long as it's in my power, I'll give my life for yours. No harm will come to you as long as I live."

It wasn't a promise Kilían could make—not really. But he felt like it ought to be; like his feelings for Kennett were so strong, they could transcend distance and time.

Kennett bit his lip. He shivered, and Kilían felt a shudder pass through his own body, as if, in this instant, the two of them were one. "I don't understand." His voice was a hoarse whisper. "Why would you do this for me?"

Kilían's chest heaved. The words were a logjam in his throat, fighting for release. But all he said was, "My reasons are my own. But believe me when I say I speak the truth. I swear it on my sverd and my honor."

Kennett's eyes scanned his face, as if searching for the answer there. And for a moment, Kilían let his masks fall. He let Kennett see him for who he really was, let everything he felt shine clear in his eyes. Let Kennett make of it what he would.

"You could come with us," Kennett said, searching Kilían's face. "Leave, too."

It was tempting. But with Kilían gone, who would look after the infant that everyone except the Executor and that midwife believed to be dead?

Slowly, he shook his head. "No," he said, his voice as hoarse as Kennett's. "I couldn't." He dropped his hands from the other boy's shoulders and clenched his fists tight, trying to hold onto the feeling of Kennett's warmth against his palms. "My place is here. But as long as I can, I will watch out for you."

Kennett stepped backward, his spine hitting the shelf behind him. The moment shattered, the odd intimacy between them evaporating into the musty coldness of the room.

Kilían didn't trust his voice, but it came evenly, devoid of emotion, the way he'd been trained. "I have to go," he said. "I'll be back, with her."

There was an odd expression on Kennett's face, something Kilían hadn't seen there before and—even with all his training in micro-expressions as a bellator—didn't understand. The other boy rubbed the back of his hand across his mouth, as if at a loss for words. Finally he said, his voice businesslike, "Miri...she won't trust you. You'll have to give her a code phrase—you know, like the Brotherhood does. Tell her—" His eyes darted toward the books, then back toward Kilían's face again. "'But to return, and view the cheerful skies, In this the task and mighty labor lies.'"

It wasn't a line Kilían knew, but this was not the time to question such things. "Fine," he said, reciprocating Kennett's businesslike tone. "You'll stay here. Don't open that door for anyone but me; I'll call out to let you know I'm back. If someone comes in and you can get away, then go through the tunnels. If you can't—take this." He slid a blade from his belt and handed it to Kennett, hilt first.

Kennett looked appalled all over again. "You expect me to stab someone with this?"

"You're a medic," Kilían said, his voice impatient. "You cut people all the time."

"To heal, not to hurt," Kennett insisted, holding the knife as if it were doused in poison.

Worry made Kilían's voice harsher than he meant it to be. "By the Architect, Kennett, now is not the time to be squeamish! You know where people's vital organs are, no? If someone comes in here and threatens you, strike without hesitation, and strike to kill. Because if I come back here and find your blood soaking the stones, I..." His voice trailed off. None of the endings he had in mind were appropriate to voice: *Because I can take a lot of things, but not that. Because if you die, even if I save your precious Miri, then all of this will be for nothing. Because I wasn't lying when I said I would give my own life to save yours, and I can't protect you if I'm not by your side, so you damn well better protect yourself.*

Shame washed over Kennett's face, darkening his eyes. "Kilían, I know the risks you're taking for me—for us. I won't let you down," he said, gripping the hilt of the knife. "I promise."

Kennett's gentle nature was one of the things Kilían loved about him; it was a piece of himself he'd lost long ago, if it had ever been there at all. The thought of abandoning Kennett to fend for himself against whatever might come through that door made Kilían ill. And then there was the other reason, the deeper one: Every moment he spent apart from Kennett now was a moment he'd never see him again.

"I don't want to leave you," he said, each word feeling as if it was being tugged from his throat.

Kennett gave him a heartbreaking half-smile. "I'll be fine. Just...get Miri."

Jerking his head in acknowledgment, the weight of all that he'd left unsaid heavy on his chest, Kilían stalked from the room, locking the door behind him.

THE BELLATORS ON DUTY—ASHE AND HALVAR—NODDED AT KILÍAN when he emerged from the hospital's stairwell. "Bryndísarson," Halvar said. "Come to interrogate the subject, have you? I think you'll find she's asleep." A smirk crept across his broad face.

Arrogant, ignorant fool, Kilían thought, returning the smirk with a simulacrum of a genuine smile. Crossing to Halvar, he clapped the other bellator on the shoulder. "That's no impediment to me," he said, using Halvar's body as a shield to conceal the syringe he drew from his pocket. Still smiling, he slid the needle into Halvar's bicep and pressed the plunger down.

He stepped back to find Ashe staring at him suspiciously. "What—" he began, but before he could get out another word, Kilían closed the space between them and pierced Ashe's arm with the second needle.

It was quick work; thirty seconds later, both bellators sat unconscious, their heads lolling on their chests. Clearly, just like Traalf and Ungar, they hadn't expected an attack to come from within their ranks. Kilían vowed never to make the same mistake.

He glanced at the window at the end of the hall; it was still dark outside. Still, he could feel the passage of time, as if his body was an hourglass, sand slipping through his veins where the blood should be.

Taking the ten steps to the room where Miriam lay, he pushed the door open to find that she was, indeed, asleep. His nostrils flared, taking in the copper scent of blood—but he could hear the steady ebb and flow of her breathing, and as his eyes adjusted to the darkness, he saw her yellow hair feathered across the pillow. She looked very young, and very alone.

Despite himself, Kilían felt a pang of sympathy. Drawing his blade in case they were interrupted, he crouched by her bed and shook her by the shoulder, more delicately than had been his original intention. "Get up."

Miriam blinked, focusing on his face. Her eyes were puffy, as if she'd been sobbing—and perhaps she had. She'd just given birth, had her child taken from her, and was about to be put to death in a few short hours. Kilían supposed he couldn't blame her for crying.

"Who's there?" Her voice was a croak.

Edging a little closer to the bed, Kilían cleared his throat. "Bellator Bryndísarson."

Miriam struggled up to her elbows, peering through the gloom at him. "All right," she said. "I won't fight you."

Despite everything, Kilían found himself amused. What an odd thing to say—as if a weakened, half-asleep citizen would be a match for an armed bellator. Perhaps the girl had courage.

The thought made him like her a little more. Bravery was no small quality to a bellator.

"You'd better not," he said. "I've come to help you escape."

He expected Miriam to ask questions, or to leap from the bed —though perhaps the latter was unreasonable, given that she'd just given birth to a child. But instead, she fell straight back down onto the mattress as if insensible, and shut her eyes once more.

Even for an untrained citizen, this seemed like absurd behavior. Exasperated, he shook her again. "Get up. We don't have much time."

She opened her eyes and peered over the side of the bed at him. "Is this some kind of trick?"

His respect for her ratcheted up another notch. Most citizens were sheep, ready to accept whatever was told to them. But this girl, even in extremis, was skeptical. He admired her discernment —though at this late juncture in the proceedings, he couldn't imagine what he thought it would gain her.

He yanked her upright, and she sucked in a sharp breath. Perhaps he'd hurt her? He felt a flash of remorse, but suppressed it quickly. There was work to be done.

"Kennett said you wouldn't trust me—although what you think you've got to lose, I can't imagine—so he made me memorize something for you." He took her by the elbow and levered her upward, onto her feet. Letting his hand fall, he recited the lines Kennett had confided to him: "'But to return, and view the cheerful skies, In this the task and mighty labor lies.'"

Bellators were trained to hear the beat of another's heart; he could hear hers start to pound. She stared at him, her dark eyes huge. Whatever these words were, Kennett had been right; they meant something to her.

"Do you believe me now?" He shook her a third time, trying to jolt her into action. "I mean you no harm. Quite the contrary. But we've got to go."

But still, she didn't move. Instead, she set her feet like a balky animal and looked up at him, refusing to budge. "Why would you help us?" she said.

He heaved a sigh of exasperation. How was it that Kennett, who was so trusting, had allied himself with such a skeptic? Worse still, how was it that she'd asked the one question he could never, ever answer?

Kilían met her gaze and gave her the only version of the truth he could. "Because if we were allowed such things, Kennett would be my friend." He swallowed hard. "Now, move."

❄

MIRIAM WAS CLEARLY IN PAIN, BUT SHE FOLLOWED HIM NONETHELESS —through the door of her hospital room and into the hallway, where Bellators Ashe and Halvar were still out cold. She stared, incredulous. "What did you do to them?"

The girl was full of questions—maybe because she was a scholar. It occurred to Kilían that under other circumstances, she would've made an excellent interrogator. Right now, however, her queries were merely inconvenient.

He shrugged, sparing a glance for his comrades. "You can thank Kennett. There are unanticipated advantages to having a medic's knowledge of drugs and herbs. They went to sleep like babes in the nursery. And Kennett swore that when they woke up, they'd have no memory of anything beyond the moment they took their places for their shift." They had better not, or there would be hell to pay. Kilían was staking his life on the fact that Kennett was right.

Miriam eyed them, a fierce look on her face. "What a pity," she said, sounding like she meant anything but.

A smile tugged at Kilían's lips. She had fire—and she would need it, to endure what lay ahead. "You'll have to move fast," he said, flicking his eyes over her gown. "Can you do that?"

The girl straightened, and her eyes narrowed, like the question offended her. "I can do anything I need to do," she said, as if daring Kilían to challenge her.

Kilían wasn't going to argue. If worst came to worst, he'd carry her, but he really hoped he wouldn't have to; it would slow them down. Keeping a close eye on her, he led the way down the back stairwell and out onto the street. She stayed right by his side as they made their way toward Marketour Square. He could see it hurt her to move, but she kept pace with him.

He heard her hiss when she saw the steep gradient of the staircase that led down into the tunnels, but she didn't complain. Instead, setting her mouth in a determined line, she grabbed hold of the railings that flanked the slippery steps and made her way down. He could hear the clink of her shoes on the metal stairs as he stepped onto the top rung and then slammed the trapdoor shut above them—slow but steady enough.

There was a thud as her feet hit solid ground, and he doubled his speed, stepping off the last rung and pulling his flashlight from his weapons belt. Time wasn't on their side; there were only two hours left until dawn, and he'd have to be back at his post before then, giving all indications of preparing for Kennett's execution.

"Come on." He shone the beam into the gloom of the tunnel that led toward the Outside, then set off at a brisk pace.

Miriam limped along behind him. He could smell her blood again, stronger this time, and when he turned to look back at her, she was bracing herself upright, one palm on the wall—but she wasn't whining or demanding that he help her. She was soldiering onward, despite the fact that she was wounded. It was an attitude worthy of a bellator.

"Are you all right?" he asked her, the words tasting strange in his mouth.

"I'm fine." She lifted her chin. "Keep going."

Worthy of a bellator, indeed. Despite himself, Kilían smiled. "Kennett said you were tough. All right; I'll take you at your word. It's not too much longer now."

A SHORT TIME LATER, THEY REACHED THE ROOM THAT LED TO THE tunnels beneath the forest. Sending up a prayer that Kennett hadn't been killed in the intervening forty-five minutes, Kilían gave a sharp knock. "It's me."

For an instant, there was no reply, and he felt his heart skip a beat. But then, "Thank the Architect," he heard Kennett say. Breathing a sigh of relief, Kilían pulled the key from his pocket and unlocked the door.

As soon as Miriam saw Kennett, she threw herself at him. Kilían felt a spark of irritation—where had her ability to move so quickly been when they were fleeing for their lives through the tunnels?

He looked away, allowing them their moment, even as it tore at him. When he turned back, Kennett had disengaged himself from Miriam but was touching her face, staring into her eyes as if no one else in the world existed. "Miri, I heard about the baby," he said. "I'm so sorry."

Miriam sniffed. "There you go, apologizing again," she said.

"I wish I could've been there." Kennett looked as if he were about to cry. "Maybe I could have saved him."

"It's not your—" Miriam started to say, but Kilían had had enough. He couldn't stand here and watch Kennett grieve for a child that was still alive.

"About the infant," he said reluctantly, "I have reason to believe Bellator Stinar might be mistaken."

Miriam whirled on him, her dark eyes so wide, he could see the whites all around them. "What are you saying?"

Curse her and the hold she had on Kennett, which had led the three of them to this damnable place. "Efraím told you what he knew to be true," Kilían said, careful not to let his feelings show in his voice. "But I have reason to believe otherwise."

Miriam had no such compunction. "Our baby is *alive?* By the nine hells, what are we doing down here, then?" She turned to Kennett, her expression pleading. "We have to go back. Kennett, we have to find him, take him with us—"

This, right here, was exactly why Kilían hadn't wanted either of them to know the child lived. It was just like a citizen to put their emotions before their own survival. And Kilían hadn't come this far so Kennett and his impetuous companion could get themselves killed.

"There's no way," he said flatly. "I don't know where they've taken the child, and tracking him down would take more time than we have." He rested a hand on his weapons belt, shifting his weight so the blades would clink against each other, reminding Miriam of who held the knowledge of surveillance and combat.

"The sun will be rising in an hour, and you need to be well clear of here by then."

But she didn't back down. "To the Sins with the sun! You got Kennett out, and me too. Surely we can rescue Lucien. I'm not leaving him behind." Her voice trembled, as if she, too, were about to cry. "I can't. Kennett, tell him."

She had *named* the infant? Kilían spared a glance for Kennett, hoping that of the two of them, he would be the more reasonable. But he wished he hadn't, because now Kennett was truly crying—albeit silently. Tears leaked from his eyes, coursing down his bruised cheek. "Miri," he said, "this is wonderful news. But Kilían's right—how are we supposed to find him in time? If we go back, we'll all die—together."

The headstrong girl made a concerted effort to hurl herself through the door and go back the way they'd come. "You leave, then. I have to go back—I have to find him—"

Aggravated, Kilían prepared himself to restrain her, but Kennett got there first. He wrapped his arms around her, pulling her back. "I'm sorry, Miri. I really am," he said. "But his best chance at life—and ours—is for us to go."

The girl was a fighter. She struggled against Kennett's grip, shooting Kilían a glare so filled with hatred, it was all he could do not to act on his training and put her in her place. "Let me go!" she howled.

But Kennett, to his credit, would not. "I can't, Miri," he said, his tears flowing harder now. "I wish I could. Seeing you this way —leaving him behind—it kills me. If I thought we had the slightest chance, I'd go back for him in a heartbeat."

"So you're not even going to try?" She kicked at him. It had to hurt, but Kennett didn't let go.

"Please don't hate me," he begged her. "I can't lose you, too."

The girl wailed and sobbed, and Kilían fought the urge to wrench her bodily from Kennett's arms and toss her into the tunnels that led to the Borderlands. What was *wrong* with her?

Did she want to make so much noise, it would bring the entire Thirty running?

After the longest five minutes of Kilían's life, she wore herself out and leaned against Kennett's chest, sniffing. He stroked her hair, with a patience Kilían couldn't have possessed if it was all that stood between him and the abyss.

"It's the right choice," Kennett told her. "The only one."

And still she argued. "It might be the only choice. But that doesn't mean it's right."

Oh, by the Architect. At this rate they would still be standing here when Sondheim and twenty-nine more like him ploughed straight through the door. "Miriam," Kilían said, realizing he'd never actually said her name aloud before. "I'll look after the infant."

"What?" She lifted her head from Kennett's shoulder and stared at him as if he'd just suggested trading in his hard-earned blades for a position in the Commonwealth's dairy.

Kilían sighed. What difference did it make at this point? He'd already made the promise to himself; maybe it would give the girl and Kennett some comfort to hear him say it out loud. "You have my word. I'll do all I can to make sure he comes to no harm."

Miriam peered at him suspiciously. "Swear it," she said, her voice a croak. "On your honor as a bellator."

He almost laughed. Here he stood, a traitor and an accomplice to two sinners' escape. Where was the honor in that? Still, if this was the promise she needed to disappear into the tunnels with Kennett, he would give it to her. "On my honor as a bellator and the strength of my sverd, I do so swear."

She considered him for a long moment, her hand in Kennett's. And then, at last, she said, "All right, I'll go."

Thank the Virtues. Conscious of time ticking away, he turned to Kennett and went over the details of their escape one final time —where they were to go, what they were to say. And this time, when Kennett said, "A wolf does not bite a wolf," he held Kilían's gaze and his voice came clear and sure.

It was enough. It would have to be.

"I have to get back," Kilían said, taking Kennett in one final time. His eyes flicked over every line of the other boy's face and body, memorizing him. "May the blessings of the Architect be with you both. Stand strong."

He expected Kennett to turn away, to pull the door open and walk through, Miriam at his side. But instead, he lingered. "Thank you, Kilían," he said, sincerity resonating in every word. "For our lives. And for your promise to our son."

Kilían opened his mouth to say something—what it would be, he had no idea—but then Kennett dropped Miriam's hand and stepped forward, wrapping his arms around Kilían, and every word he'd ever meant to say drained right out of his head. He could feel Kennett's whole body against his, feel the roughness of Kennett's cheek against his own. Carefully, afraid if he moved too quickly, the moment might pop like a soap bubble, he returned the favor, holding on to Kennett so tightly, he heard the other boy gasp. Close as they were, he felt the passage of Kennett's breath, hot against his face.

"Don't waste it," he whispered, and felt Kennett nod in response, his fingers spreading against Kilían's back, holding him close.

He closed his eyes, imagining that this embrace portended something else. That it meant the same thing to Kennett as it did to him. That it wasn't the end of something, but rather a beginning.

It took every ounce of his training, every bit of willpower that he possessed, to let Kennett go. But he did it, forcing himself to step away, then turning on his heel to leave. He couldn't watch Kennett slip into the tunnels, leaving him behind forever; that would take more strength than he had.

But he waited on the other side of the door, his eyes closed, listening. He breathed, counting to sixty, pacing his heartbeat as he had been trained to do. And then he blinked, and opened the door.

The room was empty. Kennett and the girl were gone, as if they had never been there at all.

Kilían stood there for the space of one breath. Two. And then he squared his shoulders, feeling the weight of the infant's life settle onto them, and went to learn what had become of Kennett's son.

SLOTH

"A HEART BRUISED BUT UNBROKEN"

Kennett Gundarson sat on a log in the encampment of the Brotherhood of the Wolf, Miri at his side, listening to a group of rebels explain the impossible.

The forest smelled of dirt, pine needles, and honeysuckle, from the vines that twined around the trees edging their clearing: familiar scents that reminded him of the Commonwealth where he and Miri had been raised, the place they'd lived until twelve hours ago. Every breath was bittersweet; it was comforting to feel that, in this foreign world, at least something remained the same.

Then again, if they'd stayed in the Commonwealth, they'd be dead now, at a bellator's hands. The Borderlands might be unknown and terrifying, but at least here, Kennett and Miri were alive.

Their newfound companions sat in a semicircle, on the tree stumps that edged the area where they'd made camp. There was Cordelia—the leader, though she looked about Kennett's age— with her watchful, oddly amber eyes. Next to her was Janus, a study in contrasts with his ink-dark hair and pale skin. He moved in her shadow, always on her left, as if guarding her weak side. When she stirred, he did the same, like an invisible cord connected them. Sitting on the stump next to hers, his hands dangling between his knees and his eyes on the ground, Janus still seemed attuned to Cordelia somehow. It made Kennett uneasy.

Then there was Majun, one of the group's scouts, his shaved head shining umber in the moonlight. His voice was always gentle, despite the constant tension in his body—even now, at rest. Next to him was Bridgette, whose bared forearms were covered in ink—vines and wolves and symbols Kennett didn't recognize— and, finally, Tia, whose cascade of braids fell to her waist. She sat, peering into the darkness beyond the clearing, stroking her gun absentmindedly, as if to reassure herself it was still there.

They didn't have guns in the Commonwealth, but Kennett had seen images of them in the vids of how things were before the Fall, when people were mowed down in battle en masse. The Priests and Executor had always told them that such gratuitous violence was evidence of untethered wrath and a perilous lack of self-control; it was why bellators only fought hand to hand, with blades. But Tia was quiet and reserved, not feral. She petted her gun the way Kennett had seen small children pet the communal teddy bears in the Nursery—as if it brought her comfort.

Miri shifted her weight, trying to alleviate the discomfort Kennett knew she felt from giving birth to Lucien—their son. The word seemed impossible, filling him at once with a desperate, clawing love, a forbidden rush of pride, and a deep, aching grief that he couldn't imagine would ever be sated...because it wasn't as if either of them would ever see Lucien again. In the Commonwealth, people weren't allowed to love, let alone do the things that led to getting their lover with child. These were the crimes for which he and Miri had been doomed to be executed; lust was one of the Seven Deadly Sins, verboten in the Commonwealth, and the punishment for it was death. They'd been sentenced to pay for their love with their lives—and instead, had bought their freedom by leaving their son behind.

Leaving Lucien had been their only viable choice. In his head, Kennett knew that. Trying to save him would've doomed all three of them. But knowing something in your head and your heart weren't the same things, and restraining Miri when she'd fought to go back for their son had been the hardest thing he'd ever had to do. He wasn't sure if she'd ever forgive him. At least Kilían had promised to keep Lucien safe—and if there was one thing Kennett knew about the bellator who was the closest thing he'd ever had to a friend, it was that Kilían always kept his word.

A trained warrior and assassin, Kilían could've killed Senior Scholar Joseph the moment he found the man colluding with a member of the Brotherhood, and dragged the rebel Cordelia herself before the Executor for interrogation about the resistance that existed outside the Commonwealth's fence. Such an act would've earned him accolades beyond measure, the approbation of Lead Bellator Sondheim, and guaranteed entrance to the Bellatorum's elite Thirty the moment a spot became available. But he hadn't done that. He'd kept their secret, trading his silence for Miri's and Kennett's lives. And then he'd promised to look after their son.

Kennett owed him the kind of debt that could never be paid. The bellator had taken this risk for *him,* and Kennett just wished he understood why.

Thinking about Kilían confused Kennett, not least because when he'd looked into the bellator's eyes in the room that led into the tunnels—when he'd held Kennett close, before they escaped—Kennett had felt something flare to life between them, a spark he'd only felt before with Miri. The strength of Kilían's arms around him, the way he'd gripped the back of Kennett's shirt—it was as if Kilían didn't want to let him go.

And in that instant, Kennett hadn't wanted to let go, either. He'd breathed in Kilían's scent of sweat and steel, feeling at once completely safe and horribly vulnerable. He'd felt the bellator's heart racing, his body pressed so tight against Kennett's that he wasn't sure if the heartbeat he felt was Kilían's or his own…or maybe both of theirs, pounding in synchrony.

And then Kilían *had* let go. He'd turned his back and walked away from Kennett, without even saying goodbye. Kennett didn't know why this bothered him so much—what did he want from Kilían? The bellator had already put his life on the line to save them—but Kennett couldn't deny that it did…or that he missed the boy who, in another existence, would have been his friend.

As bewildering as all of this was, Kennett hadn't had the opportunity to dwell on it until now. He and Miri had been on the move ever since they'd emerged from the tunnels that led from the Commonwealth into what Kennett had been raised to think of as the Borderlands. Cordelia Navarro, the Brotherhood's leader, had met them at the exit, but there hadn't been much time for conversation then—just hasty introductions and the expectation that he and Miri would carry their share of supplies. Now night had fallen, though, and they'd stopped to rest.

Kennett was glad of this, for more reasons than one. After

being locked in that damn Commonwealth dungeon for weeks, he was weaker than he realized—but that was nothing compared to Miri, who'd given birth to Lucien just yesterday. He could see from the stiff way she walked, the way she struggled to keep up, that she was in pain—but she'd never uttered a word of complaint. He wanted to check her, to make sure she wasn't bleeding too badly—not that he knew what he'd do to stop it out here; it wasn't like he'd had time to grab anything from the pharmacy before they escaped—but they didn't have any privacy, and besides, there were things that needed to be said.

This was how he and Miri had found themselves sitting on the log in the encampment, sharing a dinner of dried fruit and meat with the Brotherhood as the rebels explained the incomprehensible: They weren't just members of the resistance; they were devotees of people they called the skúmaskot—shapeshifters who could slip their skin and assume an animal form. And it was the Brotherhood's goal to restore those shifters to power, destroying the restrictive, prejudicial society of the Commonwealth once and for all.

Kennett had heard the term skúmaskot before. Children in the Commonwealth heard stories about them, in the form of cautionary tales in the Nursery. Moralistic fables, to teach the little ones of the dangers of sin. But stories were one thing. The idea that these creatures were real—that they were a key element of the organized resistance into which he and Miri had stumbled—was unfathomable. Yet there Cordelia sat, telling them about the skúma as calmly as if she was explaining what they planned to have for breakfast.

Not for the first time, Kennett wondered if when that cold-eyed Bellatorum bastard Stinar had punched him, he'd jarred something loose in Kennett's brain. Maybe Kennett was hallucinating; as a medic, he knew well enough what head trauma could do. He didn't care what he and Miri had read in the books they'd shared during those hours in her Library, all those stories about Sirens and Cyclops and Minotaurs. Such creatures didn't exist.

Then again, two days ago, he would've sworn a resistance to the Commonwealth's way of life didn't exist, either. That the world inside their fence was all there was, and outside it, in the Borderlands, lay only vicious cannibals who prowled the ruins of what was left of the Empire.

He didn't know what was real anymore.

His eyes flicked between each of the members of the Brotherhood. They stared back at him—at *Miri*—their expressions implacable...not hostile, exactly, but not welcoming, either. Not for the first time, he wondered what kind of bargain Kilían had negotiated to get the rebels to take them in.

Miri found her voice before Kennett did. "You want to overthrow the Commonwealth," she said, ignoring their blather about shapeshifting completely. "To destroy it? Is such a thing possible?"

Cordelia lifted her chin. "Of course it is," she said with perfect confidence. "Every system has its flaws. We will find theirs, and exploit it. That's the point of our mission—why we're here."

Miri scooted forward, wincing at the pain. "Kennett and I will help you," she said with conviction. "We'll tell you everything we know. I am—I *was*—a scholar. Kennett is a medic. Any knowledge about the Commonwealth's ways we have is yours."

"Miri," Kennett said, doubt heavy in his tone. Surely he and Miri ought to have discussed such a thing before declaring their unbridled allegiance to these people. Yes, unlike their Commonwealth brethren, the rebels weren't currently endeavoring to chop off their heads—but that didn't mean they were Kennett and Miri's friends. Especially when Cordelia was feeding the two of them a line of virtueless nonsense about being able to change shape at will.

Miri turned to him, hope bright in her eyes for the first time since she'd realized she was bearing their child. "Don't you understand what this means, Kennett? If the Commonwealth is destroyed, then we can see Lucien again. We can get him back. He'll be raised by *us*, not those despicable monsters. I would do anything in the world to make that happen. I never imagined it could."

Her joy was contagious, and despite himself, Kennett smiled at her. He'd never imagined such a thing, either. The thought seemed too fragile to sustain itself, a dandelion puff that would scatter to the ends of the earth with the slightest gust of wind.

"So we'll help," Miri repeated, turning back to Cordelia. "Anything you need. But the rest of what you said, about the skúmaskot—I don't understand. We know the term, Kennett and I—but those are just stories. Not real, any more than the myths I've studied are real. Not to insult you, but I've never read of such a thing." She looked from Cordelia to Janus and back again, as if their faces would somehow reveal the answers she sought.

"We wouldn't expect you had," Cordelia said, her voice kind. "In fact, the Commonwealths have a vested interest in keeping such knowledge to themselves. So instead, we're prepared to show you."

A mutter of dissent went around the circle. Kennett saw Bridgette's lips draw tight a moment before Janus sat forward, bracing his hands on his denim-clad knees. His dark hair was tied back with a rawhide band, and the moonlight fell on his face, illuminating the firm set of his jaw. "Cor," he said, "are you certain you want to do this? We've got a long road ahead of us. And shifting—you know it takes a toll."

Cor, Kennett thought. In Latin, it meant 'heart.' They'd studied such things in the Commonwealth—ancient, crumbling languages, anachronistic ways of seeing the world that must seem bizarre to this group of people, who were free to roam as they chose...and yet had chosen to help him and Miri. He knew little of romantic love—but the way Janus and Cordelia behaved toward each other didn't seem to indicate that they desired each other that way. Still, *something* existed between them beyond the bond of leader and follower. He couldn't define it, but he knew it was there.

Cordelia turned that intense gaze of hers on Janus. "I wouldn't ask this of you if it wasn't necessary. We need to trust each other. And for them to trust us, they need to believe what we say."

"It's not about me," Janus said, bunching the material of his pants in his fists. "Or at least, not entirely. You're our strongest asset. Is it wise to compromise you?"

"I agree with Janus." Bridgette stood, pacing the small clearing. "You lead us, Cordelia, and you know I respect you. But this—we're not bound to perform for them. You owe them nothing. We're already risking ourselves to get them safe away."

Bridgette shoved her mass of wavy, black hair back from her face, combing her hands through it in frustration. The rebels hadn't dared to light a fire, but the moon was almost full, and in its light Kennett could see the vines of ink that climbed from beneath her shirt, twining around the column of her neck. He couldn't understand why someone would mark themselves this way—for surely it had been deliberate? Had such a thing been forced upon her, to indicate her alliance to the Brotherhood, or had she chosen it? In the Commonwealth, using one's body as a canvas in such a way would never have been allowed.

"I gave my word to the bellator," Cordelia said, her tone grave. "If he had given me away, we'd likely all be dead now. And as for owing them nothing—is it not the Brotherhood's mission to destroy the Commonwealths, to expose them for the evil, soul-sucking dictatorships they are and free their citizens from the brainwashing that has defined their lives? These two"—she gestured at Kennett and Miri, who had slipped her hand into his —"were to be executed for loving each other and bearing a child. Such a thing should be occasion for joy, not murder. Now their child is abandoned, an orphan subject to the Commonwealth's vicious and deluded ways."

Her voice rose, and her hand lifted, toying with the charm that hung from a gold chain around her neck. It was an Ouroboros—the serpent that devours its own tail.

"You say we owe them nothing? I say they are the very reason we exist—the reason we are here in these woods, so far from home. Yes, this was meant to be a reconnaissance trip—a scouting mission, before planning a larger offensive. But if we can save even two souls from the horror of that place"—she dropped the charm, pointing back the way they'd come—"then I consider it our duty and our pleasure, the risks be damned."

In the wake of her speech, silence fell. Miri gripped Kennett's hand tight, her small fingers cold in his despite the fading warmth of the day, and he squeezed back, reassuring her that he was here —that he wouldn't leave her again, no matter what happened to them. Beneath the icy deluge of fear engendered by being in a strange place, ill-equipped and unwanted, he felt the unmistakable anchor of her presence, keeping him steady. It seemed a miracle that they were here together, that they were alive. Perhaps next to that, the idea that human beings could change shape wasn't so surprising after all.

Bridgette dropped her head, abashed. "You're right," she said. "And it is, of course, your choice."

"Yes, it is." Cordelia's voice had grown deeper. There was an odd note to it, something Kennett couldn't quite place. "And I've made it."

Next to him, Miri tilted her head sideways, like an inquisitive bird—the way she did when she was truly curious. Her eyes widened. "Are you saying that you intend to demonstrate this mysterious gift of yours for us right now—in this clearing?"

"I am," Cordelia said, but she wasn't looking at Miri. Her eyes were on Janus, who stared right back at her. Kennett had the oddest sense that the other boy couldn't look away, even if he wanted to.

But what existed between them? Janus acted as if he was Cordelia's defender, but he wasn't particularly well-built, the way the bellators were—as if their entire form was honed for battle. His gaze wasn't filled with fierce tenderness, the way Miri's had been when she'd seen Kennett again, in the room that led to the tunnels. Nor was it the simple obeisance of leader and follower, as Kennett had often seen between Lead Bellator Sondheim and his black-clad warriors—Kilían included. This was something else, something Kennett had no words for. It reminded him of gravity—the way the Instruktors had explained to them that the earth was tugged in its inexorable orbit around the sun…as if one of them was somehow dependent upon the other.

Janus's slender shoulders rose, then fell again. Breath hissed between his teeth, a long susurrus of air echoed by the rustle of wind through the trees. He drew himself upright, his back straight. "My skúma speaks," he said, each word distinct and slow, "and I answer."

At that, Tia and Majun stood in unison, backing away from the stumps where Cordelia and Janus sat. As Majun passed Kennett, he said, "You better get up too, exiles. Don't want to be in the middle of…that."

Alarmed, Kennett tugged Miri to her feet, an arm around her shoulders to support her. She leaned heavily against him as they joined Tia, Majun, and Bridgette in the clearing.

The wind picked up, carving its way through the forest, bending the small saplings in its wake, and Miri shivered against him. He hoped it was from anxiety, and not from the fact that she'd lost too much blood. All he wanted was to lie down next to her and curl himself around her, using the warmth of his body to heat hers. To brush her tangled blond hair back from her face, comb the leaves and burrs from it with his fingers, and watch over her as she relaxed into sleep. To heal her, body and soul, in whatever limited way he could. But instead they were standing in this clearing, waiting for Cordelia to prove whatever point she thought she had to make.

Kennett wanted to tell her he didn't care what she thought she needed to show them. That nothing mattered so much as letting

Miri rest. But if she wouldn't listen to Bridgette, then why would she give a virtueless fig about what he had to say?

So instead he watched as Janus rose and came toward Cordelia, kneeling in the dirt at her feet. She extended her hands to him and he took them, bowing his head.

"You are mine," she said, her voice guttural. Kennett heard that other note in it again, stronger than ever, and recognized it for what it was—a growl.

"I am your familiar," Janus said, his head still bowed. "No harm will come to you while I am here."

The words resonated with the force of ritual, reminding Kennett of the oaths that citizens swore during their Choosing. Around Janus and Cordelia, the night air seemed to tremble.

Cordelia stepped back from Janus. Then, to Kennett's shock, she began to strip, peeling off her clothes with an unselfconsciousness that bewildered him. He could feel his face heat. In the Commonwealth, such an action would have been unimaginable; he'd never seen anyone naked except Miri, and even that, during stolen moments. In his job as a medic, his patients had been covered, other than the parts of their bodies on which he'd worked. Yet here Cordelia stood, nude in the moonlight, as if the act of removing all her clothes was no more significant than shucking her shoes.

He didn't know where to look, or what to do—but a quick glance around showed him that everyone else was treating this as normal...even Miri, who'd always brazened her way through every situation. His cheeks burning, he endeavored to do the same.

Cordelia folded her clothes and stacked them in a neat pile on the stump behind her. She unbraided her hair, letting it fall loose over her shoulders, and set the tie on top of her clothes. Then she did the same with her necklace, unclasping it with care and dropping the charm atop her folded shirt, and turned back to Janus. "Now," she said, and placed her hands in his once more.

Janus braced himself, as if for an impact, but none came—at

least, none that Kennett could see. Instead, Cordelia's head went back, baring her neck, and her whole body shuddered—an undulating movement that traveled through her torso, down her arms, and into Janus. He jerked, a tremor running through him, and when he spoke, his voice was as rough as hers. "Give yourself to me, my skúma," he said.

Miri was gripping Kennett's hand so hard, it hurt. "What's happening?" she said to Tia, who was back to stroking her weapon again.

Tia shrugged, her waterfall of beaded braids rattling. "Cordelia wanted you to watch. So, watch," she said, laconic as usual. The whole time they'd been hiking through the woods, the only word longer than two syllables Kennett had heard her use had been Cordelia's name.

"But—"

"Watch," Majun said. "And then you won't have to ask."

Not wanting to argue, Kennett did—and blinked in amazement. One moment, Cordelia was sitting on the ground, her body arching backward in an unnatural bend, her hands ripping free of Janus's. The next moment, her form shimmered, her face elongating and her bones reshaping themselves. The way her nose and mouth were reforming into a muzzle—the way her lips pulled back, revealing razor-sharp canines that were longer than they had any right to be—such things shouldn't have been possible. You didn't have to be a medic to understand that.

Miri sucked in a breath, leaning hard against him. He expected to see his dismay mirrored on her face, but when he glanced at her, her eyes were bright with fascination. "Kennett, look," she breathed.

He wanted to tell her that he *was* looking—in fact, he couldn't imagine tearing his eyes away—but then an eerie howl escaped Cordelia's throat, filling the night. It wasn't a human sound.

On his knees in the dirt, Janus grabbed for her again, gripping where her shoulders ought to be. "Now, my skúma," he said.

Kennett was hard-pressed to explain what happened next, except that one instant he was looking at someone who was recognizable as a human being—bizarrely altered, but human nonetheless—and a moment later, that person was gone. Instead, there was an awful crunching sound, and then a huge gray wolf lay in the pile of pine straw next to Janus, panting.

"By the Architect," Miri whispered, sounding stunned.

Kennett didn't say anything. Truthfully, he was beginning to wonder if when Stinar had cold-cocked him and blackened his eye, the bellator had driven him right into a coma. Maybe all of this was a hallucination, the last gasps of a failing mind. His heart pounded, beating hard in his wrists, his ears, his chest.

The wolf lifted its head, regarding them. Its eyes came to rest on Kennett, and he realized they were the same color as Cordelia's —that peculiar, lucent shade of amber. All that time, she'd been looking out of her human face with a beast's eyes.

The Brotherhood of the Wolf, he thought numbly. No wonder. Suddenly the words Kilían had made him memorize—the ones that gave them safe passage into the rebels' midst—made sense: *Speak of the wolf, and she will come.*

Well, here she was. And here *Kennett* was, completely unable to protect the mother of his child—first from the threats inside the Commonwealth's fence, then from the outside world, and now, from a monster within the very group that was meant to offer them sanctuary.

With a sinking feeling, Kennett remembered what he'd said to Kilían when the bellator had told him the call-and-response necessary to guarantee them safe passage: *I'm not a wolf. Not even a little bit.* And his reply: *You may not be a wolf, but I am. No harm will come to you as long as I live.*

Even as Kilían had spoken the words, his eyes glittering with a peculiar intensity, both he and Kennett had known the bellator was making a promise he couldn't keep. Kennett had begged him to come with them—and now, more than ever, he wished Kilían had agreed. Because standing here in this sins-forsaken clearing, his son abandoned to the devices of the Priests and an impossible beast glaring at him from the dirt yards away, Kennett felt more helpless than he ever had in his life.

Miri, on the other hand, looked as if a miracle had been performed for her benefit. "How does it work?" Her voice was reverent, awed. "What—what did Janus do?"

"He's her familiar," Bridgette said. Kennett didn't think he was imagining the grudging respect in her tone, as if Miri had impressed her by not being afraid. "He anchors her, so she can shift—pulling energy through the earth for her to use it."

Kennett supposed it shouldn't surprise him that where he felt consternation and terror, Miri was merely intrigued. Her curiosity had always been what had driven her forward, even when it spelled her doom. "I've read so much," she said. "But never did I envision—never did I possibly imagine—"

Before Kennett could stop her, she pulled away from him, her face lit with wonder. She took one step toward the wolf, then another. The creature growled, clearly displeased by her approach, but Miri was undeterred. She stepped closer still, and the wolf froze, its eyes narrowing as if in warning. Its head tilted, like it was listening to something none of them could hear. It sniffed the air. Drool dripped from its massive jaws, puddling onto the dirt as it bared its teeth, which glistened in the moonlight. And then it got to its feet, coiling to spring.

Kennett's heartbeat ratcheted up another level, to a speed that was in no way sustainable. He grabbed for Miri and missed, his fingers skating across the back of her tattered shirt. The wolf growled louder, the rumble an unmistakable warning, but Miri didn't stop. Desperate, he lunged for her just as the animal leapt, its eyes shifting from Miri into the dark woods beyond—and then the night exploded.

There was a tremendous *boom*, so loud Kennett didn't hear it with his ears but rather with his whole body. The air was suddenly filled with flying debris, pelting his face and arms, sending him flying. He landed hard, the breath knocked out of him, and when he managed a rough inhale, he tasted bark and dirt and blood. He tried to scream for Miri but it was hopeless; all that came out of his mouth was a shattered croak, or maybe he just couldn't hear his own voice: a high-pitched warble echoed in his ears, drowning out everything else.

Terror shot through him, sharp and sickening. He raised his head and for an awful moment thought he had gone blind; all he could make out was darkness. Desperate, he scrubbed at his eyes and discovered he wasn't blind after all: the moon was obscured by smoke that fogged the clearing, the night gone pitch-black. He coughed, trying to clear his lungs, and spat blood—he could taste it, coppery on his tongue.

He called for Miri again, her name ripping from his throat, like tearing a protective layer of skin from a wound. She didn't answer, but he told himself that it wasn't because this—whatever had just happened to them—had taken her life; it was because she couldn't hear him. Or maybe she was calling back, but he was the one who couldn't hear *her*.

Grimly, he started to crawl forward on his belly in the dark, stopping every few inches to pat around himself. To his horror, after thirty seconds of crawling, his hand encountered a body, covered in the slick hot ooze of blood. He didn't have to be able to see to identify it—he'd cared for enough injured people to know what blood felt like. His heart bolted into his throat, and he ran his hands over the person's form, trying to find the source of the injury. He couldn't; the blood was flowing from multiple wounds, and when he found their throat, he shuddered—an object was embedded in it, and he could feel arterial blood pumping onto his fingers. Whoever this was, they were alive—but not for long. If Kennett was at home, in the Infirmary, he might have been able to save them...but not here. Not like this.

By the Architect, he prayed, *let this not be Miri. Please, please, not her.*

He forced himself to keep going, feeling his way up to the

body's head. He was terrified that his fingers would find Miri's long blond hair—but instead, he encountered only stubble. This was Majun, then—with his gentle voice and ever-vigilant air. But all the vigilance in the world couldn't save him from something none of them saw coming.

Kennett wanted desperately to find Miri—but he was a healer by passion and profession, and Majun was still alive, if only barely. He couldn't leave him to die in the dirt like an animal, alone and terrified. So he gripped the scout's hand, which was icy, and talked to him, even though it was agony to speak. The fingers of his free hand pressing on the erratic pulse at Majun's throat in a vain effort to stem the flow, Kennett told the scout he was there. That he'd stay with him to the end. That it would be quick, and he didn't have to be afraid.

Blood pumped onto Kennett's fingers in jerky spouts—once, twice, three times. And then it stopped. Majun's hand went limp in Kennett's. He was gone.

Rage surged within Kennett. No one deserved this kind of death—the sort of heedless violence the Commonwealth had warned them they'd find in the Borderlands. Who had done this? Had he and Miri escaped one nightmare, only to plunge headlong into another?

Kennett wiped his fingers on the grass—it felt wrong to be so cavalier about Majun's lifeblood, but what choice did he have?— and kept crawling, straight into a tangle of vines. As he struggled to free himself, his fingers snagged on something else, out of place in this world of rocks and twigs and leaves: a thin metallic chain. He ran his fingers over it to be sure and found what he knew would be there: the circular symbol of the Ouroboros.

This was Cordelia's necklace. Which meant that Cordelia herself—and Miri—shouldn't be far away. She had been walking toward the wolf when—when—

He couldn't finish the sentence, not even in his own mind. Instead, he yanked himself free of the vines' grip, crawling faster

—and almost sprawled face-down into the dirt when a hand reached out through the smoke, closing on his.

He would have known that delicate, strong grip anywhere. He'd felt it on every part of him.

"Miri," he whispered, and spun, pulling her into his arms.

Her chest heaved against his own. She smelled of blood and bone-deep fear and fire. And he'd never been so happy to hold someone in his life.

He ran his hands over her, searching for wounds, but all he found were scratches, already starting to clot. Weak with relief, he dropped his head to her shoulder. Her mouth moved against his ear, and he made out every other word through the receding whine that still dogged his hearing. "Thought—lost you—so scared—happened?"

He pressed his lips to the shell of her ear and spoke as clearly as he could. "I don't know. Thank the Architect you're all right." He didn't say anything about Majun; she'd find out soon enough.

The two of them sat there, clutching each other, and slowly the ringing in Kennett's ears began to clear. The smoke stung his eyes, making them tear—but it was thinning, just a bit. He could see a little better—but what his eyes took in didn't make any sense.

He and Miri were in a scrum of brush and trees, twenty or so yards from the clearing. A few feet from them lay Majun, a sharp chunk of wood embedded in his throat and his eyes wide open, his body covered in blood from more wounds than Kennett could count. The clearing itself was filled with smoke, the trees on the other side of it aflame. As he watched, a smoldering branch came loose and hurtled to the ground, barely missing Tia, who lay in a heap, keening. Even Kennett's impaired hearing could make out the sound—an animal sort of wail, broken and agonized.

The branch fell next to her, missing her by inches—but the wind blew and the flames leapt, catching her shirt on fire. She rolled feebly, trying to put out the licking flames—and then hands grabbed her, hauling her to her feet. Kennett followed them to their source and saw Lead Bellator Sondheim, his craggy face unmistakable, gripping Tia by the shoulders, heedless of the flames inches from his fingers. Another black-clad figure stood at his side: Bellator Traalf, one of the Thirty. At their feet lay something Kennett's brain refused to make sense of—fragments of a human form. Whoever that used to be had nearly been vaporized.

"What should we do with you, hmmm?" Sondheim said to Tia, his tone cavalier. "Let you burn? Slash your throat? Put out the flames, then interrogate you and light you on fire again and again until you give us the answers we want?"

Next to Kennett, Miri gasped, and he clapped a hand over her mouth, trying to process what he was seeing. The bellators—the Commonwealth—were behind this atrocity? The very thing the Executor and High Priests had always told citizens was so abhorrent—wrath so great, it extinguished human lives without consideration or cause—was what they'd just perpetrated. Was there no end to their hypocrisy?

On the heels of Kennett's shock came crushing guilt. Was it their fault—his and Miri's? Was the Commonwealth punishing the Brotherhood for taking them in?

The wolf must have heard something right before the explosion. The way it had tensed and growled—how its eyes had slid to the forest a moment before it sprang—it hadn't been coming for Miri at all. It had been trying to attack the bellators, to protect the Brotherhood's camp. But one animal, no matter how powerful, was no defense against a blast like that.

Miri peeled Kennett's fingers off her mouth and pressed her lips to his ear again. "We have to run," she hissed, her voice cracking.

He shook his head. They'd already left Lucien behind; there was no way he'd desert the people who'd risked their lives to save him and Miri. If there was any way he could help—anyone left whose wounds he could stanch or bind—he was going to make sure he was still here to do it.

He could feel Miri trembling beside him, taut with impatience, but she didn't say anything else. They watched in silence as Sondheim smothered the flames eating Tia's shirt. He shook her, and she moaned in pain.

"Got nothing to say for yourself, you traitorous bastard?" the lead bellator said with disgust. "Need a little encouragement to speak? Because I'm only too happy to help. Traalf, the honors, please."

Bellator Traalf stepped up and pulled his dagur, holding his blade to Tia's throat. He smiled, a slow, easy grin. "My pleasure, sir," he said.

These sick bastards, Kennett thought, no-longer-forbidden fury coursing through every inch of his body. *Bellators are supposed to live by an inviolate code of honor. Where is the honor here?*

"Speak, then," Sondheim said, bunching Tia's braids in his hand and yanking her head back so that Traalf's blade pressed into her smooth brown skin. "Or die."

A gurgle came from her throat, and suddenly Kennett couldn't take it anymore. If he didn't do something, right here, right now, the bellator was going to kill her. Kennett wasn't any kind of warrior—but he couldn't be complicit in her death, not when he might well be the reason she was in this situation to begin with. He let Miriam go and started to rise to his feet. If he had to sacrifice himself in the process, even if Tia died too, at least he'd know he did everything he could.

But before he could stand, a hand grabbed his shoulder roughly and shoved him to his knees again. For a moment he thought it was another bellator, for surely there were more here than just Traalf and Sondheim—but when he twisted his head, he saw blue-inked vines on his captor's muscled forearm. It was Bridgette, her face smudged with dirt, a bloody gash gouged into her forehead, and her dark eyes red-rimmed. "Stay down," she hissed, gripping Kennett tighter. "You can't help."

He opened his mouth to protest, just as Tia lifted her head—

not struggling to get away from the blade, but leaning into it. "Not much of a choice," she rasped…and cut her own throat.

Kennett's stomach roiled as blood poured down her torn shirt, soaking it. Her eyes met Sondheim's, victory blazing in their depths—and then they dulled as the life left them. She slumped in his grasp, and he flung her to the ground with contempt, as if she was nothing more than a marionette that had outlived its usefulness. She landed, crumpled, in a pool of her own blood.

Bridgette's grip on Kennett's shoulder was so tight, it hurt, but she didn't make a sound. Next to him, Miri stared, her eyes huge in her pale face.

Miri had been right—they should have run when they'd had the chance. Because with Tia and Majun killed, whoever that was torn to bits by the force of the blast, and Cordelia dead or gravely wounded, as was surely the case—Kennett couldn't imagine she'd let her people suffer like this without trying to save them—the bellators would come looking for the survivors next. And when they found the three of them, they'd either kill them right here in the woods, or drag them back to be executed in Clockverk Square.

In some of the books Kennett and Miri used to read, the authors had written about the Fates—the idea that your destiny was predetermined. No matter how hard you tried to thwart it, it would always find you. And kneeling there, bruised and bleeding in a tangle of thorns, Miri's hand clutched in his, Kennett was inclined to believe this was true.

If Kilían were here, Kennett thought, *he'd know what to do. He'd find a way out, a form of concealment, a strategy of escape.* But he wasn't. Kennett was alone, and the vague sense of missing Kilían that had troubled him earlier coalesced into a hard, painful ache below his breastbone. The bellator had risked so much for them, and for what? So they could be killed anyhow, a day's walk from the Commonwealth, rendering his sacrifice useless?

As Kennett tried desperately to think of a solution, Sondheim nudged Tia's body with his boot, then prodded at the pile of ash and bones next to her that was once a human being. "Pathetic, slothful excuses for soldiers," he muttered. "Too lazy to hide their tracks. Is this what's left of their sins-forsaken leader? Too bad the dead don't speak, eh, Traalf?"

"It could be, sir," Traalf said. "Or perhaps she survived, and those are the remains of another virtueless fool."

Bridgette was crouching next to Kennett now, using the brush as cover. She looked murderous. Slowly, he unfolded his fist, where Cordelia's necklace was concealed. Both she and Miri stared down at it, and Kennett was sure they were all thinking the same thing.

Cordelia hadn't been wearing the necklace when the blast went off—but it had been right next to her and Janus, on top of the stack of clothes. The rest of their party was all accounted for. Which meant that either the pile of ash in the clearing contained the remains of both Cordelia and Janus, or one of them was out here, with Kennett, Bridgette, and Miri—in the place where the necklace had wound up. And if that was the case, Kennett couldn't imagine they wouldn't have found the body—dead or alive.

Sondheim's lip curled as he stared down at the heap of ash. "They're vermin. Fitting that they should be exterminated as such." He heaved a put-upon sigh. "Well, better find out if there are any other roaches left to stamp out. The Executor will want to make sure we got them all."

Kennett's heart plummeted, as if down a length of piping, straight into his guts, which churned. Miri clung to him; Bridget palmed a knife she'd drawn from somewhere; Traalf opened his mouth to reply.

And then the unthinkable happened.

As if Kennett had summoned him, Kilían stepped into the clearing. In his black gear, studded with weapons—the flames blazing behind him, haloing his red hair—he looked like a cross between an avenging angel and one of the Architect's fire-demons: his blue eyes arctic and empty, his face set in the stern expression that was his default. With a pang, Kennett wondered if he'd imagined the boy who clutched him with desperate intensity when they said goodbye, as if he never wanted to let Kennett go.

"Bryndísarson," Sondheim said, with alarming jocularity. "How goes your first sojourn into the wilds beyond the fence?"

Kilían's expression didn't change. "Eventful but unproductive, sir. I saw no others on this side of the clearing."

Sondheim gave another aggravated sigh. "Well, check the far side, then, will you? I'd like to report back to the Executor that we've taken care of things, and then wash the dust of this poor bastard off my shoes." He scuffed his boots on the ground to rid them of the rebel's ashes, as carelessly as if he was wiping mud on a doormat. Beside Kennett, Bridgette dug her fingernails into her palms, hard enough to draw blood.

"Yes sir," Kilían said, and stalked across the clearing, in the direction of where the three of them hid.

Kennett's heart pounded as the bellator strode toward them. Had Kilían betrayed them on purpose, so he could engineer this massacre? Would he grab them by the scruffs of their necks and haul them out to suffer Sondheim's brand of justice?

He should have known better. Between one moment and the next, as Kilían pushed through the brambles on the far side of the clearing and caught sight of them huddled in the brush, his face changed, breaking open. The façade cracked, and Kennett saw the relief that swept over it, melting the ice in Kilían's eyes and permeating every line of his body. He took one stride, two, coming level with Majun's corpse and then stepping over it, as if the scout was no more worthy of notice than a log. His eyes were fixed on Kennett's, and in them Kennett saw all of the worry and desperation that they'd held when Kilían had said he would always protect him, even if the cost was his life.

Shoving the clinging vines away, Kilían reached them and fell to his knees, weapons belt and all, as if his legs refused to hold him. "Thank the Architect," he said, his voice a rough whisper. "I thought—I thought you were—" His throat moved as he swallowed. "Kennett, I couldn't stop them. There was nothing I could do. I'm so sorry."

Tears stood in his eyes—Kilían, who was rumored to have withstood the worst torture the Bellatorum had to offer as part of his initiation, without so much as a whimper. Kennett wanted to comfort him, but how? He was trained in healing wounds of the body, but this—Kennett was so far out of his depth, it was laughable. Was Kilían crying…for him?

"Are you hurt?" Kilían said, his gaze sliding from Kennett to Miri and Bridgette and then back again.

"No." Kennett forced the word from his torn throat. His bruises and abrasions hardly signified. "Kilían, it wasn't your—"

"We don't have time for this." The bellator squared his shoulders. "I told you I would protect you, Kennett, and I will. When I say, the three of you—run. And whatever you do, don't come back."

Kennett wanted to ask him again to come with them. To free himself from the world that held Kilían prisoner, just like it had once held them. But then who would watch out for Lucien, ensure that no harm came to him? And so he only nodded, giving Kilían the assurance he sought.

Satisfied, Kilían's eyes slid from his and fixed on Bridgette. "Look after them," he said.

And then the bellator rose to his feet, pulled his dagur from his weapons belt, and slashed his own arm. Blood dripped onto the leaves as he ripped his way through the tangled brush and ran for Majun's body, smearing the blood from his arm across the neck wound, so as to make the rebel's death appear fresh. Then he bent, picking Majun up as if he weighed nothing and hurling his body against a spruce with a thud. As Majun collided with the tree, Kilían turned his head, his face impassive except for the pain that still shone in the depths of his eyes, and mouthed, "Run."

They burst from their crouch and obeyed, the noise they made as they crashed through the brush obscured by the commotion Kilían was manufacturing. Kennett glanced over his shoulder once to see the bellator drape Majun's body over his shoulders in a fireman's carry and charge back into the clearing, bellowing for Sondheim. Then, though it made his heart twist to do it, he turned his back on the boy who'd saved his life twice and locked his hand with Miri's. Bruised but unbroken, they left the wreckage of their old life behind, fleeing as fast as they could toward an uncertain future.

PRIDE

"THE HEART IS A BLADE"

CHAPTER ONE

SIXTEEN YEARS LATER

Gentian is not a violent person—not to mention, in the Commonwealth, wrath is forbidden—but when the High Priest comes into view, marching Ari Westergaard toward the whipping post in Clockverk Square, it's all he can do not to break free from the crowd and put a fist through the Priest's face.

He doesn't do this, of course. He doesn't even move. The Executor and the Priests have deemed this Ari's punishment, and to protest would be treason. Maybe it would be brave to object, the way that girl did years ago, at Gustavson's execution. Or maybe—probably—it would just be stupid.

Gentian isn't stupid—at least, he doesn't think he is. He does well enough in the Instruktors' classes, even if he spends more time than he should staring out the window, watching the birds flit through the trees and wishing he was out there with them.

Here's a secret: Sometimes, he wishes he was one of them.

He envies the birds their freedom, their ability to soar over the gray buildings of the Commonwealth of Ashes, the endless days of sameness and the rigid expectations, the small cruelties. He's jealous that they can take to the sky, flying over all of it: the concentric circles of the City and the woods where the bellators train; the drop of the rapids and the dense forest where the

Bastarour roam, waiting to devour them if they're exiled; the threat of the electric fence that surrounds the Commonwealth, protecting them from the hordes that roam the Borderlands.

Try as he might, he can't escape the feeling that they're all just animals in a trap.

Envy, along with wrath, lust, pride, greed, gluttony, and sloth, is a terrible sin, so Gentian isn't stupid enough to admit any of this aloud. But he isn't brave, either. If he was, Ari wouldn't be here in the Square right now, clad in a thin, regulation green shirt despite the freezing weather, taking step after step across the cobblestones toward a wooden whipping post dark with other people's blood.

He's here because of Gentian, because he stood up for him. He's here because of a bird.

No matter what Ari says, this is Gentian's fault.

Flanked on either side by a bellator—those stone-faced, black-clad men charged with keeping order and enforcing punishment—Ari walks toward the whipping post. The frigid wind pins his shirt to his body, emphasizing its long, lean lines. His chin is lifted, his back stiff, his eyes fixed straight ahead, his face as expressionless as the bellators'. He looks every bit as prideful as the Mothers and Priests accuse him of being—but inside, he has to be scared. Doesn't he? Gentian would be terrified.

Ari knows that. He has to. It's why he covered for Gentian, saying the bird the other boy rescued was his. He is taking the punishment that, by rights, should be Gentian's—and when Gentian tried to argue with him, he wouldn't listen. He stood between Gentian and Johannes, who is an insufferable bully. He lied for Gentian, straight to Mother Trondheim's face. By then Gentian had already run away, the way Ari'd told him to, like the coward he was. But he hadn't gone all the way back to the dormitory. He'd hidden in the shadows, something he's good at— no one ever notices stammering, shy Gentian, much less in the middle of the night when the halls are deserted and they're all supposed to be asleep—and he'd heard every word.

They're right, Ari is prideful, and maybe that's a sin. But he's also something else, something that, as far as Gentian is concerned, is far more important: Beneath his arrogant, take-no-prisoners exterior, he is kind.

He doesn't let many people see this; for one thing, kindness isn't valued in the Commonwealth, and for another, it's all too easily exploited. Ari's advantages are his strength and speed, his wits and his charm. The night of the bird, Gentian heard Mother Trondheim call him silver-tongued. Gentian is Ari's exact opposite —stuttering and clumsy, though he scores all right on exams. But when Johannes and the others try to push him around, Ari stops them, every time.

He is the only one.

Ari and his entourage reach the post, and he stops in front of it, waiting. Gentian scans his features, looking for any sign of fear, but there's nothing—he looks calm, as if he isn't about to be whipped and humiliated in front of the entire Commonwealth. The gathering is massive—they've even brought the little ones out for this, the children who still live in the Nursery. They mean to make an example of him. But Ari doesn't turn to look at the crowd, doesn't even acknowledge it. He might as well be alone in the Square, aside from the bellators and the Priest.

Gentian wishes he would look. If he did, he would see that there was at least one person here who cared what happened to him. Who thinks that this is wrong. But he doesn't turn his head.

High Priest Erlich looks Ari over, an expression of grim satisfaction spreading across his thin, beaky face. Gentian thinks —and not for the first time, either—that he *likes* these occasions, far more than he should. "Take off your shirt, boy," he orders.

Without a word, Ari obeys, pulling the green shirt over his head and dropping it at his feet. His skin is a blank, unmarked canvas, his muscles rippling as he moves, and Gentian feels a shudder go through him at the sight. By the time he leaves the Square, the smooth expanse of his back will be marred forever.

Gentian doesn't know if he can stand to watch; but he has no choice.

The wind gusts, and another shudder rips through Gentian, this one of sympathy; even with his coat and scarf on, it's brutal out here. He doesn't know which is worse—a winter whipping, where the cold adds to your troubles, or a summer one, when the blood attracts flies. Maybe the icy temperatures will numb Ari's skin, make it hurt less.

"Lift your arms," the Priest says in that same implacable voice.

When Ari does, the Priest chains his wrists to the post. Ari tugs on the chains, testing them, and Gentian sees his lips set in a thin line when he realizes he can't move more than a few inches.

High Priest Erlich clears his throat and pitches his voice loud enough for all of us to make it out. "So it begins," he says.

Now, for the first time, Ari turns his head to look at the crowd. Gentian wills the other boy to see him, standing next to Johannes —the bastard has finagled his way next to Gentian, with his lackey, Arik, on his other side, in what Gentian is sure is meant to be a threat: *this is what happens to the people who protect you.* But Ari's eyes skate right over Gentian's face, and as the wind kicks up, rustling the needles of the pines and sending fallen leaves skittering over the ground, Gentian sees him shiver for the first time.

Hatred slices through Gentian, sharp as one of the bellators' blades. Ari deserves far better than this.

"Ari Westergaard," the Priest says. "You have been found guilty of the sin of pride, and sentenced to a public whipping in consequence. Do you accept your punishment and await justice with an open heart?"

Ari's jaw tightens. "Yes, High Priest," he says, his voice low but clear. "I do."

Next to Gentian, Arik snickers. "About time," he whispers, quiet enough so that if Gentian wasn't standing next to him, his words would be swallowed by the wind. But Gentian hears him, as he's meant to, and so does Johannes, who smirks in response.

Gentian's hands fist in the pockets of his coat, where no one can see. He adds the two of them to the list of people he would like to punch—if he had any clue how to do such a thing without breaking his fingers.

"Then let it be," the Priest says. His tone is serene, at least on the surface—but Gentian detects a hint of that same gleeful anticipation lurking beneath it.

The taller bellator steps forward, pressing the whip into Priest Erlich's hand. The breeze gusts as the Priest lifts the whip, his crimson robes billowing in the wind—but not loudly enough to conceal the whistling noise the leather makes as it cuts through the air, or the awful sound it makes when it strikes Ari's skin. Gentian sees him brace himself a second before it strikes. Then his body jolts with the force of the blow, driving him forward, his face nearly striking the post.

Gentian winces as blood starts to flow from the cut, trickling down the skin of his back. As the Priest's arm comes down again and again, opening multiple wounds, the trickle becomes a stream. He glances away from Ari's face—paler than its usual olive hue, sweat studding his hairline despite the cold—and, to his horror, sees the blood puddling on the stones beneath Ari, staining the shirt at his feet.

Ari's head drops with the next lash. Gentian can't see his face anymore, but he hears the grunt the whip drives from him—a telling admission of pain. Next to Gentian, Johannes chuckles under his breath. "What do you think of your hero now?" he says, elbowing him. Hidden as they are in the crowd, no one can see Johannes—and Gentian isn't so sure they'd stop him if they could. "He's not so t-t-tough now, huh?"

Gentian ignores the way Johannes mocks his stutter. After sixteen years, he's used to it. He only cares about Ari, who has lifted his head and is scanning the crowd again. Tears fill Gentian's eyes—not because of Johannes' pathetic attempt to bully him, but because of the pain that's etched on Ari's features. *He* isn't crying—no matter what Johannes says, he's stronger than most people Gentian knows—but Gentian can't help himself.

If he hadn't rescued that stupid bird and tried to nurse it back to health, if Ari hadn't kept his secret, none of this would be happening. Ari insisted the bird wasn't to blame, that they were whipping him because of his pride—but finding him out of bed in the middle of the night with a contraband creature was the last straw. Gentian doesn't care what Ari says. This is happening because of him.

The bird died, anyhow. Gentian has seen long-ago vids from before the Fall, when baby birds were only born in the spring, when it was warm outside. Afterward, when climate change brought storms and floods, the seasons turned upside down. Now, you're just as likely to find a nest in the middle of winter. He did his best to keep the bird warm, tucking her into a box filled with scraps, but it wasn't enough. Ari helped him…for nothing. And now he'll bear the scars for the rest of his life.

Ari bites his lip, and his teeth sink through it, sending a gush of blood down his chin. He hangs from the chains, wrapping his hands around the post so he won't fall—but he doesn't make a sound.

High Priest Erlich counts the lashes aloud, his voice growing hoarse: *Fourteen. Fifteen. Sixteen.* The wind shifts, bearing the metallic reek of Ari's blood toward the crowd, and Gentian's stomach twists, nausea washing through him. There has to be something he can do to fix this. Some way to help, to pay Ari back for what he's done for him today. He wracks his mind, but can't think of a thing.

The Priest's face contorts, and for the moment, he stays the whip, his fingers white-knuckled on its handle. "Why do you not cry out, boy?" he says, his eyes narrowing. "Why do you cling so tightly to your pride? It gives me no pleasure to mark you this way. Only show some humility, and all of this will be over."

He's addressing Ari, but he's talking to them, too—the crowd of witnesses. Gentian wonders how many people here think Ari is getting exactly what he deserves—and how many, like him, think this is a terrible sight. He'll never know; to do anything other than affirm the will of a Priest is treason. But part of him thinks Priest Erlich is lying—that he likes this just fine. It's Ari's defiance, his refusal to buckle, that's the problem.

Ari shakes his head. He spits onto the cobblestones, spattering them with blood. "This isn't pride," he manages, contradicting the Priest, and I hear Johannes suck in his breath. "It's discipline. Whip me if you must. I'll not beg for you."

"Stubborn fool," Priest Erlich hisses in disgust, and the whip comes down again.

Gentian wants to be brave, like Ari is. He wants to make a difference, to show that he stands for more than what the Priests tells them they should believe. But how?

Ari lifts his head again—but this time, instead of roving aimlessly over the crowd, his gaze finds a single point and holds. Curious, Gentian follows its path—and sees a girl, her face pale above the navy collar of her coat, her dark hair bound in a glossy braid. Her lips are pressed into a stern line that reminds Gentian of Ari himself. She stares back at Ari, her gaze not sympathetic or horror-struck but rather…what? Determined, Gentian decides. As if she's trying to convey something to him with the force of her stare.

The girl is familiar, but Gentian can't place her. He knows he's seen her before, and for some reason he associates her with Ari. This is absurd; they have all of their classes together, and he's never seen Ari so much as speak to a girl, unless it's to pass her a pencil or excuse himself as he brushes by her on the way to his seat. But something tickles at the back of Gentian's mind as he looks at this one.

The black braid…that determined expression…the intensity of her stare…

He looks at Ari, who's staring back at her as if he's absorbing strength from her gaze. At her. At Ari again.

And then he has it.

This is Eva Marteinn, the girl the High Priest called onto the stones the day Gustavson was executed. Gentian had been standing next to Ari that day, and when the Priests removed the man's blindfold, he remembers wondering if his dorm-mate felt as horrified as he did. Just the week before, when he and Ari had been assigned to weed the gardens, Gustavson had taken the time to bring them glasses of cool water and bunches of grapes, straight from the vine. When no one was looking, he'd even helped Gentian move a few of the worms he'd uncovered into the shade, so they wouldn't shrivel up in the sun.

Watching Gustavson wait next to the Priest for his sentence to be carried out—the bellators standing at the edge of the Square, marking time until they were called to unsheathe their blades—Gentian had felt just as helpless as he did now... wanting to stop what was happening, but knowing it was impossible. And then a small girl dressed in white had defied the Priest, refusing to accede to his demands. She'd called the bellators to action herself, and they had decapitated the man at her feet.

The girl had been bold—but frightened, too. Her eyes had roamed the crowd, but no one had been willing to look back at her...except for Ari. He'd held her eyes as Gustavson's blood bathed the stones, even knowing that if the Priest caught him, he'd face a fate worse than kneeling on the stones of the sacristy for hours with a bar of soap between his teeth, the way he had the night before.

Well, now she is returning the favor.

But the way Ari is looking at her—the fierceness of his gaze—there's more to it than support given and received, Gentian is sure of it. There's *need* in Ari's eyes, as if whatever she's offering him is all that's holding him upright.

Friendship is forbidden in the Commonwealth, much less love and desire. They are a society of children bred in petri dishes and borne by surrogates. In the vids from Before, Gentian has seen the dangers of what the world once called 'dating'—flattery, flowers, and food meant to encourage the commission of lustful sins. Such things are beyond verboten here.

But *something* exists between Ari and Eva—he'd bet the lives of every animal he's ever rescued on it.

Watching them, an unfamiliar sensation wakens in his belly, uncurling like a cat in the sun. He can't label it, can't name it. But he knows it's nothing he's ever felt before. The fear he feels for Ari is still there, but intertwined with it is a feral need of his own—to intercept Ari's gaze, unlocking the secrets it holds. HIs skin feels suddenly too tight, the blood blooming beneath it. His breath hitches as he watches them watch each other, feeling as if he's eavesdropping on a private moment but unable to look away.

The Priest's hoarse voice calls a halt to the whipping at last and the bellators unchain Ari, looping his arms over their shoulders to hold him upright. Gentian hazards a glance at Eva and sees that she's staring straight ahead, looking not at the bellators or Ari but at some remote point beyond the Square— maybe the pines, where shadows twist and shift in the flickering light. It doesn't matter; he knows what he saw.

The cat-in-the-sun sensation floods through his whole body, alarming, exhilarating. And just like that, he knows, too, what he can do.

If what exists between Ari and Eva Marteinn is outside the bounds of propriety, he will keep their secret. He will protect Ari, no matter what it costs him.

His flaws—his stuttering, his clumsiness, his shy demeanor— render him invisible to most people. He'll take his weaknesses, and transform them into his strengths. He'll watch, and wait, and do what he must when the time comes.

Seeing Ari grin at High Priest Erlich, his lip split and his back a red ruin, Gentian knows this: He may not be fast or charming or witty, the way Ari is. He may not have what it takes to sustain thirty lashes without screaming, then quote Latin to the Priest through a mouthful of blood.

But he pays his debts.

He can—he *will*—be brave.

CHAPTER TWO

THREE YEARS AFTER THAT

Rain pours down, drenching Gentian to the skin. Lightning splits the darkening sky, a fearsome flash that illuminates everything around him—birches, mud, wild blackberry thickets— a minute before thunder booms, loud enough to scare away any animals in the path of the storm. The air is filled with a mélange of scents—leaf mold and petrichor, the sweet aroma of jasmine and the bite of pine.

Gentian doesn't usually like loud noises—maybe because, throughout his childhood, they usually presaged some dreadful prank Johannes and his acolytes played on him—but out here in the woods, the thunder doesn't bother him. It's part of nature, the cycle of death and rebirth. If he gets struck by lightning, at least his death will make sense—instead of being executed for failing to follow what have increasingly come to feel like a series of arbitrary rules, created to keep the Commonwealth's citizens obedient and contained.

It's the *contained* part that disturbs him more than anything else. If he thinks too much about the fact that they can't go beyond the electric fence—that they're penned in here as surely as the livestock he's spent the past two years tending—his chest starts to tighten, making it hard for him to breathe. One time, when he

"

couldn't get the idea out of his head, he wound up hyperventilating until he nearly passed out. He sat with his head between his knees for ten solid minutes before he trusted himself to stand again, and when Instruktor Tiagen found him, he had to make up a lie about getting lightheaded because he hadn't eaten enough breakfast. Voicing the alternative—that living in the Commonwealth makes him feel like a rat trapped in one of the gen lab's mazes—would have been unthinkable .

This is one of the reasons he loves storms. There's something wild and untamed about them, and when he's outside during one —even if it's not overly sensible—he feels wild and untamed, too. He doesn't feel like Gentian Halvorson, nineteen-year-old vet tech, who spends most of his time tending to animals destined for the slaughterhouse. Here, under the open sky, he feels like he belongs—like he is free.

This is how he comes to be in the woods where the Bellatorum Lucis trains, even though night has long since fallen and the storm is raging. He didn't bring a light with him; he didn't want to advertise his presence. Wandering in the woods isn't prohibited, but he doesn't feel like having to justify his behavior to anyone whom he might encounter. Luckily, the woods are deserted. Most activities in the Commonwealth are utilitarian, and explaining to a patrolling bellator that he's out here to commune with nature in the midst of a storm is sure to evoke suspicion.

Though he has no interest in—or talent for—the Bellatorum, he feels a forbidden trickle of envy at the camaraderie they share. He craves to belong to something larger than himself, to have a purpose greater than grooming ill-fated animals who are destined to wind up as his next meal. Once, he'd thought the promise he'd sworn to protect Ari would provide that for him, but it's turned out to be no more than the empty delusion of an idealistic boy.

Over the years, he's spent enough time in the woods that he can make his way with relative ease, even at night. Between the gleam of the moon and the flashes of lightning, he can see well enough. His usual clumsiness fades away; he moves quietly, though with the cacophony of the storm, he doesn't have to be too cautious. As long as he doesn't trip over a root and wind up face down in the mud, he'll be fine.

He's winding his way around the edge of a clump of blue spruces when he hears voices. So someone else is out here, after all—and close by, too. Listening harder between rolls of thunder, he realizes that it's a boy and a girl—and their voices sound familiar. He strains to hear, and then he recognizes them: For some Architect-forsaken reason, Ari Westergaard and his apprentice, Eva Marteinn, have chosen to train at night in the woods—in the middle of a storm.

Ari's been a member of the Bellatorum Lucis for as long as Gentian's been a vet tech—two years, ever since the Choosing, which takes place when Commonwealth citizens turn seventeen. Ari swore his oath a year after his whipping, and the next time Gentian saw him, he was dressed all in black like the rest of them, a sverd strapped to his back and a weapons belt hanging from his hips. Efraím Stinar, the lead bellator, even took Ari on as his apprentice—a rare honor, and one reserved for the most talented among their brotherhood.

Ari and Gentian haven't spoken in a long time. Bellators aren't encouraged to fraternize with citizens. But he always smiles at Gentian whenever he sees him—not his trademark sarcastic grin, but a real, open smile.

For Gentian's part, he does his best to avoid Ari. Whatever he felt that day in the Square was dangerous. He notices things about Ari—about other boys—that he shouldn't: the way they move, the fall of their hair, the way their towels cling to their hips when they step from the shower. But only when it comes to Ari does he feel something more, an unmooring sort of desire that tugs at his heart as well as his body. When they happen to be in the same room together, Gentian tries not to look at Ari unless he has to. He's afraid it's stamped all over his face, afraid Ari will see.

If Ari knew the truth, would he regret helping Gentian so

many times? Would he still smile at Gentian, or would he be too disgusted to even look his way?

Gentian's had no cause to keep the promise he made three years ago in the Square; he's never seen anything untoward pass between Ari and Eva. As far as he can tell, the two had never even spoken until this past Choosing Eve, when Ari and Bellator Riis were assigned to guard an Instruktor doing penance in the breakfast line. Eva had taken issue with the Instruktor's fate, and Gentian had watched covertly from his table as she gave Ari a hard time. She seemed to rattle him, in a way Gentian had never seen anyone do before.

The next morning, the unthinkable happened: At the Choosing Ceremony, when it was time to call Eva's name, the Executor announced she would be the first female bellator to serve the Commonwealth. Gentian felt the shock wave reverberate through the Great Hall as she stepped onto the dais—and then Bellator Stinar called Ari up to swear an oath as her mentor. He would train her, guide her through her apprenticeship until she was ready to serve as a full-fledged member of the Bellatorum Lucis.

Watching Ari and Eva standing side by side on the dais, Gentian thought of Gustavson's death, of Ari's whipping. He remembered the way the two of them had looked at each other. And he had the oddest sense of the Executor as a giant spider, spinning a web in which they were all innocent flies. Then the vision passed, and it was just Ari and his apprentice-to-be, holding each other's gaze as Efraím's blade came down, piercing her arm for the blood sacrifice that sealed her oath.

Gentian didn't think Ari would interrogate him if they stumbled upon each other here—or even demand an explanation —which means that Gentian would owe him, yet again. Still, that doesn't mean he wants to encounter Ari and Eva, and not just because being around Ari undoes him. If they're training, that means they're likely using something for target practice. Gentian doesn't want to accidentally add himself to the list. He debates the best course of action just as lightning flashes again, illuminating the clearing on the other side of the grove of spruces.

And then he freezes.

Ari and Eva stand in the clearing, the tip of her blade beneath his chin. Her fingers are locked around the blade's handle, her body tense. Surely Ari could disarm her, but he does not. Instead he stands there, her knife nicking his throat, as still as Gentian is. His face is guarded, but Gentian knows him well enough to recognize an expression he have never seen on it before: Fear.

Of what? Her? He's at least fifty pounds heavier, with the advantage of two years' experience. Gentian doesn't understand.

The flash fades and the clearing goes dim again. Gentian can't see them well anymore, other than outlines in the gloom—but when Ari speaks, he can hear him clearly.

"What do you want from me?" Ari's voice is husky, as if the words pain him to speak. "Do you want me to beg? I will, if that's what you need. Just tell me, so I can get it over with and we can get the hell out of here."

Now Gentian is more puzzled than ever. Ari's greatest sin is his pride. Gentian has never heard him offer to beg anyone for anything before. In fact, he's barely heard him *ask* anyone for anything. In all the time Gentian's known Ari, he's been self-sufficient to a fault.

"That's an interesting proposition." Eva sounds amused. "Go ahead and beg, then. I'd like to see you try."

Thunder rolls, so Gentian misses what—if anything—they say next. When it stops, Ari's voice comes again, lower than before. There's a note to it Gentian's never heard, an intensity he can't place. "You wanted me to beg, yeah? Then come here."

Gentian hears rustling, as if they're stepping on the soggy carpet of leaves and pine needles that covers the ground of the clearing. Alarm paralyzes him—what if they're moving this way? He squints, peering into the shadows, but he can't see enough to tell. He can hear Ari whispering, too quietly to make out the words, and then Eva says his name, her voice laden with alarm.

What is happening? Should he try to leave? But if he does—and they catch him—what will the consequences be? Ari will overlook Gentian roaming in the woods; but if he and Eva are doing something they shouldn't, and he knows Gentian's seen them, he can't imagine Ari will be able to afford to let that—let *him*—go.

He has to stay here, to hide. He has no choice.

"Eva." Ari's voice comes again, sounding as if he's been running—but Gentian is sure he hasn't moved; he would have heard it. "Do you like this? Do you want me to stop?"

What is he talking about? Surely they aren't—

Lightning splits the sky again, and this time, what Gentian sees in the clearing tears a gasp from his throat. He covers his mouth, horrified—but neither of them have heard a thing.

They are *kissing*—leaning up against a tree, Eva's hands knotted in Ari's hair, his mouth covering hers. The rain beats down on both of them, but neither of them seem to notice. As Gentian watches, Ari lifts her, and she wraps her legs around his body, pulling him closer. Their absorption in each other is total, which is a good thing, because Gentian's stumbled backward, tripping over a fallen log. He lands on his rear in the dirt and sits there staring.

Gentian has never seen two people kiss before, of course, but he knows what it looks like, from the vids they show citizens to warn them of the perils of lust. If anyone found out about this transgression, the punishment would be swift—exile, at the least. Maybe worse. There are few sins in the Commonwealth more serious than this.

The unfamiliar sensation he felt three years ago, the cat-in-a-sun one, is back, curling low in his belly. He watches Ari's hands move over Eva's body, slow and sure, watches him bend his face to hers, and realizes he is jealous. Gentian wants Ari to touch *him* that way. He wants to know whether Ari's dark hair is soft or rough, feel what it's like to hold Ari in his arms, hear Ari speak to him in that husky, undone voice: *What do you want from me? Do you want me to beg?* Remembering how beautiful Ari looked when he took off his shirt that day in the Square, Gentian's filled with an all-consuming need to skim his fingertips over Ari's skin, to press his lips to Ari's the way Eva is doing right now and make the bellator shiver in his arms.

A pure, desperate *want* courses through him, followed quickly by shame. He can't feel like this. He can't even think it. What in the nine hells is he supposed to do?

He has to get out of here.

Scrambling to his feet, he waits for the next clap of thunder. When it comes, he moves as quietly as he can through the underbrush, then runs full out, heedless of the branches that scratch his face or the mud that cakes his shoes. He'll go back to the dormitory and change his clothes, and he'll forget this ever happened—

The next second, he smashes headlong into something solid and bounces off it, tumbling face-down into the muck. When he sits up and blinks to clear his eyes, he sees two bellators standing over him—Jakob Riis, who was with Ari that day in the breakfast line, and his apprentice, whose name Gentian can't recall.

Damn his sins-cursed luck.

To say Riis has a face like a ferret would be doing the ferret a disservice. In the moonlight that filters through the trees, Gentian can see rain dripping from his pointed chin. His beady eyes narrow in suspicion as he prods Gentian with the toe of his boot.

"Care to tell me what you're doing here, citizen—and where you're off to in such a hurry?"

Gentian's stomach lurches. Thankfully, this is one occasion on which his stutter comes in handy; it's all too easy for people to underestimate him—if they don't get sick of listening to him first. He peers up at Riis and—what the devil is his name?— endeavoring to look as pathetic as possible, which, under the circumstances, isn't difficult. "I-I-I—"

As expected, Riis heaves a sigh of disgust. "What's the problem, citizen, did you get too much mud in your mouth?"

"I recognize this one," his apprentice says, sounding equally repulsed as he wipes rainwater from his face. "He can barely complete a sentence. If you want to get a straight answer out of him, you'll be standing here all night."

Riis' head tilts, considering this, and for a moment Gentian feels relieved—maybe they will just walk off and leave him here in the mud, without further interrogation. But then he remembers his promise.

If Riis and his apprentice go further into the woods, following the path Gentian took—it would be hard to miss, even in the dark, and surely they'll be curious about what sent him crashing through the woods like a deer in rut—they will doubtless come upon Ari and Eva. And if they find the two of them in a compromising circumstance, there's no way they'll keep it to themselves. Bellators are cutthroat competitors by nature. These two will report what they've seen to Efraím Stinar, who will go right to the High Priests or even the Executor himself—and then the next execution Gentian's forced to witness in the Square might be Ari's own.

He cannot let that happen.

Watching Ari and Eva together, he'd thought his heart was a finely-blown glass, shot through with cracks and about to shatter—but he'd been wrong. His heart is a blade, and with it, he will cut whoever he need to. Ari can't be his—that's not possible—but if being with Eva is what he wants, then Gentian will protect him.

His mind races, trying to come up with a strategy, a way to distract the bellators, as Riis shrugs. "Maybe you're right, Karsten," he says, contempt giving way to boredom. "Let's leave mudmouth here to his own devices. We have far better things to do than to waste our time with him. Count your blessings, citizen; today's your lucky day."

He turns to go—and, desperate, Gentian reaches out, snagging the pant leg of his gear. "W-w-wait," he chokes.

Riis stares down his nose at him, his expression incredulous. "Let go of me," he says, each syllable a warning.

By the Architect. He's laid hands on a bellator. Such things aren't done. They're untouchable, above such things.

Well, it's too late to take it back now—and at least Gentian has his attention. He unfurls his fingers and looks up at the bellator, wrapping his arms around his knees. "S-s-sorry, Bellator Riis," he manages, exaggerating his stutter, and is gratified when the man's expression settles into something that resembles satisfaction. Men who crave power as he does are petty. The fact that Gentian has bothered to learn his name will go a long way.

"Your apology is accepted," he says with an air of magnanimity. "What do you want?" He folds his arms across the chest of his rain-slick gear, waiting.

"I'm lost," Gentian says, widening his eyes. "I t-thought I remembered that there was a b-b-blackberry thicket near the edge of the w-woods. But when I t-tried to f-find it, I couldn't…and then it started to r-r-rain. I've been w-wandering for hours. I'm wet, and I'm c-c-cold. Please, can you h-help me?"

Riis stares down at him, expressionless, and for a terrible moment Gentian wonders if he's gilded the lily. But then the bellator laughs, and Gentian remembers what he should have known all along: Bellators like him expect the rest of them to make idiotic choices, and have no concept of how to rescue themselves from the consequences. Citizens are the sheep, and they the dogs that guard the clueless flock. By those lights, it's totally reasonable that Gentian would venture into the woods in the middle of a thunderstorm, searching for a ripe crop of berries.

As if he's summoned it, lightning flashes again, illuminating the four of them: Riis and Karsten, their arsenal of blades—enough to qualify as an entity unto itself—and Gentian, sitting in a mud-soaked, ignominious heap. For good measure, he wipes his eyes and sniffles, as if he's started to cry—it's not as if anyone could tell the difference, in this sins-forsaken storm.

Riis gives an irritated snort and hauls Gentian to his feet. "Unbelievable," he mutters. "Passing up an opportunity to track those useless excuses for bellators so we can shepherd a citizen foolish enough to misplace his path, two hundred yards from his own front door."

You know I can hear you, Gentian wants to snap—but instead, he melds his features into the obsequious chump Riis expects to see...never mind that he's just discovered that the bellator's only here, in the woods, to follow Ari's trail. Now, more than ever, Gentian needs to play his part.

"So you'll h-help me? Th-th-thank you so much." Gentian reaches toward the bellator with shaking fingers, as if overwhelmed by his gratitude. "May the Architect b-b-bless you—"

Riis dodges backward, evading his grip, looking more put-upon than ever. "Enough of your blather. This way. Let's go."

Thunder rolls again as Gentian complies, his heart pounding in triple-time. Tonight, he's done three incredible things. He's discovered a secret that threatens the life of the boy he's sworn to protect. He's fooled a bellator and his apprentice, and tricked them into helping him, in the name of upholding his promise. And he's learned that, though he once allowed Ari to take the whipping that was meant for him, he can, indeed, be brave.

Then and there, he makes a decision. He refuses to be ashamed of the way he feels for Ari, how his desire for him sears through his veins where the blood should be. The Priests say it's wrong, that feeling like this about anyone, let alone another man, is a terrible sin—but it doesn't feel wrong. It feels...beautiful.

Gentian may not ever have the freedom he dreamed of, soaring above the Commonwealth and leaving it behind forever, but he can have freedom within himself—to love who he wants, and make Ari's world better because of it. Gentian can be true to his heart, even if no one knows it but him.

Loving like this will free him.

Head held high, he follows Riis and his apprentice out of the woods.

CHAPTER THREE

The sirens blare, a piercing sound that hurts Gentian's ears. He wants to cover them, to protect himself from the invading noise that feels like a needle, penetrating the soft center of his brain—but that would draw attention to a weakness he's learned to keep hidden, so he refrains. He has enough problems without giving people ammunition.

If he's forced to, he can cope with the sirens. What he can't do when they're going off like this, though, is *think*—and he needs to do that now, desperately.

Usually, when the sirens go off like this, it's a drill. In fact, he's never known it to be otherwise. They're for alerting citizens to invasion from without, not threats from within—but the latter is exactly what's happening tonight.

Gentian did his best to protect Ari, but his best wasn't good enough. He and Eva got caught. Gentian doesn't know who Informed on them, or how, but three days ago, the Executor gathered everyone in the Square to announce that Ari had been exiled and Eva was imprisoned, awaiting her sentence. He didn't say why—all he alluded to was "transgressions against the Commonwealth"—but Gentian can think of only one reason.

Ever since then, Johannes has been insufferable. Through some unfortunate twist of fate or deliberate affront, Gentian's cot is next to his. For the past two nights, all he's done is harangue Gentian about how he'd always known Ari was a traitor, how the Bastarour will rip him apart, et cetera ad nauseum.

And on the third night, the sirens began to blare.

The only advantage of this is that Gentian can't hear Johannes's diatribe over their incessant bleating. But neither can he think—which is what he needs to do, if he's going to find a way to keep his promise.

The sirens are blaring because—after they exiled Ari—he's somehow managed to return. Gentian doesn't understand how he survived the Bastarour, but if anyone could manage it, it's Ari. What's truly beyond him, though, is *why* Ari would come back. He must know there's nothing for him here—that the bellators will happily put a knife through his throat the moment he shows his face. He'd have better luck with the hordes.

Gentian sits on his cot, ignoring Johannes, trying to figure out what to do. He refuses to admit defeat, to acknowledge that saving Ari is hopeless. Ari hasn't given up—so neither will he.

In the pauses between the siren's shrieks, Efraím Stinar's voice rises, coming through the speakers strategically located throughout the Commonwealth: "Bellator Marteinn. Exile Westergaard. Show yourselves. It will be easier for all of us if you do."

Bellator Marteinn. Exile Westergaard. They're together, then?

Now Gentian understands. Ari didn't come back out of fear of what lay beyond the fence. He came back for her.

Gentian can't decide if this is the bravest thing Ari's ever done —or the most foolish. What he does know is that Ari's out there, with Bellator Stinar's Thirty on his trail, and nothing to stand between him and certain death except the blades he and Eva carry.

Gentian may not be much, but at least he is *something.* And anything he does will be better than sitting here like this. He knows he can't have Ari the way he wants. But knowing that Ari's out there somewhere—even if it's not with Gentian—makes his gray world livable. Losing Ari to Eva and the Borderlands is bad enough; the thought losing him to death at the hands of the bellators carves a yawning chasm inside Gentian, where his heart should be.

Saving Ari isn't selfless; quite the opposite. It's an act of self-preservation.

Gentian gets to his feet and edges past Johannes, who grabs his wrist and mouths, *Where do you think you're going?* But Gentian doesn't bother to answer. Instead he wrenches his wrist free, slipping past Johannes and their oblivious dorm-mates, who are fixed on the spectacle outside—luckily, Gentian's cot is by the door—and then out into the hallway. He listens, but Johannes doesn't follow. The bully is full of bluster, but under all of that, he's a rule-follower and a coward. If the dormitory is supposed to be under lockdown, with his longtime enemy roaming armed and dangerous in the streets, then in the dormitory he'll stay.

Keeping to the shadows, Gentian makes his way down the stairs and out into the storm that's raging outside, the thunder competing with the sirens to create an indescribable cacophony. The moment he steps out of the dormitory and onto the concrete walkway, he's drenched. Thirty seconds later, he starts to shiver.

Why, when it's time to make good on his promise to Ari—the one the bellator doesn't even know about, more's the pity—is it always pouring?

The streets are deserted. When he makes his way around the corner of the dormitory and onto the path that leads to Clockverk Square, he sees no one. But he also needs to make sure that no one sees *him*—every citizen in lockdown probably has their faces plastered to their windowpanes, wanting to be the one to catch a glimpse of the traitors and Inform on them. Pride in one's accomplishments is verboten, but you can dine off the notoriety that comes from committing an act of patriotism in the name of the Commonwealth for weeks. And there's never been an opportunity like this—not since Gentian was born, anyhow.

Rain splashes the sidewalk, seeping through his shoes. He can't just stand here. He needs a plan.

The siren stops, and he rubs his temples, blinking rainwater out of his eyes. *Thank the Architect.* But his relief is short-lived, because now he hears voices—and the sound of feet pounding through puddles, coming his way. Heart thumping, he steps back into the alleyway that cuts between his dormitory and the machine shop, at the very edge of the Square.

"What do you mean, you don't know what they'll do?" The voice is sharp-edged, impatient—and familiar. It belongs to Kilían Bryndísarson, the Commonwealth's lead interrogator—a ruthless bellator who will stop at nothing to extract the truth from a sinner. When Gentian was small, the children were told that if they didn't live virtuously enough, Kilían would snatch them from their beds in the night.

An icicle of fear stabs Gentian's heart. He flattens himself against the wall of the machine shop, the wet stone rough against his back, and prays Kilían doesn't decide to come this way.

"It's obvious," Kilían continues. His voice is closer now—he's paused at the mouth of the alley. Suppressing a whimper of terror, Gentian presses himself even closer to the wall, wishing he could meld into it completely. "They've already done for Eleazar. Who knows how Riis will fare—you took him to the infirmary yourself. There's only one option left to them. Please tell me you're bright enough to figure out what it is."

"Escape." It's Riis' apprentice's voice—Karsten, that's his name. "Through the forest. They're going to try to get beyond the fence."

Kilían gives a grunt of approval. "The boy survived the Bastarour the first time around. He's wagering he can do it again. Let's hope his companion doesn't demonstrate similar fortitude."

Karsten snorts in response. Then, to Gentian's immense relief, he hears the thud of their footsteps again as the two of them move on.

Gentian's mind spins. Ari and Eva have killed one bellator,

and injured another. If there ever was a possibility that either of them would be reintegrated into the Commonwealth, it's gone now. Kilían's right, the only option is for them to brave the Bastarour and then try to disarm the electric fence—though how such a thing might be done, Gentian has no idea.

He can't do anything about the fence. But he does know how to deal with the Bastarour.

He waits a full minute, counting to sixty to be certain. Then he pokes his head out of the alley to make sure Kilían and Karsten are gone.

He sees no one. Not in the Square, not on the streets.

Moving as fast as he dares, keeping to the shadows, he steps out into the rain and runs for the vet tech center. He presses his palm against the pad that gives him access; someone will see the data logs later and know that he's entered the building when he was supposed to be in lockdown, but there's nothing he can do about that. There's nothing he can do about the muddy footprints he's leaving all over the floor, either. It's not like he has time to stop and clean them up.

He races for the pharmacy, where they compound the drugs that they use to treat their livestock. As a tech, he has access to them—including the tranquilizers. He knows the dosage needed to sedate the Bastarour; last year, two of them got into a vicious fight with each other, and the bellators needed to use dart guns to subdue the animals, so the techs could treat them. Only the senior techs were allowed to go; they cared for the Bastarour right in the forest, not wanting to risk bringing them into the clinic. But Gentian had been the one to prepare the darts.

His hands shaking, he fumbles for his keys, unlocks the drug cabinet, and draws up the dosage. There are six of the animals in the forest. He fills nine syringes, just in case he misses. The dart gun holds seven; he caps the remaining two syringes and stuffs them into his pocket.

If he misses, the animals will kill him. Maybe he'll wind up using one of these on himself, to put an end to his misery if they get hold of him.

He'll just have to lure them close enough that missing isn't a possibility.

Water drips onto the floor—another telltale clue as to his presence here—as he loads the darts into the gun, straps it across his chest, relocks the medicine cabinet, and runs for the stairs. Back out into the rain he goes, toward the path that leads into the woods where he saw Ari and Eva kissing. He crashes through the trees, the dart gun banging against his back, branches catching on his clothes, water slicking his face and stinging his eyes.

He can't let himself think too much about what he's about to do. If he keeps moving, if he just focuses on taking the next step, and then the next and the next, then eventually he'll reach his destination, and there will be no turning back.

Because if he thinks about it—the fact that he's stolen tranquilizer darts and is running through the bellators' training territory, on a mission to tranquilize the Bastarour and abet two traitors' escapes—he'll turn around and go back. And if he does that, there's no way he could live with himself.

He bursts through the last copse of trees and emerges on a hillside, fronting a meadow. In the distance, he can see the edge of the forest, the one that contains the Bastarour. They can't leave—their shock collars prohibit it—but there's nothing to prevent citizens from entering. Who would want to? Except—obviously—Gentian. And the people he's trying to save.

There are multiple entry points to the forest. It surrounds the entire Commonwealth—first the City, then the wooded training territory, then the hills and gorges, then the forest, then the fence. He has no idea where Ari and Eva will enter it…but the Bastarour roam the forest in its entirety, and they are trained to sense—and hunt—unwelcome humans.

The beasts will find him; there's no doubt in his mind. It's just a matter of which of them will strike first.

But Gentian knows animals—he's worked with them all his

life. He doesn't mean the Bastarour any harm; it's not their fault that they were bred and raised as weapons. Maybe somehow they'll sense that. And if not, all the tranquilizer will do is knock them out for a few hours. It won't hurt them.

A buzzing sound fills the air, and he rubs his ears, trying to make sense of it: Is it a weapon of some kind? Is he hyperventilating from sheer terror? Then lightning streaks from the sky, striking a tree in the middle of the meadow. For a moment he sees the forest beyond it clearly, a forbidding tangle of limbs and foliage. The air fills with the acrid scent of ozone, searing his nostrils. Then the flash fades, cloaking the meadow in darkness once again.

He's far enough away that the strike doesn't hurt him, but every hair on his body stands at attention nonetheless. It's foolish to be outside during a storm like this—but what's even more foolish is what he does next: break from the safety of the treeline and race across the meadow, in the wake of the lightning strike, in plain sight of whatever bellators might be watching from the shadows.

He's panting hard when he makes it to the other side of the meadow. Bellators train every day, but Gentian's exercise lately has been limited to citizens' mandatory twice-weekly fitness sessions. It doesn't matter much; if a bellator had seen him, they wouldn't have had to catch up to him to kill him. They're experts at distance bladework; Gentian's seen the demonstrations, a warning to citizens that someone is always watching, and the consequences of their actions may be both swift and unseen.

His chest heaving, he takes the first step into the forest. The blackness encloses him, terrifying and absolute. There's no trail here; the best he can do is to push his way through brambles and thickets, one arm up to protect his face from the lash of branches. It's only partially effective—he feels a sharp, slashing pain a moment before warm blood begins to trickle down his cheek.

Well, maybe it's for the best. The blood will summon the

Bastarour. No matter where they are in the forest, they'll smell it and give chase.

He hears the sob of his own breath under the rolling boom of thunder and the steady patter of raindrops on the canopy above. Grimly, he pushes deeper into the forest, thorns catching his clothes and vines twining around his ankles. The gun smacks against his back as he moves, reassuring him that it's still there.

Then, as he steps into a rare clear spot, bare enough that the dim light of the moon reaches the forest floor, he hears what he's been both hoping for and dreading—the crash of something large through the trees, heading his way.

There's no point in going to meet it; it will find him, and soon. Instead he pulls the strap of the dart gun over his head. His finger trembles on the trigger.

A low growl reverberates from the shadows, vibrating in his chest, his limbs, his head. It is the single most menacing sound he's ever heard, and Gentian shakes so hard, he almost drops the gun. But he doesn't. He hangs on to it, scanning the spaces in between the trees for clues as to what shouldn't be there—what doesn't belong.

He's focusing as hard as he can. But even still, he doesn't see the Bastarour until it steps from between two trees, detaching from the shadows like a piece of the night come to life. Gentian catches his breath. The creature is monstrous—ink-dark and massive, with the streamlined body of a panther, the bulk of a tiger, and the elongated muzzle of a wolf. As it tilts its head to regard him, the moonlight falls across its face, and he can see the stripes it inherited from its tiger ancestors. Its wolflike ears prick, listening for further invaders—and then its lips draw back, revealing its teeth, as it scents the air.

It is monstrous, all right—but it's also beautiful and powerful, in its own way. And it's trapped here, just as much as Gentian is.

"Hello," he says to it, keeping his voice low, soothing.

It assesses him with its flat green eyes, as if trying to determine the most effective way to vivisect him. And then it lifts its head and howls, telling its brethren that it's located their prey.

This is the best chance he'll have. As the creature bunches its hind legs, about to leap, he raises the tranquilizer gun and fires. To his amazement, the dart lands true, sticking in the beast's shoulder. It yelps, takes one wobbling step, then another…and then falls in the brush at Gentian's feet.

He hardly has a moment to savor his victory before another beast bursts from the trees, this one even bigger than the first. Rain streams into his eyes, clouding his vision, but he knows he'll only get one shot. If he misses, he'll die.

Gentian prays to Ari, rather than the Architect—what has the latter ever done for him? *Help me. Guide my aim.* His finger tightens on the trigger, and when the dart flies, it sinks into the beast's flank. Its eyes widen, as if it's as surprised as Gentian is. It growls, a guttural sound that trails into nothingness as its knees give and it collapses.

Then a third one leaps from the shadows, knocking him onto the ground with an impact that drives the air from his lungs. It growls and snaps, its jaws closing not on Gentian's neck but on the dart gun. It seizes the weapon, strap and all, and rips it from his grasp, hurling it into the trees.

Despite the fact that Gentian's probably about to die, he can't help but be impressed.

The Bastarour stands over him, growling and snapping. Thick ropes of saliva drip onto his face. Its breath floods Gentian's lungs, stinking of old blood, as it lowers its head, teeth coming closer and closer.

It could kill him in an instant, but instead it's toying with him, extending the pleasure of the hunt.

Gentian's instinct is to struggle, to fight to break free. With an effort, he suppresses it. The moment he fights back, it will snap his neck. And so he doesn't move, nor does he look away; they're in a battle for dominance, he and the beast, and if Gentian drops his eyes, it will see that as the final white flag of surrender.

He can't move his right arm; the beast has pinned it, sharp claws digging in. But he can move his left. Slowly, he inches his fingers toward his pocket and the backup stash of tranquilizer darts.

The beast growls again. It paws at his chest, ripping through the fabric of his shirt and drawing blood. Gentian worries that the scent will drive it into a frenzy, but instead it lowers its head and licks the blood from his chest, its tongue rough, as if savoring an appetizer before a particularly delectable Idle Day meal.

It's disgusting. But it's also a distraction.

As the Bastarour laps at his blood, its claws digging into his arm and its saliva drying on his face, Gentian feels his fingers close around one of the syringes. He draws it out, slips off the cap, and fumbles for the plunger.

The beast must sense danger. It lifts its head and roars, then lunges for his throat. He tries to get his free arm up, to protect himself, but it's no use. Its breath is hot on his neck, its teeth inches from his jugular. He rolls out of the way a second before it pinions him with a giant paw, drawing even more blood. It roars again in triumph—just as Gentian wrestles one arm free from beneath its bulk and stabs its shoulder with the syringe.

The needle sticks, but his thumb slips off the plunger, and now the creature is more enraged than ever, lunging and snapping. His fingers fumble across its rain-soaked hide, desperately searching for the syringe. For a moment he thinks it's hopeless, that he'll never find it in time. *At least I took care of two of them for you,* he thinks. *I did the best I could.*

But Lady Luck smiles on him, and his hand closes on the syringe. He seizes it and jams the plunger down. The beast stiffens in shock—and then collapses on top of him, going limp.

Panting and dripping blood, he wriggles out from underneath its bulk. He half-expects another one to come hurtling out of the woods—but then he hears it howl, far away, and realizes the rest of the beasts have found what they're after.

He's cut the pack in half, given Ari and his apprentice a

fighting chance at freedom. It's far more than he'd hoped for, and as he eases off his shirt and rips it in strips to stop the bleeding, he allows himself to feel a fierce, forbidden sense of pride in what he's done.

The beasts lie at his feet, unconscious but breathing steadily. He'd give anything to be able to examine them, to rid them of their taste for human flesh and be able to set them free. But such a thing is beyond his grasp. So instead he yanks the syringes from their bodies and turns his face to the sky, letting the rain wash the blood and saliva away.

"May the Architect speed your way, Ari Westergaard," he whispers, the words coming clear and even, though there's no one to hear him but the trees and a pale slice of moon.

He has been the hero of Ari's story more than once, even though the bellator didn't know it. Now the only thing left is to be the hero of his own.

Shoulders squared, he turns and goes back the way he came, resolved to face his fate.

GREED

"HEART OF SHADOW AND FLAME"

The sky is the color of a fading bruise as Gentian makes his way out of the forest, which is fitting. Everything hurts: His right arm, from where the Bastarour dug in its claws; his chest, from where it pawed at him as he struggled to reach his backup stash of tranquilizer darts; his heart, which aches like a black-and-blue mark that he's pressed his fingers into again and again.

He knows what he did was the right thing, even if it might cost him his life. He's tired of living in the shadows as stuttering, invisible Gentian, who loves a boy even though love is forbidden, has been bullied since he could walk, and is doomed to pass his days caring for utilitarian animals, not allowed to so much as rescue baby birds that tumble from their nests, lest that be seen as an unholy sign of attachment.

In the Commonwealth of Ashes, people live and die by the rules of the Seven Deadly Sins—pride, greed, lust, envy, gluttony, wrath, and sloth—and attachment is the first step on the thorny road to sin. But Gentian can't help but wonder: if you can't stop yourself from becoming attached, if connection is what you crave —to the natural world, to the animals you care for, to the boy who's always stood between you and the worst of your tormentors—then have you already sinned?

It's not a hypothetical question. From the moment he splinted the leg of a hurt mouse he found in the Nursery when he was a child and Ari Westergaard discovered him tending it, his heart hasn't been his own. He'd expected Ari to report him, to go running to the Mothers with irrefutable evidence of his sins—but instead the other boy had leaned in closer, examining the twig Gentian had tied to the mouse's leg using a scrap of yarn. Ari's eyes, the color of a ripe green apple, had widened, and as he'd extended a finger to stroke the mouse's tiny head, it had stilled under his touch. "Poor little thing," he'd said, and Gentian couldn't help but wonder if Ari meant *him*, as well as the mouse.

All the rest of that day and into the next, Gentian had braced himself for the repercussions—but none came. And he realized that, for no reason other than the fact that—inexplicably—he'd wanted to, Ari had protected him.

Looking back, that was the moment Gentian fell for him.

In the Commonwealth, love of any kind is forbidden, so it took Gentian a while to realize that was what he felt for Ari. At first, it just seemed like a dangerous obsession, one he needed to guard against at all costs. It wasn't until he placed Ari's happiness and safety above his own—not just once, but again and again—that he realized the true nature of his feelings. Now here he is, sneaking out of the forest that's all that lies between the Commonwealth and the horde-infested Borderlands, the remains of his tranquilizer darts in his pockets and his clothes in tatters from the Bastarour's claws.

No one other than the Bellatorum's Thirty goes into that forest and lives—except apparently, Gentian…and, hopefully, Ari. Stealing a tranq gun from the vet clinic where Gentian works, running toward the mutant beasts rather than away from them, risking the wrath of the Bellatorum's warriors and the Priests—it all adds up to a recklessness that's the opposite of how he usually behaves. But Ari is in that forest, fleeing for his life, and Gentian wants to give him the best chance of survival.

Part of him is furious with Ari. He'd been exiled for mysterious "transgressions against the Commonwealth" that no one would name—though Gentian can guess well enough. He could have been free; if anyone could find a way to escape the Bastarour and survive in the Borderlands, it's Ari. He's a bellator —a trained fighter and a skilled killer. But what did he do? Somehow, someway, he survived the Bastarour the first time around…and the lunatic came back. For *her*.

As far as Ari's concerned—and by extension, Gentian—there's only one *her*. It's Eva Marteinn, his apprentice in the Bellatorum and the girl Gentian caught him sinning with months ago…not that Ari knows that. They were in the woods, kissing—an act that's punishable by death. Gentian had been shocked when he'd found them, but heartbroken, too. It's not that he expected Ari to share in the way he felt. But seeing him risk his life to touch Eva that way, hearing the tone of his voice when he'd spoken to her—tender, pleading, the way Gentian had never heard him speak to anyone else—it had shattered something inside him.

But just as quickly, his resolve had hardened. Ari had taken a whipping meant for Gentian. He had protected Gentian, again and again. If the only way Gentian could return this favor was to guard Ari's secret with his life, then that's what he would do.

Gentian didn't know if Ari and Eva's sinful relationship was finally discovered, or if something else altogether occurred—the inner workings of the Bellatorum aren't something to which typical citizens are privy. But three nights ago, Ari was exiled, and Eva was imprisoned in the dungeons beneath the Commonwealth. Gentian had felt sick; exiles were released into the forest, where the Bastarour prowled. They were never seen again, unless the beasts dragged what remained of their bodies to the edge of the woods to show off their prizes.

He'd clung to the hope that Ari still lived. And sure enough, the other boy had—because the next thing Gentian knew, the sirens were blaring, and Lead Bellator Stinar's voice was booming over the speakers, demanding that Ari and Eva give themselves up.

Desperate to do something, anything to save him, Gentian had crept out of the dormitory and into the rain, hiding in the shadows, racking his brain for what he could do to help. And then he'd heard Kilían Bryandísarson, the Bellatorum's terrifying lead interrogator, say that Ari and Eva would surely head through the forest, to disarm the electric fence that led to the Borderlands and escape.

Gentian himself is the furthest thing from a warrior imaginable. He's clumsy, he's shy, and he stutters when he tries to speak. But one thing he does know well is animals—how to help them, how to heal them, and how to render them less of a threat. Which is what brought him to where he is right now—having tranquilized half of the Bastarour's pack to give Ari the best chance of escape; stumbling out of the woods, bruised and bloodied from his encounter with the beasts.

He lost the dart gun somewhere along the way, and there was no hope of finding it. It flew out of his hand and into the foliage when one of the beasts attacked him. With luck, it'll stay hidden in the underbrush; there was no time to search for it in the dark and the rain. His only hope is to return the remaining darts to the clinic—if he's found with them on his person, he'll likely wind up at the hands of Kilían himself, and the Lead Interrogator's touch is far from gentle.

Stepping clear of the forest, he shoves the sopping mass of his hair back from his face and peers into the fading darkness. He's facing the meadow that separates the forest from the woods that ring the Commonwealth's City. Though the woods don't house any creatures more dangerous than raccoons or, at worst, coyotes, that doesn't mean they're safe. They're the Bellatorum's training ground, and while Gentian is sure most of the warriors' elite Thirty are in the forest he just left, hunting down Eva and Ari, that doesn't mean there aren't a few still stationed in the woods he's about to enter.

Well, it doesn't matter. This is the only way home, so he has to take it. He knew the moment he shut the door of his dorm behind him and stepped out into the rain that his life might be the price.

Grimly, he takes the first step into the meadow. The mud squelches underfoot with a sucking sound, threatening to swallow his shoes whole. He can't see well enough to even make the attempt to step in anyone else's footprints; the sun is still well below the horizon, and thank the Architect for that. So he relinquishes stealth in favor of speed and races across the meadow, his body trembling with adrenaline. Rain pelts him, stinging his eyes and plastering his ripped clothes to his body, but he keeps going, crashing at last into the woods on the other side of the meadow.

There are trails here, as opposed to the forest. Still, it's too dark to make them out. He fumbles his way through the woods, branches catching on his clothing and scratching his face, vines twining around his ankles and threatening to ensnare him. It's as if the woods are alive, as if they want to trap him and keep him here until the bellators find him and drag him before the Priests for justice.

The thought sends a chill through him, and the roar of thunder that sounds overhead and shakes the trees doesn't help matters. Terror makes his teeth chatter. They clip his tongue, sending blood flooding into his mouth. He spits again and again, trying to rid himself of the coppery taste.

At long last he fights his way free of the woods and finds himself standing at the edge of the grounds that lead to the City. He knows his way from here; there's no need of light. In fact, the less of it, the better. He makes his way past the path that leads to the vineyards, where the workers grow the grapes for the Priests' ceremonial wine, then skirts the edges of Clockverk Square and slips into the alleyway that runs between the stone buildings of the Library and the Education Center.

The streets are empty—suspiciously so. His neck crawls with the sensation of the bellators' eyes on him...because surely they are watching.

But perhaps they aren't. Perhaps all of their attention is trained on Eva and Ari, because he manages to make his way back to the clinic without incident. His heart begins to slow as he presses his palm against the pad and creeps inside.

It's a relief to be out of the pounding rain—but in the stale, bleach-scented air of the clinic, he begins to shiver. He can't tell if it's cold or the after-effects of shock, but either way, he shakes as he creeps down the darkened hallway toward the pharmacy, where he'll need to expel the tranquilizer from the darts and then restore the empty syringes to the cabinet. Water splatters from his clothes and his hair, leaving a trail along the tile floor, and he forces his brain to function, to remind himself that he'll need to get a towel and wipe it up. What a pity it would be if he managed to subdue six Bastarour and survive the forest, only to find himself on his knees for the executioner's blade because he'd forgotten to sop up a few puddles.

Keep it together, Gentian, he tells himself sternly. *Now is not the time to surrender to your fear.*

The strange thing is, the voice in his head doesn't sound like himself—stuttering, cautious, fearful Gentian Halvorson. It sounds confident, calm.

It sounds like Ari.

Heartened by the idea that he'll be able to keep some part of the other boy with him, even if it's just a voice inside his own head, Gentian makes his way to the pharmacy and fumbles in his pocket for the keys. Inside, he knows the place well enough that he can navigate without turning on the lights. He heads for the sink, pulling the darts from his pocket and setting them on the counter. *Almost done,* he tells himself. *Almost safe.*

Thunder booms again, rattling the windows and making him jump. The rain is a steady patter, pelting the glass. He tries as hard as he can not to think of Ari out in it, facing the remaining three Bastarour and the Bellatorum's fearsome Thirty with only Eva at his side. Gentian did his best to help, but he knew it wasn't nearly enough. How could it be? There are only two of them, and a battalion of warriors.

He consoles himself with the thought that not *all* of the Thirty made it into the woods. When he'd overheard Kilían earlier, he'd said that two of them had already fallen. But that still leaves twenty-eight. What if they've killed Ari? What if right now, as Gentian stands here emptying syringes into the sink and congratulating himself on a job well done, Ari is bleeding out onto the forest floor?

Stop it, Ari's voice says in his head, sounding exasperated. *This isn't helpful. You have a job to do—so do it, and stop whining.*

Ari's right, of course. Gentian's done everything he can. The other boy will either survive, or he won't—but Gentian has never been good at compartmentalizing. At the thought of Ari's body lying in the mud, studded with blades and fodder for the Bastarour, nausea sweeps him. His hands shake as he picks up another syringe and presses the plunger down.

"In a hurry?"

The familiar voice comes from behind him, sardonic and low, cutting through the drumming rain as cleanly as a blade. Gentian almost stabs himself with the syringe, but somehow manages not to—thank the Virtues. Instead he clutches it tight and spins around to find Kilían standing behind him in the gloom of the pharmacy, his short red hair soaking wet, his black bellators' uniform plastered to his body, and his hand on the hilt of his dagur.

By the nine hells.

Perhaps it was greedy to imagine he might save both Ari's life and his own. Perhaps he has asked for too much.

Gentian's heart skips a beat and then starts speeding, beating so quickly, it makes him dizzy. He's only seen images of deserts in the vids from before the Fall, but that's his mind right now: barren, empty, and desolate. He opens his mouth, but nothing comes out.

Kilían looks him over—his torn clothes, the cut on his cheek where a branch slashed him, the rainwater dripping from his body onto the tile floor—and the bellator's lips rise in a sneer. "Nothing to say for yourself, boy?"

The short answer to this question is *yes*. Gentian's ability to speak, which is faulty at best, seems to have failed him utterly. But then he hears Ari's voice in his head. *He's just a man, Gentian. So he's found you. So what? The worst thing he can do is kill you, and you knew that was a possibility when you started down this road. Are you going to let him bully you? I'm not here to stand up for you anymore. You'll have to do it for yourself, or die trying.*

It's ridiculous, given that Ari's voice is no more than Gentian's imagination, but somehow this gives him the courage to straighten his spine and clear his throat. "D-don't c-call me boy."

His voice sounds just as terrified as he feels, but at least it comes. "My n-name is Gentian."

The sneer morphs into an assessing expression—like Kilían's weighing what a stuttering boy who would talk back to a bellator is made of. Either that, or perhaps the man is determining the most efficient way to rend him limb from limb. "Gentian, then," he says, his lips twisting as if the name tastes foul. "What brings you to the veterinary clinic in the middle of a Commonwealth-wide lockdown, with two armed and dangerous traitors on the loose? Why aren't you tucked up in your dormitory with the rest of the sheep?"

The contempt in that last word is clear; the bellator isn't trying to hide the way he feels about the Commonwealth's regular citizens. Why would he bother? Gentian is at his mercy.

"D-duty calls," he gets out. It's no more or less than the truth.

The bellator snorts. "Indeed. I've tracked you for the last ten minutes, *Gentian*. You've met no one. Cared for no creature. So what *duty* brings a vet tech out on a night such as this?"

Gentian *knew* someone was watching him—that it hadn't just been his imagination. Fear shudders through him, but he holds on to the idea that Kilían could have killed him whenever he wanted to, if that's what he was after. Bellators are silent and surefooted, plus there's the storm; he could've come up behind Gentian at any point in his trek out of the forest and put a blade to his throat. But he didn't. He let Gentian live—because he wanted to see where the boy would lead him: a predator, tracking his prey. He's doing the same now; Gentian draws breath at his pleasure, and they both know it.

Steady, says Ari's voice in Gentian's head. Clinging to what remains of his composure, he lifts his chin and says, "M-my own."

Kilían gives a disbelieving huff. "Does your *duty* include aiding in the escape of an exile and a condemned prisoner? Because that's the only reason I can think of for your presence here." Those arctic eyes of his bore into Gentian, the intensity of his gaze visible even in the dimness. "Don't bother lying. I just came from the forest, where three of the Bastarour hunted down the exile Westergaard and his apprentice. The pack numbers six, yet the rest were nowhere to be found. Now here you are, emptying syringes into the sink. One hardly needs to be the Bellatorum's Lead Interrogator to draw the connection."

He takes a step closer, menace clear in every line of his body. "So, little Gentian. Tell me. What. Did. You. Do?" The words are a hiss, their syllables lingering in the air long after his voice falls away.

Hunted down. By the Architect, what does that mean? Is Ari dead? Gentian wants more than anything to ask, but to do so would give away the fact that he cared about Ari's fate. And here in the Commonwealth, caring about anything but your responsibility and your virtue is not allowed. "What I h-h-had to," he tells the bellator.

"Hmmmm." Kilían looks him up and down, his eyes lingering on the syringe still gripped in Gentian's hand. "A timid thing like you, venturing into the forest. Confronting the Bastarour. I'd lay odds if I went back right now, I'd find three of them lying unconscious in the muck." He steps closer still, so that Gentian has to look up at him. It's an intimidation tactic, and it works just fine. The bellator is taller than Gentian, broader. Not to mention, he's got a huge blade strapped to his back and a belt around his hips hung with more weapons than Gentian can name.

"Do you want to know what that tells me, little Gentian?" he says, his voice barely above a whisper. "Either you value your life not at all, or you value one of the traitors' more. If it's the first, you're of no use to me. But if it's the second . . ."

He lets his voice trail off, and as Gentian's sure he intended, the boy finishes the sentence on his own. *If it's the second, I will bleed the answer out of you. If it's the second, I will take pleasure in carving you up, piece by piece, until you tell me everything I want to know.*

He's watching Gentian closely, a cat toying with a mouse. "You tranquilized half the pack. Do you deny it?"

Say nothing, whispers Ari's voice in his head. *If you speak, you incriminate yourself.*

Gentian's teeth sink so deep into his lip, they draw blood—again. But somehow he manages not to say a word.

"Come now," Kilían says, his voice measured. "You expect me to believe that if I made my way back into the forest, I wouldn't find a dart gun somewhere in the underbrush? Your trail would be easy enough for me to follow, as soon as the sun rose. And unconscious animals or no, that would be all the proof I'd need. Because I'm sure you didn't go out there armed with a couple of syringes, expecting to get close enough to stab the beasts."

He knows, Ari says, his tone a warning. *He's playing with you. Keep your silence. And don't retreat, or he'll pounce.*

Gentian tries to hold Kilían's eyes, but it's hard. The bellator's gaze is blue and slippery—cold as ice, and just as impenetrable. The way he's looking at Gentian reveals nothing, except perhaps that the boy is an idiot to have placed himself in this regrettable position.

Kilían waits, one hand resting easy on the hilt of his dagur, like they can stand here for the rest of what remains of the night—at least, until he loses patience and carves out Gentian's tongue for refusing to speak. It reminds Gentian of a stare-down between two creatures as they try to determine which one holds the alpha position; he's dealt with this enough with the beasts in the veterinary practice to recognize it.

In the end, Gentian lets his gaze slide from the bellator's. He may be an idiot, but he's not foolish enough to believe that of the two of them, he is the dominant animal. Sure, he might be able to muster the courage to hold Kilían's eyes...but that would be a Pyrrhic victory. He'd see it as a challenge, and either way, Gentian would be just as dead.

He drops his eyes to the floor, hoping the bellator will see this as the sign of submission it is and let him go. But instead, Kilían exhales slowly, as if it's all he can do not to reach out and strangle him. "Speak, boy," he says, making no effort to disguise the irritation in his voice. "My patience is growing thin."

Oh, by the Virtues. "Wh-who am I to s-say what you'd f-find in the f-forest?" Gentian says, his eyes fixed on the tile between his feet. "It w-would be the g-greatest arrogance to imagine a l-lowly citizen like myself is c-capable of predicting a legendary b-bellator's capacity."

As soon as the words leave his mouth, Gentian wants to rewind time and stuff them back inside. What is *wrong* with him? Does he want to die right here, his blood hosed off the tiles like that of the wounded pig he stitched up just last week?

He braces for the kiss of Kilían's blade against his throat. But instead, he hears the low rumble of the bellator's laughter.

Disbelieving, he flicks his eyes up to Kilían's face. The bellator's still standing with one hand on the hilt of his weapon—but those frosty blue eyes have warmed, and the corners of his mouth have curved upward.

There's no mistaking it: Kilían Bryndísarson, Lead Interrogator and merciless killer, is *smiling* at him. And despite himself, Gentian can't help but notice that when he does, the granite planes of his face smooth out into something almost...beautiful. For one peculiar moment, he imagines he can see what Kilían looked like when he was young like Gentian, before life in the Bellatorum hardened him, robbing him of everything but the icy, emotionless control he needed in order to survive. Then that image is gone. His face smooths into its usual stern expression—but Gentian swears he can still see the ghost of Kilían's younger self peering out from behind those ice-chip eyes.

"I know you're acquainted with Bellator Westergaard," Kilían says. "I watched you watch him, the day he took that public whipping years ago. You watched him, and he was watching her." The words curl into the air, deadly by their very nature—but his tone isn't threatening. Gentian can't fathom it. Together with finding him here tonight, Kilían has everything he needs to destroy him. But he makes no move to slit Gentian's throat.

Three years ago, when Ari and Gentian were sixteen, he was whipped because of Gentian—because he took the blame for something Gentian did. It's true Gentian's eyes lingered on him that day in the Square, wanting to give him strength. And equally true that Ari's gaze skimmed over him, fixing instead on Eva Marteinn. It had taken finding the two of them in the rain-soaked woods, kissing against a spruce, for Gentian to understand why.

"You went into the forest for *him*," Kilían says, and it isn't a question. "You risked your life for Westergaard. And even now, you keep his secrets. Why would you do such a thing?"

They say that Kilían is such a gifted interrogator because he can see inside you before you speak a single word—that he knows the inner workings of your mind and heart better than you do yourself. That before he's done with you, you'll confess things buried in the deepest recesses of your subconscious. There is no hiding from him, and so Gentian doesn't try. Instead, he lifts his chin and meets the bellator's gaze again.

"If you know," he says without a hint of a stutter, "then I would be even more of a fool than you believe me to be if I bothered to deny it."

Kilían's eyes fix on his face, but this time the way he's looking at Gentian is different. He can feel the bellator's gaze assessing him—an unwrapping of sorts, as if he has peeled back Gentian's skin to reveal not muscle and sinew, but something deeper: the boy's thoughts and intentions, the motivation that has brought him to stand before Kilían today. It is exquisitely uncomfortable, but Gentian doesn't look away.

A minute passes. An eternity. And then, to Gentian's shock, the bellator begins to laugh again. It isn't cruel, though. It's... amused, and bitter, and somehow, surprised.

Gentian knows he should keep quiet. He should be grateful that the bellator seems to find this situation funny, rather than cause for decapitation. But instead, a fierce red thread of fury winds its way through his veins. It yanks taut, taking his mouth with it.

"He could have d-died!" he says, feeling traitorous tears burn his eyes. Kilían will probably laugh at them too, but at this point, he couldn't care less. He is so tired of apologizing for and hiding who he is. "Y-you and your f-fellow B-bellatorum attack d-dogs p-planned to s-s-slaughter him. F-for all I k-know, you *d-d-did*. All I did was g-give him a f-f-fighting c-chance."

He expects Kilían to mock him, but when the bellator speaks again, his voice is soft. "He lives, Gentian. Perhaps thanks to you."

Relief bolts through Gentian, weakening his knees. He reaches out, steadying himself on the counter. "And the girl?"

"Does it matter?" he counters.

Gentian sets his jaw. "She m-matters to him," he says, his voice soft but determined. "He c-came back for her. And so she m-matters to me, as w-well."

Kilían says nothing—but the strangest expression flits across his face before he schools it again to blankness. It looks oddly like...recognition.

Gentian doesn't understand this, either. But the bellator doesn't seem to be intent on killing him at the moment, so emboldened, he presses on. "H-how?"

The bellator's mouth presses into a thin line. "The girl," is all he says.

Outside, the rain is beginning to slow. It streaks the windows, dripping down the glass. A faint hint of light seeps through the fading night, setting Kilian's red hair aflame. Gentian peers up at him, and sees what he couldn't before—the bellator's black gear is soaked with drying blood, and the water that drips to puddle at his boots is red-tinged. "Are you h-hurt?" he says, so appalled at the quantity of it, he forgets he's speaking to the Commonwealth's Lead Interrogator, a man who has the power to break him with a word. "I'm not a m-medic, but I c-can treat you—"

Kilían glances down at himself in puzzlement, as if just noticing the state of his gear. "It's not my blood," he says absently. "Or Ari's, in case you're wondering."

Gentian sucks in a sharp breath. "Then whose?"

"Well," the bellator says, plucking the fabric of his sodden shirt away from his body with disgust, "some of it belongs to one of the beasts. The girl stabbed it, when it threatened Westergaard. Almost severed its spine. As for the rest, that belongs to Efraím Stinar. Apprentice Marteinn managed to open the electrified gate and tempt one of the beasts into charging through. Bellator Stinar followed—and then the girl programmed the gate to close again, just as lightning struck. Efraím was trapped with the beast. He couldn't—well." The bellator closes his jaw with a snap, leaving Gentian to follow his story through to its logical conclusion.

This doesn't take much imagination. Having just survived an up-close-and-personal tussle with one of the beasts before he managed to sedate it, Gentian knows full well just how vicious they are on their own—let alone while compounded by an electrified fence in the middle of a lightning storm. Still, his eyes widen. "Are you t-telling me Lead Bellator Stinar is *d-dead?*"

His jaw tight, Kilían gives a barely perceptible nod.

By the nine hells. Ari and Eva conspired to kill the leader of the Bellatorum—a vicious, stone-cold killer who Gentian had always thought seemed more machine than man. And as head interrogator, Kilían was his second-in-command. Which means—

"The Bellatorum is y-yours now," Gentian says, awe clear in his voice. "You l-lead the T-thirty. So w-why are you standing here, wasting your time with m-me? Why n-not just k-kill me or h-haul me away to the d-dungeons?"

The bellator draws himself up to his full height, looming over Gentian again. "I don't have to answer to you," he says.

Of course, he doesn't. As the de facto leader of the Bellatorum, he answers to no one but the Priests and the Executor himself. But though he may refuse to tell Gentian anything, the bellator can't stop him from thinking—and his mind is racing, putting the puzzle pieces together. He thinks about the unexpected gentleness in Kilían's voice when the bellator told him Ari lived. Of the recognition on his face when Gentian said Eva mattered to him because she was important to Ari. Of the way he laughed when Gentian told him there was no point in denying why he'd risked his life in the woods. A spark of knowledge flares inside Gentian, fanning into a flame.

"Y-you w-wanted him to escape," Gentian says. "Y-you watched me w-watching him, that day of the whipping. Why would you do either of those things?"

He doesn't expect the bellator to answer him. But Kilían does. "Those are two very different questions," he says, his tone wary.

Ari's voice speaks in Gentian's head, insistent this time. *Press him*, he says, and so Gentian does. "Are they?"

The bellator takes a step back, his hand tracing the hilt of his dagur, like the weapon is one of the communal teddy bears Ari and Gentian used to share as children in the Nursery. And then he sets his shoulders, as if girding himself to speak. "I noticed you watching him," he says at last, "and him watching her in turn, because—once, I stood in your shoes. And like you, I made a choice."

Gentian's heart starts to pound again, this time with excitement and shock. "You...c-c-cared for someone? And you h-helped them escape?"

The bellator's eyes narrow to blue slits. "Such a thing would be high treason. Punishable by death."

Gentian ignores this. There is no one to overhear but the two of them; he might not be aware of another's presence here, but Kilían surely would be. The man is a warrior and a hunter, trained to detect the slightest of threats. "S-so it has been d-done before," he says. "I'm n-not the only one who t-thinks things could be d-different. B-better."

The bellator's silence is the only answer he needs.

"You p-protected Ari," he says, the certainty settling over him with the same instinct that guides him to approach wounded creatures without fear of getting bitten or scratched. The instinct that allows him to heal. "You w-wanted h-him to get away. And you followed m-me because you know I w-wanted the s-same thing."

Kilían swallows hard, his throat working. Gentian watches his Adam's apple move above the collar of his blood-soaked gear, watches the way a muscle twitches in his jaw. And for a moment, they aren't a pitiless assassin and a helpless vet tech. They are just people who share a secret, standing on the tiled floor of the vet clinic as the rain comes down.

"I promised to protect him when he was born," Kilían says finally, his voice so low Gentian can hardly hear it. "I swore on my honor as a bellator and the strength of my blade. And though that arrogant attitude of his hasn't made it easy"—he heaves an exasperated breath; the sin of pride is Ari's worst flaw—"I've done my best to keep my vow."

Gentian's mouth falls open. Of all the things he expected Kilían to say, this wasn't it. "Who did you promise?" he asks before he can stop himself.

Unsurprisingly, Kilían doesn't answer him; but it doesn't matter. Here in the Commonwealth, where attachment is verboten, Gentian can think of only one thing that would make a bellator make such a commitment: Love, the same thing that led Gentian to risk himself for Ari tonight. Whoever Kilían cared for, they are connected to Ari, and have been since his birth. Gentian has no idea how or why; in the Commonwealth, children are carried by artificially inseminated surrogates and then raised by Caretakers in the Nursery. But he would stake his life on the fact that whoever Kilían loved—the person that made *him* risk everything—is the reason behind the vow he swore.

A powerful surge of hope crests in Gentian, sweeping away the fear in its path. He imagines a world where people don't have to hide their feelings, where a boy doesn't get whipped in a public square for rescuing a fallen baby bird. "Are w-we the only ones w-who have d-dared to defy the P-priests and the Executor?" he asks. "Or are we p-part of s-something l-larger?"

The Lead Interrogator mask settles over Kilían's face again, any hint of vulnerability sealed away. "I don't know what you're talking about, *Gentian*. And I would advise you refrain from sharing any of your misguided suppositions with others, lest you find yourself in the regrettable position of parting with your head."

Normally, this would cow Gentian. But this time, he doesn't retreat. He doesn't need the echo of Ari's voice in his head to tell him the bellator is lying; he feels it in his bones. And if this is Gentian's only chance at a life other than what the Commonwealth has to offer him, he will lunge for it with both hands, or die trying.

"I'm not going to tell anyone. And I know you understand exactly what I mean." Gentian's voice is fierce. For once, he doesn't stutter. "I might not look like much, but over the years, I've found that to be an advantage," he says, refusing to fold. "I won't betray your cause. Take me. Use me. I want to fight."

For a long moment, Kilían regards him, his gaze impassive. The rain comes down and Gentian's heart pounds and he watches the bellator watching him, the way Kilían must have done so long ago, in the Square. He waits—for the man's knife to slide between his ribs, for Kilían's blade to carve out his tongue, so he can never speak of their exchange. A strange calm has settled over Gentian; time drips, slow as honey from the hives the little ones tend.

Gentian has made his choice. He made it years ago, when he gave his heart to Ari, without regard for whether the other boy could keep it safe. In the end, it wasn't what Ari could give to him, or whether he returned Gentian's feelings—not that it would have mattered if he had. It was about the strength Gentian found in himself, the resilience and power that loving Ari gave him.

It was about the person he wanted to be.

He sees the decision cross Kilían's face an instant before the bellator speaks. The man's arm moves, and Gentian braces himself for the bite of his blade. But instead of pulling his dagur from his belt, Kilían extends his hand. It hangs in the air between them—a question asked and answered, a risk taken and another promise made.

"Welcome to the resistance, Wolf's Brother," he says.

SHADOWS OF THE SEVEN SINS IS SET IN THE UNIVERSE OF THE AWARD-winning Seven Sins series, which also includes a free prequel novella and a trilogy.

SUBSCRIBE TO EMILY'S NEWSLETTER AT EMILYCOLINNEWS.COM FOR insider updates about the world of the Seven Sins and bonus stories!

If you're brand-new to the series (other than this short story collection, of course!), start with Book 1, *Sword of the Seven Sins*.

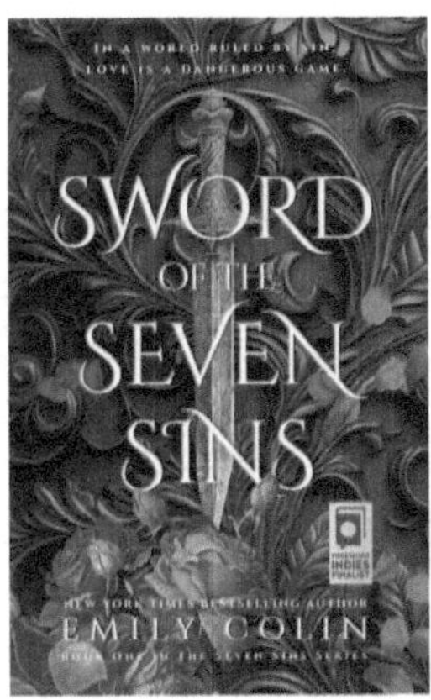

In a world ruled by sin, love is a dangerous game.

WINNER of the **2021** N**orth** C**arolina** I**ndie** A**uthor** A**ward** in Young Adult Fiction

FINALIST for the 2020 Foreword INDIES Award in Young Adult Fiction

SHORTLISTED for the The Manly Wade Wellman Award for Science Fiction and Fantasy

WINNER of the 2022 Gold Moonbeam Award for Best Book Series

T**heir forbidden love could save them.** O**r kill them.**

Tech prodigy Eva is resigned to life in the Commonwealth, as long as she's behind a computer screen. To her horror, the Priests Choose her to train as a bellator, one of the Commonwealth's enforcers. She's eerily good at it. If only she weren't taunted at every turn by her deadly mentor, Ari, to whom she's bound by a blood oath. She's falling for the magnetic Ari, but in the Commonwealth, love is punishable by death.

Thrown into the life of a bellator, Eva is no longer a sheep of the Commonwealth, but a wolf, learning to patrol and kill. Her inexplicable strengths make her a top bellator, drawing unwanted attention. Meanwhile, as she and Ari train together, their antagonism becomes grudging respect.

But the more time they spend together, the harder it is for Eva to resist the lure of his green eyes, his grace and power with a sword, and the charm beneath the sarcastic front he shows the world. Things take a treacherous turn when a heated night in the woods reveals a dangerous secret—Ari has loved Eva for years.

Their feelings put their lives at risk, but their love is too powerful to deny. Meanwhile, Eva's mysterious physical gifts heighten to a terrifying degree. Soon, Ari uncovers a secret that could take down the Commonwealth itself. Will Eva set aside her fears and fight for freedom with the boy she loves, knowing it might destroy them both?

AUTHOR'S NOTE

If you love fierce girls with swords, infuriating guys with hearts of gold, forbidden love between a mentor and apprentice who can't keep their hands off each other, and star-crossed lovers who fight to the death by each other's sides, then this is the book for you.

LEARN MORE ABOUT THE SERIES AND WATCH THE BOOK TRAILER AT thesevensinsseries.com.

BOOKS BY EMILY COLIN

THE SEVEN SINS SERIES

Sword of the Seven Sins: A Novel

Sacrifice of the Seven Sins: A Novella

Shadows of the Seven Sins: A Story Collection

Siege of the Seven Sins: A Novel

Storm of the Seven Sins: A Novel

YOUNG ADULT FICTION

Wicked South: Secrets and Lies: Stories for Young Adults

Unbound: Stories of Transformation, Love, and Monsters

FICTION FOR ADULTS

The Memory Thief

The Dream Keeper's Daughter

NONFICTION

The Long Way Around: How 34 Women Found the Lives they Love

The Secret to Our Success: How 33 Women Made their Dreams Come True

The Changing Face of Justice: A Look at the First 100 Women Attorneys in North Carolina

facebook.com / emilycolinbooks
x.com / emilyacolin
instagram.com / emilycolinbooks
amazon.com / author / emilycolin
bookbub.com / authors / emily-colin
goodreads.com / emilyacolin